A Watch in the Night

BOOK III
Snare of the Fowler

ROSEANNA LEE

This book is a work of fiction. Names of characters   places and incidents are products of both the author's imagination and based on certain historical facts. Any resemblance to actual persons, living or dead, business establishments, events or locales are entirely coincidental.

Copyright 2019

ISBN: 978-1-945190-74-2

FV-1

Cover Design and Layout: Isaac Rivera
www.isaacsifontes.com

First Edition: December, 2019

www.IntellectPublishing.com

For all of those who fought the losing battle and won!

Arise, cry out in the night, as the watches of the night begin; pour out your heart like water in the presence of the Lord.
Lamentations 2:19

A WATCH IN THE NIGHT

PROLOGUE

Remember that the storm is a good opportunity for the pine and the cypress to show their strength and stability. Mao Tse Tung

Funny thing about a river, Bud thought, it's always moving, but it never really changes. It rises, it falls; but at some point in time, it always goes back to its banks.

Bud stood watching the swift water of the river meandering along before it turned and disappeared into the wilds of the swamp upstream.

Today would tell the story on this river. He studied the currents; he checked out the banks. If he was going to survive, he needed to be prepared. He needed to know, really know, this river.

As he studied the river, a strange thought occurred to him—peace like a river—Bud remembered he had heard this in church: *Peace like a river; the Lord will give you peace like a river.*

But what the hell did that mean? That phrase—peace like a river—had struck him as odd then, and it struck him as odd now. A river was anything but peaceful.

Maybe, just maybe, if he had stayed around that preacher, long enough, the preacher could have eventually explained that conundrum to him.

But he rarely went to church—only the occasional visit on Christmas and Easter. In his family, Sunday was just another work day. Church was a luxury for a man trying to find enough time to keep his family fed.

Bud believed that if God existed, he had, thus far, done a pretty good job of keeping his presence hidden, at least from him. The *Lord* and his peace like a river had never shown up in his life. A man made his own way in life; at least as far as Bud could tell.

Oh sure, a river could look peaceful enough—about like it did now. But looks are always deceiving, Life, not a preacher, had taught Bud that truth.

The thing any good river man could tell you is that the peaceful flow of a river is nothing more than an illusion. What appears calm on the surface is always churning beneath.

You might jump into the river on a hot day to cool off, and a gator, barely submerged below the surface of the water, could grab your leg and drag you to the bottom. Life could happen just like that. Peaceful one minute; over the next. And you never see it coming.

Look at Tommy Long. Hadn't he gone out to the river that day for some fun? Hadn't the river lured him in only to spit him back out—dead? Sure, you could argue that Trey egged him on. But it wasn't Trey's words that killed Tommy. It was the river's current.

A river's current is a strange thing. Depending on the level of the water, it can be swift or it can be gentle. The current can be a roaring, merciless torrent, destroying everything in its path; or the current can be a sweet, steady stream, something that playfully tickles your feet as it filters the sand through your toes.

The only real truth about a current is its deceptive nature. Just like life. What you think you can handle, what you think you can manage, is more often than not, the very thing that does you in. And you don't see it coming.

The only way to manage a current is to swim along with it while slowly angling yourself out. Every river man knows that. Fighting and floundering will wear you out, and then you lose.

And wasn't that the way life worked? You jump into a problem, thinking you can handle it, then the current drags you off course. If you allow yourself to flow with the current, most times you can maneuver your way out.

Few people did that! Most people, more often than not, struggle and swim against the flow until it does them in. Being sheriff had taught Bud a few lessons about people and how they took on life.

Hell! That very thing was happening to him. He had jumped into that big old murky mess of a river—called Trey Hillman's life—and now he was fighting to survive.

When he took the initial plunge, it looked appealing enough. It looked like a way to the other side. A tough swim and he could leave poverty and all of the ugliness that goes with being poor behind. A tough swim and he could walk right out on the other side, a successful man.

That was an illusion. Like the river, appearances had been deceptive. What started out as a peaceful swim, a way to refresh himself as life heated up, turned out to be anything but refreshing. Bud knew without a doubt that he was now fighting for his life.

The current of Trey's life had dragged him under, time after time, and then sent him bobbing back to the top only to be dragged under again.

While Trey occasionally appeared to be calm on the surface, Bud now knew the truth. Trey was always churning underneath the surface, always unpredictable, always a moment away from disaster. The current in Trey's life had this time pulled Bud way off course.

Bud knew he needed to get out. He knew that he needed to make his break with Trey. But just like Tommy Long, the swim had exhausted him. The strength to swim out alive was diminishing. Bud feared he would be swept along until he found himself in a disaster that would simply overwhelm him. Like Tommy Long, he would be dragged under and spit out dead.

A lot of life fed on the river, only to realize too late that the hunter often became the hunted. Hadn't he seen a big, old peaceful bird waiting patiently on the banks of the river, beak poised to catch a fish—the predator. And hadn't he seen that same bird, in a moment's flash, snapped up in the jaws of a gator—the prey.

Bud kept staring at the river, trying to make sense of it all when a tributary caught his eye. His focus on the churning middle of the river almost caused him to miss this detail.

Still, there it was: a tiny stream, an almost indistinguishable rivulet, flowing off to the side. A stream that was going its own way; dredging its own course.

Maybe that was the answer. If he could break away from the flow, break free of the river, maybe he could set his own course. Maybe he could find some sort of peace—peace like a river; but he seriously doubted that.

He knew unless something changed, drastically changed, he would drown. Bud turned and walked up the slope of the riverbank.

Only time would tell.

Snare of the Fowler

Third Watch

A WATCH IN THE NIGHT

CHAPTER ONE

The truck roared toward Trinity, cars pulling aside at the sound of the siren, but it wasn't fast enough to suit Rodrigo. Time slowed down to a crawl as he looked down at the pale face of the woman still cradled in his arms.

He and the driver had opted to take her to the Clinic in Trinity. There was no time to get to the hospital in Cartersville.

"Hold on, baby," he kept whispering down to her, pulling her in closer to his chest. "Don't leave us. Please hold on."

They reached the outskirts of Trinity, and the guard swung the truck onto Main Street. He slammed on his brakes at the Clinic's back door, jumped out and rushed inside.

"We need help here," he shouted. Rodrigo followed him inside, with Rachel in his arms.

Karen was the first to hear them. She rushed out from the front office to see what was going on.

"Overdose," Rodrigo said. He struggled to pull the empty pill bottle from his pocket, while still clutching Rachel in his arms. "We need a doctor."

"I'm a doctor," Dr. Luke said, coming up behind Karen. "Bring her in here." Dr. Luke pushed through a set of swinging doors into an examination room.

"Put her on the table," Dr. Luke said. Rodrigo gently placed Rachel on the white sheet, and Dr. Luke pressed his fingers against Rachel's neck.

"She has a pulse," he said.

Dr. Luke leaned over Rachel and placed his stethoscope on her chest. Rodrigo and Karen watched and waited. After what seemed like a long time, Dr. Luke stood up and turned to face them. "She has a heartbeat," he announced, "but it's weak."

"Do you know what she took?" Dr. Luke asked Rodrigo.

3

Karen passed the empty pill bottled over to him. "Washed those down with a half bottle of wine," Rodrigo said.

Dr. Luke read the label and shook his head. "Sleeping pills. We'll have to pump her stomach. She needs to go to the hospital, but there isn't time. I'll do it here. Karen, you stay. You two wait outside."

"I'm staying," Rodrigo said.

"Then get out of my way," Dr. Luke replied. Rodrigo moved to the corner of the room.

"And you call the Davis wagon," Dr. Luke said to the guard.

The Davis wagon pulled up to the back door as Dr. Luke was finishing up. "We need to transport her to Cartersville," he said to Rodrigo and Karen. "Her pulse is still weak, but she's breathing. Let's pray that she'll make it."

Looking at Rodrigo, he added, "You got to her just in the nick of time. Any longer and we'd lost her. At least now, she's got a fighting chance."

"She's got two little kids to thank for that," Rodrigo replied. The Davis driver wheeled the stretcher into the room.

Karen looked at the Plantation guard, who was helping the Davis driver, recognized the uniform, and then her pulse quickened.

"Two kids?" Karen asked.

"Yeah, two kids," Rodrigo said. "Out at the Plantation."

"Are the children alright?" Karen asked. She tugged at Rodrigo's sleeve to make him pay attention to her.

"Yes, they're fine," he said, shaking Karen's hand off of his arm.

"I'm going with her," Rodrigo said to Dr. Luke.

"So am I," Dr. Luke replied. The Davis driver and Dr. Luke rolled the stretcher outside and lifted it into the wagon.

"Get in." Dr. Luke motioned with his head for Rodrigo to climb into the wagon.

"No riders," the driver said.

4

"It's alright. He's helping me," Dr. Luke responded authoritatively.

The driver shrugged his shoulders, jumped to the ground, slammed the door and rushed to the driver's seat.

The wagon lurched forward as the driver sped away, siren on, lights flashing. People on the street stopped to stare as the wagon flew through town in the direction of Cartersville.

"What in the world?" Annie said, when the wagon passed by her shop. "Call James Davis," she said to the manicurist. "Find out what's goin' on."

The ride to Cartersville was tense. Dr. Luke feared that the woman in his care was losing ground as her pulse grew so faint that she was barely alive at all. All color drained from her face.

Rodrigo feared for her as well, never letting go of her hand. "Breathe," he whispered into her ear. "Breathe."

The wagon whipped into the emergency entrance, the doors flew open and white swirled all around them. In one swift movement, Rachel was moved out of the wagon and was rolled into the emergency room. Rodrigo moved with them, still clutching Rachel's hand.

"You'll have to wait outside, sir," a nurse said to him. "Hospital policy. Wait there." She pointed to a room with straight-backed chairs and a television suspended on a rack overhead.

Dr. Luke put his hand on Rodrigo's shoulder. "Is she your wife?" he asked.

"I don't even know her," Rodrigo said.

"Do you want to wait for the outcome?" Dr. Luke asked.

"Yes, of course," Rodrigo replied.

"Then wait in the room as the nurse instructed you. I'll come out to tell you what's happening as soon as I know something."

Dr. Luke turned and disappeared behind the swinging doors, with a sign that read *HOSPITAL PERSONNEL ONLY*. His head reappeared briefly. "You need to call her family, her next-of-kin," he said. He disappeared again before Rodrigo could tell him that he had no idea whom that might be.

5

Rodrigo surveyed the waiting room. There was a phone on a small table. He should give Mrs. Brodie and Naomi a call, he thought.

Mrs. Brodie answered on the first ring. "Thank God, it's you. Did she make it?"

"So far. But just barely. We're at the hospital in Cartersville."

"I know. Karen called us."

"Karen?"

"Naomi's daughter. She works at the Clinic."

"That explains it."

"What?"

"She wanted to know if the kids were okay. I didn't put it together until now. So she's the Karen that the kids talk about so much."

"That's right."

"What did the doctors say?"

"Not much. I was told to wait. Oh, and we need to call her next-of-kin. I'm going to stay here with her. Could you do that?"

"I'll try. I will need to get the real estate agent on the phone. Or maybe security. Perhaps, they can help. Her name is Rachel Edwards. I do know that much."

"How are the kids?"

"Upset. They don't understand. But they'll be alright. Naomi took them home. I'll call her; so don't you worry about that. But please call me as soon as you have any word. I don't care how late you call. I doubt I will be able to sleep tonight."

"I will. I'll call as soon as I know anything. Bye now."

Rodrigo hung up the phone. He slumped down into a chair and dropped his face into his hands.

During the long wait, he must have dozed off because the next thing that he knew Dr. Luke was shaking him by the shoulders. "Sir, we have moved the woman into intensive care."

"How is she?" Rodrigo asked.

"It's not good. But she's alive. The next twenty-four hours will tell us a lot. Were you able to reach her next-of kin?"

6

"Not yet," Rodrigo replied. Rodrigo extended his hand to Dr. Luke.

"My name is Rodrigo," he said. Dr. Luke took Rodrigo's outstretched hand into his own. "Dr. Lucas Lowry. But Dr. Luke will do."

"Thank you, Dr. Luke." Rodrigo pumped Dr. Luke's hand.

"No thanks needed. I am only doing my job. But let's get back to our patient. Are you friends with her?"

"I don't really know her. She lives next door to a friend of mine."

"Mrs. Brodie?"

"That's right," Rodrigo replied. "Do you know Mrs. Brodie?"

"Karen is my assistant," Dr. Luke said. "Karen's mother is Naomi—the Naomi who works for Mrs. Brodie. So I know a bit about Mrs. Brodie. And I've met the twins who found her."

"Yes, Mrs. Brodie explained Karen's connection to the twins to me," Rodrigo said.

"May I ask what is your connection to our patient?"

"Really none. I am on the Brodie estate frequently—friends with Mrs. Brodie, Naomi and the twins. I have never met the patient. When the kids found her passed out, they went looking for help. I was that help."

"Lucky for her you were close by."

"May I see her?" Rodrigo asked.

"You're not allowed into the intensive care unit—hospital policy. But, if you would like, you can move into the intensive care waiting area. We usually let a family member into the unit every hour for a few minutes. However, you're not family."

"Right now,' Rodrigo said, "I'm all that she's got."

"I must get back to my office in Trinity," Dr. Luke said. "The nurses will let you know immediately if there's any change. I'll ask them to make an exception to the 'family only' rule. I will request that you be allowed to go in and see her."

"Her name is Rachel," Rodrigo said, "Rachel Edwards. Or that is what Mrs. Brodie told me."

"I'll have the nurses put her name on the chart. Thank you. The intensive care waiting room is down the corridor. First door on the left. I'll see you in the morning, if you're still here."

"If Rachel's here, I'll be here. I don't want to leave her alone."

"How about her family?"

"Mrs. Brodie is working on that."

"Good. It would be prudent to call them immediately."

"Here is my home number. Call me if you need me." Dr. Luke handed Rodrigo a card.

"Thanks," Rodrigo said, taking the card.

"No problem. And Rodrigo."

"Yes."

"If you're a believing man, I would pray. This Ms. Edwards knew what she was doing. She took a lot of pills."

Rodrigo paced around the intensive care waiting room. The only other people in the room were an older couple. They sat in the corner. The woman cried quietly, her head resting against the man's chest.

After an hour, a nurse came into the waiting room and told him that he could see Rachel. Just for a few minutes. She led him into a room where Rachel was lying on a hospital bed.

The room was cold and sterile. He scanned the monitors, and listened to the hiss of the breathing machine and the thump of the monitor that measured her heart rate. Shivering, he took the few steps needed to stand next to the bed.

As he looked down on her, he thought that she looked so small and fragile with all of those tubes hooked up to her body.

Leaning down, he whispered into her ear, "Live, Rachel. Please live."

He stood holding her hand until the nurse came back into the room. "Sir, your time is up," the nurse said. Rodrigo kissed Rachel's forehead and left.

All night Rodrigo sat in the waiting room, mostly staring at a painting that hung on the wall. It was of a tranquil scene, a sailboat cutting through the waves. Rodrigo's thoughts drifted back to his own childhood. He had always been a shrimper; but he had not always lived on Palm Island.

Rodrigo had been brought up by his father, a hard-working as well as a hard-drinking man. Together, they lived on his father's shrimp boat.

He had never known his mother. She left shortly after he was born. His father never spoke of his mother other than to say that she had left them alone.

As far back as he could remember, a black-and-white photograph of his mother—yellowed with age—sat by his father's bed in a tarnished silver frame. That photograph was all that remained of her on his father's boat—other than the boy that she left behind.

The few times that Rodrigo summoned the courage to ask his father about her, his father had always given the same answer.

"She left us, boy. That's all you need to know. Me a working man and you nothing but a baby. There's nothing more to say."

Rodrigo learned to walk on the rolling deck of his father's boat, harnessed to the deck with enough line so that he could toddle about and play without going overboard.

"That boy's got nothing but sea legs," the other shrimpers would say, laughing good-naturedly. "Put that boy on land, and he's liable to fall down."

When he was old enough to go to school, Rodrigo walked himself to school, and then he walked himself home again to the docks in the late afternoon.

If the boat stayed out overnight, he spent the night with the Torres's family, an older married couple, who ran a bait shop next to the dock. They were kind people, and for a few dollars a week, they made sure that Rodrigo had a hot meal and a place to stay until his floating home returned.

Rodrigo acquired his habit of hard work from his father, and by the time that he was seven, he had already started to earn money by doing odd jobs about the docks.

And he worked hard in school. For him, learning came naturally. While he took pride in his schoolwork, his father didn't place much value on education.

"What you need to know comes from hard work, boy; not from books. No book is gonna teach you how to smell rain or know when the shrimp start runnin'. Only time and experience will teach you that."

It was Mrs. Torres who encouraged Rodrigo in his schoolwork. "Don't pay no mind to what your daddy says about school," she often said to Rodrigo. "You get your lessons first; you can work later." Mrs. Torres even made a spot in the back of the store, with a table and a chair, where Rodrigo could go and do his homework.

After completing his homework, Mr. Torres paid Rodrigo to help out at the bait shop. "A boy needs his own spending money," Mr. Torres would say to his wife. Mrs. Torres kept Rodrigo's money for him, writing the amount in a book that she kept in the cash drawer at the bait shop.

By the age of eight, Rodrigo had saved himself enough money for his first bicycle. With the help of Mrs. Torres, he bought it from a local store.

The bicycle gave Rodrigo new mobility. He rode it to school and around the small town. It was on one these trips that he discovered the local diner, with its weekly special of a steak dinner. He'd never tasted steak, only fish.

Each day as Rodrigo passed the diner on his way to school, he eyed a picture of the steak special in the window. Finally, one Saturday morning, he requested that Mrs. Torres give him a draw from his account in the amount of five dollars.

"That's quite a sum, young man," Mrs. Torres said to Rodrigo. "Whatever are you going to do with the money?" Rodrigo typically was not a spender.

"If you don't mind, Mrs. Torres, I'll just keep this to myself," Rodrigo replied politely.

"Not at all, boy; it's your money. You earned it fair and square."

Rodrigo stuck the money down into the pocket of his jeans and rode his bike to the diner. Peeking in the front window, he saw there were only a couple of people inside.

He paced back and forth outside of the diner, occasionally stopping to glance inside through the front window, for a full thirty minutes before he garnered the courage to venture inside. This was his first time in a restaurant. Rodrigo sat down at the first table he came to, the one by the front window.

The waitress approached his table with a smile on her face. She had a young boy of her own.

"What can I do for you young fella?" she asked, pulling out her pad and pen. "If you're wanting ice cream or a cold drink you should probably sit yourself up there at the counter."

"I like this table," Rodrigo replied. The table had a white tablecloth with a vase containing one small flower in the center.

"If it's alright with you, I'll just stay here at this table," he quickly added, unsure of the proper protocol for dining in a restaurant.

The waitress looked around the room. It was almost empty. What would it hurt to let the kid sit by the window, she thought. She liked this kid.

"That's fine, son," she said. "Sit at the table. Now what would you like to order?"

"Order?" He gave her a puzzled look.

"What would you like to eat?" she said, tapping her pencil on the pad in her hand.

"Oh! I'll have that steak dinner from the sign outside," he said, looking her straight in the eye. The waitress raised an eyebrow.

11

"That's a lot of food for a boy your size, although you do look mighty big and strong. How old are you?"

"Eight. Going on nine."

"Well, you are a big boy for eight going on nine," she said, smiling down at him.

"That dinner cost five dollars," she said kindly. "Maybe you'd like to try a hamburger. That's only a dollar. Most boys your age get that. The hamburger comes with fried potatoes and a large coke."

"No, ma'am. I want the steak dinner," Rodrigo answered. He reached into his pocket and pulled out his money. He had five one-dollar bills.

"I have the money," he said. Rodrigo held up his fist to show the waitress the money.

"Alright, son," the waitress said. "If it's steak that you want, it's steak that you'll get." Rodrigo let down his guard and risked giving her a quick smile. She winked at him and then returned his smile.

As he waited on the steak, Rodrigo sat surveying the scene outside of the window. He watched as a young woman, which he guessed was a mother, came out of the five-and-dime store, holding the hands of two small boys. Each boy clutched, what appeared to Rodrigo to be, a coloring book. The young woman and both boys looked happy.

Rodrigo wondered what it would be like to have a mother. All he had of his mother was the black-and-white photograph. Before he could spend any more time thinking on this topic, the steak arrived.

It was much larger than Rodrigo had imagined. The waitress was right—the steak special was a lot of food. But, then again, he was very hungry. Rodrigo took his knife and fork and attempted to cut into the meat. The plate slipped and slid on the table.

The waitress's heart went out to Rodrigo. "Here honey," she said, "let me show you how to use that knife and fork."

She leaned over him and demonstrated the proper way to handle a knife and fork. Rodrigo followed her instructions meticulously; he never got the proper use of a knife and fork wrong again.

Rodrigo ate slowly, savoring the texture and flavor of the meat. He ate until he was full. Then he put down his knife and fork and rested until he could eat some more. It took him a while; but he managed to clean his plate. When he put his knife and fork down on the table, he was full and satisfied.

The waitress saw that he was done and came back over to his table.

"I wish you'd look at that," she said, grinning. "You ate a steak big enough for a grown man. I don't think that I would have believed you ate that much, but I saw it with my own two eyes."

As the waitress scooped up his plate, Rodrigo pushed back his chair to get up.

"Not so fast, young man. There's more." She was back in a few minutes with a large dish of ice cream.

"Your special comes with dessert. I took a chance that you might like chocolate." She sat a bowl of chocolate ice cream, with a whipped cream topping and a cherry, in front of him.

"And this is your bill," she said, putting the ticket on his table. "When you're all done, you pay that man on the way out the door."

He ate his ice cream in tiny bites, making it last as long as he could. He liked sitting at the table by the window watching the people go by.

When he finished, he took his check up to the counter and counted out five one-dollar bills.

"Thank you very much, son. And come back to see us," the man behind the cash register said cheerfully.

"I'll be back alright," Rodrigo replied, grinning at the nice man. "I like that steak—a lot! It sure beats fish every day of the week."

Once his chores were done, Rodrigo loved to read. During the school year, he brought books home from the school library.

His favorite books were about people—people different than the ones he saw every day; people who lived in distant, strange, foreign places.

He had never traveled more than ten miles from home unless it was out on the water. As he read, he dreamed of the places he would travel to one day; the people he would meet; the adventures that were his for the taking.

During the summer, he got his books from the bookmobile, which made its rounds from the county library over in Smithville. Rodrigo's life centered around books.

Working the docks made him strong and muscular, even as a young boy. With dark skin that stayed tanned a deep, olive brown all year round; jet-black hair; and dark, brooding eyes, he grew into a handsome young man.

And he cultivated a good heart to go along with his good looks and strong body. He became a favorite among his classmates and teachers. Even with all of his other responsibilities, he found the time to play football for the Easton Wildcats, first junior varsity, and then senior varsity when he enrolled in high school.

Things changed the year that he turned fifteen. He knew immediately that something was wrong when he woke up at his usual time, and he did not smell the aroma of fresh-brewed coffee. His father started each day with a cup of coffee.

Rodrigo found his father still lying in his bunk. Dead from a heart attack.

When the old circuit judge made his appearance in Easton, the county seat, he accepted the state's recommendation to let Rodrigo live alone on his father's boat. Mrs. Torres appeared at the hearing with Rodrigo and assured the judge that she and her husband would "keep an eye on the boy."

The judge listened attentively as Mrs. Torres explained that Rodrigo had pretty much raised himself.

"He has always been an 'A' student," she explained to the judge. "Not to mention that he has worked for me and my husband since he was a young boy. And worked hard, too. He has never been a minute's trouble to anyone," she added. She smiled over at Rodrigo where he sat at a table next to the state worker.

Mrs. Torres' glowing assessment of Rodrigo swayed the judge. The only alternative the judge had was to place the boy into foster care. The judge was no fan of the foster care system. Banging his gavel, he issued an order that allowed Rodrigo to remain on the boat under the guardianship of Mr. and Mrs. Torres.

Rodrigo continued on in school, working for the Torres and playing football. Folks said he was the best quarterback to ever come out of Easton High, and with a little luck, he would end up receiving a scholarship to the state university.

His senior year in high school, nobody was the least bit surprised when Rodrigo did, in fact, win a football scholarship to the state university. The entire town celebrated this accomplishment with him. He was the first student from Easton High to ever earn such an honor.

When the fall rolled around, the Torres helped Rodrigo settle his affairs and head off to college. There he played football for four years, while still maintaining an "A" average.

There was even some talk that he might go "pro" but a knee injury squelched those hoped. When he graduated with a degree in English Literature, he went straight on to law school. There he met his wife—Angelina Whitmore.

Angelina came from an old southern family. Her father was a sitting federal district court judge, and her mother was an aspiring socialite. Together, the Whitmore family proudly navigated the treacherous waters of the top social tier, their daughter firmly in tow.

Angelina's father even managed to be nominated to the U.S. Supreme Court, but he failed to make it through the Senate confirmation hearings when it was discovered that he belonged to an "all-white" club.

Unfortunately, at least for Mr. Whitmore, he failed to keep pace when belonging to an all-white country club changed from being an asset to a liability.

The membership in the country club cost Angelina's father a seat on the Court. Embittered, he gave up his lifetime appointment as a federal district court judge and ran for Congress. After being miserably defeated, he turned to the bottle and opened a private practice.

Upon graduation from law school, Rodrigo joined his father-in-law's firm, at his wife's insistence. Working at his father-in-law's firm was doomed from the start.

No matter how hard he tried, Rodrigo couldn't handle life behind a desk practicing business law. The work, although he was quite capable of keeping pace, bored him.

As much as he disliked the work at the firm, he might by sheer willpower have survived, if not even prospered. But a bigger problem, a much bigger problem, began to take shape.

Rodrigo found that he loathed the social scene, and all of the commitments it entailed. But this was not true for his wife. For Angelina, the social scene became the very bread of life. A clash was inevitable.

Angelina had grown up in the spotlight. She had waltzed her way through childhood beauty pageants, cheerleading squads, homecoming courts—including homecoming queen— and debutante balls. In college, she embraced the sorority lifestyle, with all of its prestige and accolades.

The spotlight was where Angelina thrived, and the spotlight was where she intended to be at all costs. Marrying a handsome, young lawyer, who also happened to be a former football star, was just the ticket that she needed to skyrocket herself to the top of the social heap.

Rodrigo loved, or so he thought, his wife. He wanted to please her. In the early part of his marriage, he acquiesced to his wife's demands and joined her on the torturous march up the rungs of the society ladder.

Later, looking back, he realized his efforts were doomed from the start. As he and Angelina paraded through the social circuit, Rodrigo often felt like a monkey on a leash, jerked around by every whim of his wife. The shoe never fit.

What started as a small rift between them developed rapidly into an impassable channel. They divorced the year after they lost the baby—a boy, a stillbirth.

After the divorce, Rodrigo returned home to Easton, but soon realized that everything had changed. The Torres had died the year he graduated from college, their deaths only six months apart. A condominium building now occupied the space that had once been the home of the bait shop. Easton was no longer the sleepy fishing village of his childhood, but a rapidly-developing tourist destination.

He found Palm Island quite by accident—he went there to buy a boat. Rodrigo bought the boat, but he never left the island. He had been shrimping in the waters around Palm Island ever since. The last he heard of Angelina she had married a judge. He wished her well.

CHAPTER TWO

Rodrigo waited out the night in the small room adjacent to the intensive care unit, alternating between praying for the woman he had found on the dock and pondering his own past. Every four hours, he was allowed into the room with her for only a few moments. During these brief visits, he squeezed her hand and whispered into her ear, "Hold on."

Early the next morning, he wasn't sure of the exact time, the waiting room attendant called him to the front desk. He had a telephone call, and he could take it in the small room to the left. It was Mrs. Brodie.

"How is she?" Mrs. Brodie asked.

"Holding her own, or so they tell me," Rodrigo answered. Mrs. Brodie could hear the fatigue and anxiety in his voice.

"How are things on your end?" he asked.

"The same—we are holding our own. Naomi brought the children this morning. They're listless, confused. Naomi said they didn't sleep much. She's baking. That's how she deals with stress. And she's got the children helping her. They are managing."

"And you?"

"Oh, I'm alright. Feeling guilty. Helpless. Perhaps, if we had listened more closely to what the children had to say …"

"Nobody is to blame, Mrs. Brodie. There was no way we could have known."

"I suppose that you're right. Still, I'm glad you're staying with her."

"I won't leave her alone. Do we know any more about her?"

"A little. I spoke with the real estate woman who manages the property. The house belongs to a Rachel Edwards—I thought that was her name—and a man named Peter West."

"And Peter West? Is he her husband, boyfriend, what?"

"The realtor didn't know. All she knows is that Rachel Edwards is an attorney from Miami. There were two emergency numbers listed with the agency, one in New York and one in Miami."

"Did you call?"

"I did. I called both numbers. I didn't get an answer in Miami, but I did get an answering machine in New York for Peter West. I left a message. This morning I received a return call from him."

"What did he say?"

"Not much. It was odd. He said that Ms. Edwards was his *companion*. Whatever that means. I told him what happened. That she was in the Cartersville hospital. He said that he would get there as quickly as possible. I tried to ask him about any family that she might have, but he abruptly ended the conversation. He said that he would handle matters going forward and clicked off the receiver in my ear. Nice man."

"Sounds that way. I should hang up now. I don't want to stay away from the waiting room for very long."

"Call if there is any change."

"You know I will." Rodrigo hung up the receiver as the waiting room attendant came rushing toward him.

"Sir, you're needed in intensive care."

He didn't wait to hear more. As he pushed through the swinging doors into the unit, he saw a medical team swarming around Rachel's bed. There were several nurses, the attending physician and Dr. Luke had returned. Rodrigo tried to enter her room, but an intern held him back. A nurse pulled the curtain shut.

"You can't be in here; not now," the intern said.

"What's going on?" Rodrigo looked over the man's shoulder at the drawn curtain. Dr. Luke stepped from behind the curtain and saw Rodrigo.

"Wait outside," Dr. Luke said to him. "The worst is over. I'll be right out."

Rodrigo reluctantly obeyed, pacing back and forth in front of the window until Dr. Luke came outside.

"She went into cardiac arrest, but we managed to bring her back," Dr. Luke said. He placed his hand reassuringly on Rodrigo's shoulder.

"What now?" Rodrigo asked.

"We wait," Dr. Luke said.

"I won't leave her," Rodrigo replied. "I'll wait as long as it takes."

"She's very weak," Dr. Luke said. He appeared weary to Rodrigo. "I don't think that she's been taking care of herself. Depressed people don't. I suspect too much alcohol, too many pills and not enough food. But her heart is strong."

"She runs," Rodrigo said.

"What?"

"She jogs. Through the woods next to the Brodie estate. That's how the kids met her."

"Interesting. Do you happen to know anything else about her?"

"No, not really. I wish I did."

"I'll be straight with you, Rodrigo. She has lost the will to live. She wanted to die. The number of pills she swallowed tells us that."

At that moment, the doors to the intensive care hallway flew open. A tall, handsome man dressed in a tailored suit came barreling through the doors.

"You can't go in there," the receptionist was saying to his back.

The man stopped and looked Dr. Luke over, taking in his white lab coat and his nametag, which read Dr. Lucas Lowry.

Satisfied that he was speaking with a doctor, the man addressed Dr. Luke, while managing to ignore Rodrigo completely. "I'm here for Rachel Edwards," he announced. "Where is she?"

Dr. Luke stepped forward and Rodrigo stepped back. "I'm Dr. Lowry, one of Ms. Edwards' attending physicians."

The man hesitated and then extended his hand to Dr. Luke. "Peter West," he said. "I'm Ms. Edwards' fiancé. What happened?"

"Attempted suicide. Overdose. She washed a handful of sleeping pills down with a partial bottle of wine."

Peter looked stunned. "Are you sure?" he asked Dr. Luke.

"Quite sure, sir. Two children from the neighboring estate found her passed out on her dock." Dr. Luke pointed to Rodrigo before saying, "You have this man to thank that she is alive."

Peter looked at Rodrigo. "What … ?" Peter was at a loss for words.

"I had security take her to the clinic in Trinity," Rodrigo said. "It was Dr. Luke who saved her."

"She is not *saved,* yet." Dr. Luke interjected. "I pumped her stomach and had her transported here. She has been in intensive care since last evening."

"What exactly does all of this mean?" Peter asked. He looked confused and angry.

"It means that God only knows," Dr. Luke said. "We just had a scare. Cardiac arrest. We were able to start her heart—this time."

Peter ran his hand through his hair and shook his head in disbelief. "I knew that she was not herself lately, but this?"

"Unfortunately, yes," Dr. Luke said, looking from Peter to Rodrigo. He continued, "Her prognosis is guarded, at best. We don't know any more."

"And we don't know what precipitated this event," Dr. Luke directed this comment to Peter. "Perhaps, you could be of some help to us there."

Peter was visibly shaken as he listened intently to Dr. Luke's words.

"Suicide?" Peter said. "Are you sure? I knew that she was depressed, but I never imagined that she would try something like this. She had cancer—breast cancer—but her treatments are over. The prognosis there is good."

"Perhaps, you should sit down, Mr. West," Dr. Luke said. He pointed to a chair behind the nurse's station.

Peter sat in the chair, putting his elbows on his knees and his head in the palms of his hands.

Dr. Luke and Rodrigo waited patiently, giving Peter some time to process the shocking news.

Peter looked up at them with tears in his eyes. "She had trouble at work. I thought she went to Palm Island to regroup. You know, rest and relax. I had no idea how badly things were going for her. I didn't expect this. Suicide?"

"Of course, you didn't," Dr. Luke said.

"Can I see her?" Peter asked.

"You can. But she's in a coma. She will not respond to you."

Dr. Luke led Peter through the door and walked him over to Rachel's bedside. He then left the room and stood with Rodrigo at the glass window staring into the room.

They both saw Peter flinch as he looked at Rachel. They watched as his eyes scanned the room, a room full of i.v. poles, tubes and monitors. Even outside, they could hear the purr and hiss of the machines.

Peter ran his finger across her cheek, traced her lips. He leaned down and whispered something into her ear. Nothing. No response. He stood up as he continued to softly stroke her face.

After several minutes, Dr. Luke went in. He placed his hand on Peter's shoulder to get his attention.

"You'll have to leave now," he said. "You can't stay with her. You'll have to wait in the adjacent lobby. If there's any change, a nurse will summon you immediately. Otherwise, you can visit her every couple of hours for five minutes."

Rodrigo stood staring through the glass. The whole scene made him queasy. He didn't like this Mr. West.

And then it struck him. The man was too well-groomed. A close shave, slicked back hair, a starched shirt, no wrinkles in his suit. Had he stopped to shower and meticulously groom himself before coming to the hospital?

Mrs. Brodie told Mr. West that Rachel was critical. Rodrigo was sure of this. Mrs. Brodie did not make mistakes on details. And if he was her fiancé, why hadn't he known that she was in trouble? It didn't add up.

Rodrigo turned to leave as Peter and Dr. Luke walked out of her room. Dr. Luke stopped him. "Mr. West, I apologize for not introducing the two of you earlier. This is Rodrigo ..."

He stopped. Dr. Luke realized that he didn't know Rodrigo's last name. "I apologize, sir," he said to Rodrigo, "but I don't know your full name."

"Simply address me as Rodrigo. That's fine," he said to Dr. Luke, without taking his eyes off of Peter West.

"As I told you earlier, Rodrigo saved Ms. Edwards' life. But for him, she would have surely succumbed to the overdose without ever getting off of the island. And he has stayed with her during this entire ordeal."

Peter faced Rodrigo, looked him over and then thrust out his hand. "Thank you," Peter said curtly.

"You don't need to thank me," Rodrigo said, shaking Peter's hand firmly as he held his gaze.

Peter looked away first, and Rodrigo released his hand. "I only did what any decent human being would do."

"Of course," Peter responded. "Thank you for all that you've done. You're free to go. I'll see to Rachel's care from here on out."

Rodrigo looked at Peter. His voice was low and determined as he said to Peter, "I am not your servant to be dismissed. I will leave this hospital when I choose to do so."

"You are no longer needed." Peter's voice was as strong and determined as Rodrigo's.

"Is there more that I should be told," Peter said to Dr. Luke. His voice had picked up an acerbic tone. "This man's concern for my fiancé seems to exceed the bounds of being neighborly."

"Mr. West, there is no need ..."

Rodrigo interrupted Dr. Luke before he could finish his sentence. "I intend to stay here until she wakes up. If she wants me to go, then I will go. But not before."

"Very well, have it your way," Peter replied dismissively.

"Alright, gentlemen. I have other patients to see." Dr. Luke turned and left the room. Peter and Rodrigo retreated to opposite corners of the waiting room

The hours dragged slowly by for both Rodrigo and Peter.

Rodrigo tried to sleep, but all he could manage was a series of catnaps, all ending in bad dreams.

Peter, on his side of the room, paced the floor as Rachel's condition remained unchanged.

Every couple of hours, Rodrigo and Peter, alternatively and separately, were allowed in the room with her for a few moments. Dr. Luke orchestrated that arrangement before he left the hospital.

Rodrigo was dozing when a ruckus from Peter's side of the room woke him. A woman, who vaguely resembled Rachel, had stormed into the room. She and Peter stood arguing in hushed tones. But Rodrigo could hear their words.

"Susan, what are you doing here?" Peter said, rising to meet the woman.

"I might ask you the same question, Peter," she retorted, "but first tell me how she's doing?"

"She's holding on, but just barely," Peter answered, his hostility subsiding.

"Peter, why didn't you call me? How could you let this happen to her?"

"Let it happen! You're blaming me for this?"

"You are the one who left her. You must have known how that would affect her after all that's she's been through."

"For your information, Susan, and, not that it's any of your business, she left me."

"She's my sister and that damn well makes her attempted suicide my business. I love her, Peter. Which is more than I can say for you."

Rodrigo, who stood watching the exchange from his side of the room, realized that the battle lines had been drawn between these two long before now. When Peter and Susan's voices rose to a shout, he felt that he had no choice but to intervene. Rodrigo crossed the room taking long, swift steps and placed himself between Peter and Susan.

"In case you two haven't noticed," he said, "this is a hospital intensive care waiting room. Out of respect for Rachel, whom you both profess to care about, I suggest that you sit down and shut up. Focus on her and not on some simmering animosity between the two of you, which, from all appearances, seems to predate this incident."

Susan spun and turned her wrath on Rodrigo. "And who the hell might you be?"

"I am the person responsible for bringing her here. I found her near death at her home."

"Oh, I'm sorry," Susan said. "I didn't know. Thank you for saving her."

"Madam, she is not saved; not yet," Rodrigo shot back. "She is hanging on by a very thin, very tenuous thread. So why don't the two of you bury the hatchet for now, and let's bring some civility back into this room."

When neither responded, Rodrigo said, "Because you two appear to be oblivious to anything but your ongoing feud, I will point out the very obvious to you both: there are others waiting in this room. Have a little respect for them. Either shut up or take your quarrel outside."

"Of course, you're right," Susan said.

Rodrigo didn't wait to hear more. He pushed through the doors. He needed some air; some water; some space—he needed something. This room and these people were suffocating him.

Rodrigo paced the hallway trying to regain his composure. He did not intend to operate on the level of those two piranhas in the waiting room. Even now, he regretted that he had let them bring him down to their level. When he finally returned to the waiting room, it was quiet. He took his same seat. There were now three camps.

And so the vigil continued throughout the night and into the next day. Dr. Luke, when he arrived for his morning rounds, brought Rodrigo some fresh clothes and pulled some strings to get him access to the doctors' quarters for a quick shower and change. Naomi had sent enough food into Dr. Luke's office by Karen to feed the entire waiting room, so he didn't need to leave to eat.

Rodrigo gave up on trying to understand the bond that held him in the waiting room. All he knew was that he couldn't leave her; certainly not now, with the two hyenas waiting in the wings.

Susan and Peter must have found some sort of accommodations in Cartersville. Or at least that was Rodrigo's best guess. They both left and came back in fresh clothes.

An unspoken truce enveloped the three. They alternated taking turns for the five minutes every couple of hours that somebody got to spend with Rachel in her room. Another compromise brokered by Dr. Luke. During his five minutes, Rodrigo implored Rachel, in a soft whisper into her ear, "live, please live."

At the end of the second day, Dr. Luke came into the waiting room and summoned the trio into a smaller room adjacent to the intensive care unit. Once the three were inside, he closed the door and turned to face them.

"There has been a change in her condition," he said. "A change for the better. She has come out of the coma. She's still weak and needs some recovery time, but she has weathered this storm."

"Oh, thank God for that," Susan said. She collapsed into a chair, openly weeping. "Thank God for that news."

"When can I see her?" Peter asked.

"Well, we have some complications," Dr. Luke responded. "You all need to take a seat so we can talk."

Obediently, Rodrigo and Peter pulled up chairs, next to the still sobbing Susan. Rodrigo sat uneasily on the edge of his chair, while Peter sat rigidly, with his arms and legs crossed in an air of defiance.

Dr. Luke summed up the three. "Ms. Edwards started to come out of the coma this morning. The nurse on duty summoned me as she was instructed to do. At first, she was very disoriented, which is to be expected considering what she has been through. As I said earlier, she's still very weak, although I anticipate that we can move her into a regular room later this morning."

"But when can I see her?" Peter insisted.

"We have a problem with your request," Dr. Luke said. "She can't remember a lot of what happened. We have filled her in on some of the details. She knows that all three of you are here. But, for now at least, she doesn't want to see anyone other than Rodrigo."

"Him?" Peter said angrily, nodding his head in Rodrigo's direction.

"Yes, *him*," Dr. Luke snapped back at Peter. Dr. Luke was fed up with Peter's arrogant, demanding ways. "We told her that Rodrigo is the person who found her. Other than Rodrigo, she is refusing all visitors. And I think that we should respect her request. She is distraught and depressed. The last thing that we want to do at this time is further distress her."

Dr. Luke paused and looked at the three. When nobody made a comment he said, "And, we must remember, this was a serious, calculated attempt at suicide. The authorities must be notified, and she must be put immediately under psychiatric care. While she has physically weathered the storm, the underlying problems remain. She cannot simply be released to go home and try this again. The next time she may succeed. So there are some decisions to be made. But for now, she needs rest. We'll talk later." Dr. Luke turned to leave the room.

"I won't stand for this," Peter shouted. He jumped up and grabbed Dr. Luke's arm, spinning him around.

"Sir, I would kindly ask you to remove your hand from my arm." Dr. Luke's aggressive tone startled Peter, and he dropped his grip on Dr. Luke's arm immediately. "As far as your *standing* for anything, I don't see where you have any standing here at all."

Peter stepped back. He and Dr. Luke locked eyes. "According to your own words, sir, you are or were Ms. Edwards' fiancé. You are not a family member, and unless you can prove otherwise, I suggest that you have no legal basis here to stand for or against anything."

Peter turned to Susan. "Help me out here," he snapped at her.

Susan did not have time to answer before Dr. Luke took charge once again. "She cannot help you, sir. I am Ms. Edwards' doctor, and I make the calls. Ms. Edwards has made it evident to me and the medical staff at this hospital that she does not want to communicate with you. It is my medical opinion that putting her through the ordeal of an unwanted visit from you would only exacerbate her condition. In short, you will not be allowed to see her."

"I'll call my lawyers," Peter snarled, only partially subdued by the authority with which Dr. Luke had made his last statement. "We'll see about this," he barked. "She needs some *competent* medical attention. Obviously, there is nobody with the credentials necessary to treat her in this backwoods town."

"Call anybody, lawyer or otherwise, that you choose," Dr. Luke said. His voice was now calm and controlled. "That is entirely up to you. My only concern is my patient—what is in the best interest of my patient. And, at this time, that does not include a visit from you."

"How about me?" Susan said timidly from her chair. "I'm her sister. May I see her? Only for a moment. Please."

"I'm sorry, but you cannot." Dr. Luke spoke more kindly to Susan. "Your sister is quite overwhelmed by the enormity of this situation. She needs rest. Contrary to Mr. West's assertion, we have an extremely competent psychiatrist on staff. She is scheduled to meet with Ms. Edwards tomorrow. Perhaps, as her sister, you could be of some help to the psychiatrist. If at all possible, I suggest that you stay. But you will not be allowed to see her. Not now."

"Of course, I'll stay," Susan said. "My only concern is that she get the help that she needs. She's my sister. I love her. I only want what's best for her."

Dr. Luke turned to Rodrigo, who waited quietly in the wings. "Rodrigo, if you'll come with me, I'll take you to see her now."

Susan reached out and touched Rodrigo on the arm as he turned to follow Dr. Luke. "Wait, please," she begged. "May I have a word with you?"

Rodrigo stopped. "I'm afraid that I behaved dreadfully the day that I arrived," Susan said. "I was so upset. But, of course, that's not your fault, nor is it an excuse for my actions. Thank you for being there for my sister. Oh, and please tell her that I love her."

"Sure," Rodrigo said. "I'll tell her." He felt pity for this woman, who was so obviously concerned about her sister. Rodrigo followed Dr. Luke to Rachel's room.

Rachel's head was turned on the pillow, staring out of the window, when Rodrigo walked into her room. The tubes and monitors were gone, but she still looked frail and vulnerable.

As he stood looking at her, Rodrigo wondered for the thousandth time what had brought her to this point in life. A nagging concern in the back of his mind told him that her problems had something to do with that Peter West, in his fancy suit, with his arrogant attitude.

Rodrigo cleared his throat, but Rachel continued to look out of the window. He stepped closer to the bed before he spoke. "You asked to see me," he said softly to her back.

Rachel turned her head in the bed, and for the first time, Rodrigo saw her eyes. They were a murky color, some shade between green and brown, sunk low into their sockets, outlined by dark circles.

"Are you the man who found me on the dock?" she asked.

"Yes, I found you."

"Would you please tell me what happened that day. I can't remember much. Everything is still so foggy. I was hoping that you could fill in a few of the details."

"There's not much to tell. In fact, I was hoping to ask you the same question."

"Please, just tell me what you know," Rachel said in a tired and strained voice.

"It was late on Wednesday afternoon when I found you on your dock, unresponsive."

"What day is it today?"

Rodrigo had to think. "It's Saturday."

"Go on," she said.

"The twins, Millie and Mango, they found you. Millie was acting upset that afternoon. She wanted to go back to their fort— it's a tree in the woods where they play."

"I know the fort," Rachel said.

"What?"

"Never mind about that. Tell me what happened."

"Anyway, as I said, Millie was acting strangely. I waited a few minutes, and then I followed them. I met Mango on the path, running—distraught. I couldn't make much sense out of what he said other than someone needed help."

"Poor little man," Rachel said. Her groggy eyes weighed down even more with this news.

"I ran with him back to your house—or I guess it is your house—and I found you with Millie. You were lying on a lounge chair on the end of the dock. The pill bottle and the wine bottle were by your side." Rodrigo hesitated. He didn't want to upset her.

"It's alright," she said. "I want to know. Go ahead. Tell me the rest."

"It wasn't difficult for me to figure out what had happened. I carried you back to the Brodie estate. Security met me there. We took you to local doctor in Trinity—Dr. Lucas Lowry—and then he and I rode with you in the ambulance here. I've been waiting here for the running lady to come back to life."

"*The running lady?*"

"Yes, the running lady. That's the name the twins gave you."

"Oh, really. I thought that I was the princess." For a split second, Rodrigo thought, perhaps, he saw a faint smile form at the corners of her lips.

"They call you the running lady. At first, we thought the children had imagined you. But then I saw you myself."

"And let me guess. You are Rodrigo."

"I am."

"The children are quite fond of you," Rachel said. "They spoke of you often to me."

"Really?" Rodrigo was puzzled. "The children never told us that they had actually met you."

"Yes, a couple of months ago. They would hide in the woods and watch me when I ran. At first, it was eerie. I felt as if somebody was in the woods with me, but I never saw anyone."

"The fort!" Rodrigo said, his eyes lighting up. Things were beginning to add up.

"Yes, the fort. One day I happened to spot them. Up in that big oak tree. Then they followed me home. But they didn't show themselves; they hid behind a sago palm and watched me."

"They came as far as your house?"

"Oh, yes. Although they left quickly. I got the impression that they were forbidden to go off of the path."

"You're right. Those little dickens. I can't believe they went all of the way to your house. We had no idea. We all assumed that they played on the edge of the woods."

"By we, I assume that you are referring to yourself, Naomi and Mrs. Brodie."

"That's right."

"The twins and I became friends. We met often in the woods. They only came as far as my house a couple of times."

"May I ask you a personal question?"

"Sure, I guess that you're entitled. After all, you did save my life."

Rodrigo moved closer to the bed as Rachel kept talking.

"I know that I should be grateful, but gratitude is not exactly the emotion that I feel at this moment. I tried to end my life, and I would have succeeded but for your heroic efforts."

Rodrigo shrugged his shoulders. "Guilty," he said. "But what would you have done if you were faced with the same situation."

"I don't know," she said, her voice becoming strained. "Still, now I find myself in a dilemma. Not only am I forced to deal with being alive, but I will probably be branded as crazy. You know attempted suicide has some serious ramifications in this state. I'm a lawyer. I know these sorts of things," she said.

"I know these sorts of things as well," Rodrigo said. "But who are you?"

"I am a woman who in another life was a lawyer, a lover, a daughter and a sister. I had a home, a career, a relationship and a life.

"Without giving you all of the gory details, one day that all changed. One day I woke up to the fact that my world had disappeared and nothing had moved into that space to take its place. So I decided to kill myself.

"Hence the wine and the pills. But my plan hit a little glitch. My white knight, or in this case my dark knight, came rushing in to save me. And I now find myself about to be locked away in the loony bin for what I can only imagine will be some intensive therapy."

"I'm not sorry that I found you," Rodrigo said. "In spite of what you say, I don't believe that you really wanted to die. And I surely do not think that you are 'crazy.' I think that you just wanted to put the hurt on hold for a while. And you can do that here."

Rachel looked at this swarthy man, with the piercing black eyes. She was being much too hard on him. He meant well.

"I'm truly sorry for what I put you through, and I'm especially sorry about the children. I'm fond of those two 'little dickens' as you call them. I never intended for them to be hurt. I sent them home and made them promise not to come back. How are they coping? Do you know?"

"I won't lie to you," Rodrigo said. "The children were extremely traumatized over what happened to you. They're very precocious, but after all, they are very young children. This is all extremely difficult for them to understand. But they'll recover; especially, now that I can tell them their running lady is alright."

"Forgive me, but I'm starting to get very tired. If you don't mind, Mr. ... oh, I'm sorry, I don't even know your last name."

"There's no 'Mr.' anything. My name is Rodrigo."

"Well, Rodrigo, I'm afraid that you have put yourself to a lot of trouble for nothing, but thank you for caring. Now if you will leave me to myself."

"Sure," Rodrigo said. "But one more thing. Your sister, Susan, is here. She asked me to tell you that she loves you. Also, a man in a suit."

"Yes, yes, that would be Peter. The doctors told me that both Peter and my sister are here. I'm not up to seeing either of them."

"I'm sure they will understand." Rodrigo picked up a pen and paper off of the bedside table. "Here's my phone number. If you need anything, anything at all, just call."

"Thank you, but I don't think that I'll be needing anything. But thank you again. Will you close the door on your way out?"

"I will," Rodrigo said. He impulsively reached for Rachel's hand and gave it a squeeze. "I'm here if you need me. I'm just a phone call away. Your doctor—Dr. Lowry—I know him. He can always reach me, too."

Rodrigo turned and left, closing the door behind him. He knew that it was time for him to go.

CHAPTER THREE

After Rodrigo left, Rachel turned her face into the pillow. What have I done now, she thought. I even screwed up killing myself. Not only am I alive, I'll probably be Baker-Acted; locked away in some institution with all of the other pathetic misfits. Plus, both Peter and Susan were here. The entire tawdry mess was really too much. Why couldn't she have just died?

Rachel's head was swimming. She didn't hear the nurse come into the room. "I have a shot for you," she said. "It should make you sleep."

Thank you, God, Rachel thought. Sleep was the only refuge that she had left. Rachel felt the prick of the needle and then the warm rush of the drug as her body relaxed. Her last thoughts before she drifted back into sleep were of Peter.

Rodrigo left Rachel's room and went in search of Dr. Luke. He felt some relief that Rachel was out of the woods, but he knew that the reprieve was only temporary. She was badly wounded; there was no fight left in her.

"I'm looking for Dr. Luke," he said, to the nurse perched on a stool at the nurse's station, reviewing charts.

"I'll find him for you," she said. "Go back to the waiting area, and I'll send him to you."

Rodrigo saw Susan as soon as he walked into the waiting area. She sat with her arm pressed up against the window, cradling her head. He went over to her and tapped her shoulder lightly. She jumped.

"Sorry," he said, stepping back. Susan looked up at him. She looked weary, defeated. Rodrigo took the chair next to hers.

"Did you see Rachel?" Susan asked. She felt oddly comforted by his presence. She was drowning in a sea of confusion, and Rodrigo's presence felt like a life raft.

"I did," he said. He wanted to say something reassuring to her, but he wasn't sure that was possible.

"How is she?"

"I don't really know what to tell you. Physically, she seems to have survived the crisis. But emotionally, as you can imagine, she's still teetering on the brink. She didn't say much. Mostly, she wanted me to tell her what happened after I found her."

"What did happen?" Susan asked.

"I don't know much. She was already passed out when I got to her."

"Are the two of you friends?"

"No. I don't know her."

"Oh, I just assumed that you were since you've been here the entire time with her."

"I'm a friend of Mrs. Brodie—she owns the estate bordering your sister's property. I saw Rachel running through the woods, jogging, but we never met. She kept to herself."

Susan smiled weakly. "I'm not surprised. Rachel has always been a very private person, to say the very least."

"Mrs. Brodie's housekeeper cares for two small children. The children are almost six-years-old—twins. They found her. To make a long story short, they ran to me for help. I got her to Dr. Luke's office, he stabilized her, and then we brought her here in the ambulance. You know the rest."

"Thank God for those kids and you."

"May I ask you a question?"

"Certainly."

"Who is she? I don't know anything about her other than she lives next door to my friend. It's really none of my business, so don't answer unless you want to, but do you know why this happened. Why would she want to kill herself?"

"All I know is that she is depressed. But I didn't expect this. If I had, I would never have left her alone. She said that she went to Palm Island to regroup, to recuperate. She wanted to be alone."

Rodrigo sensed Susan needed to talk. He stayed silent, hoping she would say more.

After a few moments of silence, Susan continued.

"Lately, she has not been returning my calls. Or when she did, she wouldn't say much. I intended to come see her, I really did. Then security called telling me she had been taken to the hospital; they had my number in case of an emergency. I wish I had come to see her. I am feeling so guilty for leaving her alone."

Susan wiped tears from her eyes with a tissue she had been clutching tightly in her hand.

"Recuperate, from what?" Rodrigo asked.

"Rachel was a very successful attorney in Miami until she was diagnosed with cancer. She had radiation and a series of debilitating chemotherapy treatments."

"Miami?" Rodrigo was not sure he made the connection.

"Yes. She lives, or should I say lived, there. During the treatments, she started to spend time on Palm Island. It seemed to make her feel better to be away from Miami."

"Oh, I understand that," Rodrigo interjected. "Miami, well, in my opinion, Miami is not a place I could call home."

Susan smiled. "Me either."

"Go on, please."

"The treatments ended. The doctors said she was cured; or so we all hoped. I guess it's a waiting game. If you are cancer free for five years, that is deemed a cure."

"Hold that thought," Rodrigo said. He stood up and left the room only to return a few minutes later with two cups of coffee.

"Black? I couldn't find any cream or sugar. Sorry."

"No, no, black is fine. Thank you." Susan took the cup of coffee and tried a few sips.

"Wow! Strong," she said, smiling.

Rodrigo tasted the coffee. "Really, strong," he said, making a face as he tried his cup. "Please go on with your story."

"Where was I?" Susan took another sip of coffee. "Anyway, Rachel returned to Miami and to her job after the cancer treatments ended. I'm not sure exactly what went wrong, but I know there were problems with her work.

"Then her relationship with Peter went bad. She wouldn't tell me much. Particularly, where Peter was concerned. I suppose that you have surmised by now that he and I do not see eye to eye when it comes to Rachel."

"I did detect just a hint of animosity between the two of you. Remember, I refereed your fight in the waiting room."

"Oh, that's right. I'm sorry about that. He just makes me so furious."

"For what it is worth, he seemed to be the instigator."

"And all of this talk about him being her fiancé." Susan shook her head, and her speech became quite animated. "That's the first time I have heard of *that*.

"The last I heard they had broken up. And now he shows up here claiming to be her fiancé. Maybe they were seeing one another again, but I'm quite certain they weren't contemplating marriage. Rachel would have told me that."

"Are you sure?" Rodrigo asked gently. "Apparently, there was a lot you didn't know about her."

"Agreed," Susan admitted.

"I never liked him from the start," Susan said angrily. "Then when she was sick, he all but deserted her. In my opinion, he treated her deplorably. But she made excuses for him. Said that it was his work. Work—her life was on the line! What could have been so important? We eventually just agreed to disagree on him."

Susan sat back in her chair and took a big slug of coffee. Talking about Peter had her very worked up.

"If first impressions count, I don't particularly care for him myself," Rodrigo said.

"Before her illness, Rachel was confident, determined, so sure of herself," Susan said.

"The only weak link I could see in her life was Peter. She seemed powerless over him. And then the cancer came and sucked the life right out of her. When the treatments were over, she had survived the disease, but it had taken its toll on her. Emotionally she was spent. She left her job. She just up and walked off one day. That was so not like Rachel. I only found out when her office called looking for her. On a hunch, I found her at the house on Palm Island. I came here to see her. She told me nothing other than she wanted to be left alone."

Susan sat the coffee on the table and massaged her temples with her fingers.

"We don't have to keep going," Rodrigo said. "Maybe, you need to go get some rest."

"Actually, talking to you helps me," Susan replied. "It helps me to focus, helps me to try and make sense of all that's happened."

"Then keep talking if you want to. I have no place that I need to go."

Susan smiled over at him. "Has anybody ever told you that you are a really kind person?"

"Maybe," he said, returning her smile.

"Anyway … I hoped the time on Palm Island would help her. Obviously, I was wrong." Susan's face clouded over.

Rodrigo instinctively reached over and put his arms around her as she started to cry again.

"This is not your fault; you must know that," he said. And then he just let her cry.

"I can't in my heart believe that she really wanted to kill herself," Susan sobbed. "For God's sake. She's my sister. I love her."

"She loves you, too," Rodrigo said. "She asked me to tell you that. She's simply too tired and confused to see you now." He felt sorry for this woman. A small lie couldn't hurt.

Dr. Luke entered the room and came over to Rodrigo and Susan. He exchanged a concerned look with Rodrigo.

"I am so sorry to intrude," he said.

"It's alright," Susan replied, sitting up and wiping her eyes on that same tattered tissue she still clutched in her fist.

"Here. I almost forgot," Rodrigo said, pulling some folded tissues out of his pocket. He handed the tissue over to Susan. "I brought you these."

"You really are a kind man," she said, taking the tissues. She wiped her eyes and blew her nose.

"The nurse said you were searching for me," Dr. Luke said to Rodrigo. "She told me you would be in here."

"Yes," Rodrigo answered. "I wanted an update."

"I can accommodate you," Dr. Luke said.

"And I hoped to find you here as well," Dr. Luke said to Susan. "We need to talk."

"Would you mind if I stayed?" Rodrigo asked Susan.

"Not at all," she replied.

"I suppose we need that other fellow, Peter, as well," Dr. Luke said. "He professes to be her fiancé. Perhaps, he should be included in this discussion."

"The fiancé status is uncertain," Susan said. "I would prefer to leave him out of this conversation."

"You're the only blood relative present. I'll honor your wishes," Dr. Luke said.

"For now, unfortunately, all that I can tell the two of you is basically what you already know. Ms. Edwards is a troubled woman. Physically, she will recover from this attempted suicide, but that's not her primary problem. The key is her mental health.

"For that reason, I have called in a favor from a colleague of mine. She is a psychiatrist working here in Cartersville at the mental health clinic. She travels over from the university, where she teaches, to see patients a couple of days a week. I have asked her to do an evaluation of Rachel."

"Will she do that?" Susan asked.

"I think she will," Dr. Luke said. "I simply can't release her from the hospital even if she were strong enough to leave; which she is not. She has attempted suicide. I am almost certain she will try suicide again if her mental condition is left untreated."

"Please, Dr. Luke," Susan said, "We must help her."

"Of course," Dr. Luke said reassuringly.

"Yes, please," Rodrigo added, "there must be something you can do."

"For now, she will remain in the hospital under my care. Perhaps, Dr. Artemus, the psychiatrist whom I called, can shed some light on how best to proceed from here."

One week later, Rachel was transferred to a private mental health facility close to the university. Dr. Artemus agreed to treat her there.

Rachel reluctantly accepted the arrangement. She knew that they could Baker Act her—lock her away in a state facility, for a brief period, if they chose. So she agreed to go to the private clinic. Mostly, she wanted to rest. She hoped to be released within a week. She stayed two months.

The first day that she woke up at the facility, she felt frantic—like a prisoner, not someone who was mentally ill. That label didn't sit well with her.

No matter how many times Dr. Artemis told Rachel that depression was an illness, it didn't make her feel any better. Intellectually, the diagnosis was tolerable, but she felt like a *nutcase,* locked away in a loony bin.

She wondered if others knew where she was and what they would think if they knew. Surely, Peter knew. And where was he today? At work. With his girlfriend? Parading around New York as if the world had not turned upside down.

And Nancy? The managing partner at the law firm. What was it the office had labeled Nancy? Oh, yeah—our unsinkable Molly Brown. What would Nancy think? Rachel certainly wasn't unsinkable; in fact, she had gone down like a rock.

Jonas McNeil—the rat bastard who had taken her place at the firm? Would he revel in her defeat? Now that his competition was gone, he was sure to be the next partner. She told herself that she didn't care. That she didn't care about Peter or Nancy or McNeil or that damned law firm.

But she couldn't even pretend to herself that she didn't care about Susan. A sister who had always been there for her. And the twins. Two innocent little children who called her their friend. What hell had she inflicted on Susan and the twins when their only fault was to care about her?

Reality hit her hard. Here she was in the *nuthouse*, and here she would stay, unless, of course, she could find a way to convince young Dr. Artemus, the female Don Quixote in blue jeans and a T-shirt, that she was not certifiably crazy, just tired and confused.

Tired. Why couldn't the incident be written off as extreme fatigue. That was the real problem. She was basically too damn worn out and beat up to go on. Rachel allowed herself to settle on the "tired" label as she closed her eyes and drifted off to sleep.

In the weeks to come Rachel learned that Dr. Artemus was not one to be easily manipulated. She didn't give Rachel anti-depressants and wait for the miracle. Instead, she "engaged" her.

That was psych lingo for talk therapy. In the beginning, Rachel obediently answered Dr. Artemus' questions, although all of her answers were calculated to line up with the extreme fatigue angle.

Eventually, Rachel had to accept the fact that her self-diagnosis of extreme fatigue was not going to fly with Dr. Artemus. She would need to try a different tactic. Dr. Artemus, much to Rachel's dismay, was turning out to be tougher nut to crack than Rachel had initially anticipated.

Rachel wondered why she had ever agreed to let Dr. Artemis be the deciding factor on her release. Oh yeah, because that was the only way she got shipped to this fancy clinic and not to a state institution.

So Rachel dug in; she got with the program, a program that required her to attend the group therapy sessions. While Dr. Artemus could coerce her into sitting in the group therapy circle,

Rachel decided early on that she could win this particular battle with Dr. Artemus by feigning participation.

The very idea of pouring her guts out to total strangers was one that Rachel found quite revolting. What good could this group pity party possibly do anyone? Still, she would do almost anything to leave this place—for her, it was time to go.

Over time the watch and wait strategy failed. It was not humanly possible to sit and hear others tell their stories and simply listen.

Slowly, but ever so surely, Rachel started to listen, really listen, and then talk. Without the sleeping pills and wine, the fog began to lift.

With listening and talking, eventually came learning. Rachel's first epiphany was her realization, and then her acceptance, of the futility of trying to control the world and everything in it, including people.

No matter how hard she tried, control wasn't always within her power. Some parts of life were beyond control. And trying to control, that which was ultimately uncontrollable, could prove to be exhausting, even overwhelming. It could make one very tired. Sentencing yourself to be a Sisyphus in your own life was tiring and doomed to failure.

Life could change. It always did change. Sometimes change was good; sometimes change was not so good. The really scary part for Rachel was her inability to control the change or to even know ultimately how the change would turn out.

Epiphany number two: For somebody who prided herself on being fearless on the outside, on the inside she was really quite fearful. What do you do about that?

Cope? Or so she was told. Sometimes the most you could hope for was to go with the flow. Adapt. Ride it out, learn to change with the change. Rowing upstream all of the time, can make you very—well—tired.

Epiphany number three: Other people mattered. For the first time in her life, Rachel looked around her. She really looked at other people for the first time. She looked at them as people, with all of their complex needs and emotions and not as mere objects to be used to enhance her own lifestyle.

Here, at this clinic, all pretenses were quickly abandoned. No fancy clothes, no fancy cars, no plaques, no trophies, no diplomas detailing achievements littering the walls.

Real scars, real bruises, real wounds, all exposed for all to see. Stories were told, and retold. Trauma lived and relived. Empathy and sympathy, passion and compassion acted out on a human stage.

Rachel thought about the people from her own life. How much did she know, or really even care, about them?

Mary? For several years they worked together, but all that she knew about her, really knew, was that Mary had a husband and then she didn't. That she acted happy while always looking sad. For Rachel, Mary had been a tool. Really nothing more, nothing less.

What about Nancy Kerry-Green? Nancy who needed to have two last names to make herself appear bigger than life. Was all of that false bravado just a show? Nancy had been a tool. Really nothing more; nothing less.

Jonas McNeil? What fueled his obsession with success? The same thing that fueled hers: insecurity. He was an obstacle. Really nothing more; nothing less.

The people here with her were all a story. Some far more tragic than hers; some far less. All forced to let go of control, to accept life, to change, to cope—or not.

With startling clarity Rachel came to understand that some would not, some could not, survive. Some would go home and contrive a way to keep going. Some would go home and thrive. Some would go home only to come back. Some would die trying.

It really was a choice when all was said and done. She had been so bogged down in self-pity that she had not even tried to accept, must less adapt to, a new normal.

Epiphany number five: She really didn't want to die. She wanted the courage to change, to adapt and to grow. She wanted to not just survive, but maybe—just maybe—she could thrive.

Maybe, it was time to go. But then Dr. Artemus said not yet.

So she dug in and worked some more. No more epiphanies for her: other than that's life. You can choose to live it—or not. You can choose to embrace life with all of its changes—or not.

And then she started to feel better. One day the sun came through the window, and she consciously made the choice to get up and look outside. She made a choice to look forward, not back. She made a choice to go home and try this thing called a life again.

Rachel told Dr. Artemus that it was time for her to go. Dr. Artemus smiled and said, "soon, but not yet." Rachel stayed on.

This time with a new attitude; she felt grateful. Gratitude was something new for her. Like new shoes she had to try on gratitude; walk around in gratitude; break in gratitude; and finally, let gratitude take charge.

Rachel realized that with gratitude it was possible not to lose heart. In fact, with gratitude, it was possible to corral her wild heart and take it along for the ride. Suddenly, life just didn't look doable, it looked exciting. Anticipation, that life could and would get better, took root.

It was time to go.

"Yes, it is quite possibly time to go," Dr. Artemus said, "but you must agree to some conditions for going home before I release you."

Dr. Artemus called in Dr. Luke for a consult.

"Rachel believes that she is ready to leave here," Dr. Artemus said to Dr. Luke after he had settled into a chair in her office.

"What about you, Dr. Artemus? What do you believe?"

"Honestly, I believe that she is pushing to go too soon. She has made a lot of progress. Unfortunately, I think that might conceivably translate into overconfidence in Rachel's case."

"Then why let her go?"

"Because I can't keep her here against her will. Sure, she gave me the authority to determine her release date, but we all, including Rachel, always knew that once she is no longer a danger to herself, we must release her."

"Why did you call me?"

"I think that I have a proposed compromise for Rachel. That's where I need some help from you."

"I'm listening."

"My primary concern regarding Rachel's release at this time is that she insists on returning to her home on Palm Island. I'm uneasy with that arrangement. I don't want her to be so alone."

"I am not a psychiatrist, but I share your concern."

"She might very well start to isolate herself again."

"Agreed."

"I suggested that she consider going to live with her sister Susan, but she vetoed that idea immediately."

"Okay, but I am unsure of what you are asking of me," Dr. Luke said.

"She will leave here," Dr. Artemus said, "and most likely return to Palm Island. In the short-term, she should do well. It's the long-haul that bothers me. With no support system, alone on the island, she could regress, relapse. I have an idea; I wanted to run it past you."

"Still listening," Dr. Luke said, somewhat intrigued.

"She wants to return to Palm Island. The problem is the fact that she lives alone; she lives a somewhat isolated life on Palm Island."

"That is my understanding," Dr. Luke said, still uncertain of where this conversation was leading.

"Rachel has spoken of a neighbor next door, a Mrs. Brodie. "Do you know her?"

"I know who she is, but I have never met her. She owns the estate where the twins visit."

"Rachel has bonded with the twins. I was hoping the neighbor, this Mrs. Brodie, might be of some help. If Rachel could establish a relationship with Mrs. Brodie and see the children, then I wouldn't be as concerned about her becoming too isolated."

"I have a better idea," Dr. Luke said.

"Now I'm listening," Dr. Artemus replied.

"Stay with me here. This gets a little complicated. My assistant is Karen Ivey; Karen's mother is Mrs. Brodie's housekeeper. Has been for over thirty years. Naomi—that is the housekeeper's name—is the person who brings the twins to the Brodie estate. She is a fine person as is her daughter. Are you still with me?"

"I think so."

"I personally have not visited Mrs. Brodie's home, but I'm told by Karen that it's a certifiable mansion. Plenty of room. Acres of grounds. Only a small forest of trees separates it from Rachel's home."

"I am familiar with those woods. Rachel told me some of this. She was jogging in the woods when she met the twins. But what are you proposing?"

"This. Perhaps, we could transition her back into her own home by initially moving her onto the Brodie estate. That is, of course, if Mrs. Brodie will agree."

"Will she?"

"I wouldn't have even suggested this arrangement, if I wasn't familiar with Mrs. Brodie and her character through Karen. From what Karen tells me about Mrs. Brodie, I have surmised that she is a gentle, kindhearted older lady. Lonely herself. She might be amenable to helping."

"That sounds like a workable solution," Dr. Artemis said. "Still, forgive me; but from my conversations with Rachel, I did not get the impression that she has ever even met Mrs. Brodie. Am I missing something here?"

"No. I don't think they have met. However, they both are intensely attached to the twins. The key I believe to convincing both of them to agree to this arrangement is their mutual concern for the children. This could be a healing time for the twins, both of whom were traumatized by finding Rachel after her suicide attempt. Am I on track here?"

"Yes," Dr. Artemus said, "I believe you are. But do you really think that Mrs. Brodie would agree to take in a perfect stranger?"

"For the twins, yes."

"Do you think Rachel would agree to this arrangement?"

"For the twins, yes. I think so."

Dr. Artemus and Dr. Luke stared intently at each other as each weighed in their minds the viability of what they were proposing.

"We are asking a lot of both Rachel and Mrs. Brodie," Dr. Luke said. "From what I can surmise, both appear to be fiercely independent and both appear to value their privacy."

"Very true. Perhaps, this would be a bridge too far for both of them," Dr. Artemus said.

"Under ordinary circumstances, I would tend to agree with you," Dr. Luke replied. "But these are extraordinary people and extenuating circumstances.

"Mrs. Brodie took in the twins. She has grown to love them—is very protective of them. According to Karen, this whole episode really had a negative impact on the them. You're the psychiatrist here, but wouldn't having Rachel on the estate benefit the twins?"

"Yes, I think it would," Dr. Artemus said. "I have not met with the twins, but such an episode as the one they have experienced, would typically traumatize children, especially children this young. It is very difficult for children to work through such a harrowing experience with words only. Interacting with Rachel, seeing that she is truly alright, would do so much more than simply telling them that she is alright. Yes, at first blush, this seems like a very positive initiative for the children."

"My guess is that Mrs. Brodie would take in Rachel even without the twins," Dr. Luke responded enthusiastically. "But add them to the equation, and I'm almost certain that she would agree."

"As for Rachel, she also is attached to the twins. Their company could be therapeutic for her. She is still internalizing a lot of guilt about her perceived negative impact on them."

"I am liking this idea more and more," Dr. Luke said, sliding up to sit on the edge of his seat. "Now add this to the equation. Not only would Rachel be interacting with the children, but she would have Mrs. Brodie and Naomi as well. Naomi has a nurturing spirit. And Mrs. Brodie did open herself up to the twins. These women would make Rachel comfortable, I'm sure of that.

"And Rodrigo, the man who found her on the dock the day of the overdose, is also on the estate frequently. Since he brought Rachel to my office, he and I have become friends, of sorts. Another loner, I might add."

Dr. Artemus smiled. "Go on," she said,

"Rachel knows him—well, sorta. The point I am trying to make is this: Rachel would have plenty of space and privacy— the estate is that large and more. She would be living in close proximity to her own home, with the added benefit of a built-in support group."

"Sounds like our answer," Dr. Artemus said, smiling broadly this time. "There's just one problem. Really two. Getting Mrs. Brodie on board, and more difficult still, getting Rachel to agree."

"I'll volunteer to enlist Mrs. Brodie," Dr. Luke said. "I don't foresee any real problems there. But it will be up to you to persuade Rachel. It may take me a couple of days to bring Mrs. Brodie on board, but I can almost guarantee that my job will be the easier one."

Dr. Artemus rose from her chair and warmly extended her hand to Dr. Luke. "Thank you so much. In an abundance of caution, I won't discuss it with Rachel until I hear back from you."

Later that day, Dr. Luke called Rodrigo. "I need a favor," he said. "It's about Rachel. Could you stop by my office?"

"Sure. I've been meaning to stop in and ask about her. I hadn't planned on shrimping today. How about this afternoon?"

"That's fine."

Rodrigo drove into Trinity late in the afternoon. He wanted to arrive as the Clinic was closing. He was greeted in the reception area by Karen.

"I ain't seen you since the day you brought in Rachel Edwards," Karen said. "We never got to meet proper-like. But I feel like I know you 'cause my mother and the twins talk 'bout you all the time. I'm Karen Ivey, Naomi's daughter."

"It's a pleasure to meet you, Karen. And I feel like I know you as well. You are the topic of conversation frequently on the Brodie estate. All good I might add. The twins love you, and your mama is so proud that she can't speak your name without grinning."

"Well, I don't know 'bout all of that, but it's good to meet you, too. Nice to put a face with a name. Take a seat. I'll tell Dr. Luke you're here. He's got one case of whooping cough left, and then he's all yours, 'less a 'mergency comes through the door."

"Thanks," Rodrigo said. "I don't mind waiting. I didn't make an appointment."

"There is no such thing as an appointment 'round here," Karen said, laughing. "You get sick. You go to the Clinic. That's the way it works."

Pointing to a door at the end of the hall, Karen added, "I know that he was lookin' for you to stop in. Wait in his office. He won't mind."

When Dr. Luke came into his office, Rodrigo stood gazing out of the window at the shrimp boats unloading in the harbor. He heard the door open and close and turned to face Dr. Luke, who was stripping off his white coat.

"Sit, sit," he said to Rodrigo, pointing to a chair. Dr. Luke sat down in the chair behind his desk.

"No, thanks. I'll stand if it's all the same to you. You said this was about Rachel. How is she?"

"Better. Much better, or so I'm told by Dr. Artemus, her psychiatrist. In fact, she's so improved that Dr. Artemus is recommending that she leave the facility. That's why I called you."

"Me? What does her leaving have to do with me?"

"We have a small problem. I thought you might could help."

"A problem?"

"Of sorts."

"Tell me what you need. I'll do what I can."

"The problem is this: Where does she go when she leaves the hospital? Rachel insists that she wants to return to her home on Palm Island. While Dr. Artemus agrees that returning to the island is a good place for Rachel to start, her concern arises from the fact that if she returns to her house on the island, she will be alone."

"I don't really understand where you are going with this," Rodrigo said, raising a suspicious eyebrow.

Dr. Luke forged ahead. "While she has made progress at the treatment center, her condition is still fragile, or so Dr. Artemus says. Do you remember, Dr. Artemus?"

"I have not met her, but I know she took over Rachel's care after leaving the hospital."

"That's correct. Well, it is the opinion of Dr. Artemus, and for what it is worth I agree with her assessment, that Rachel's return to her island home could prove to be traumatic. It's the scene of her attempted suicide. There is the danger that she will isolate herself there again. Dr. Artemus and I are concerned about that scenario."

"For what is worth, that makes sense to me, too. But what has this got to do with me? How can I help? Are you suggesting that I look in on her?"

"Actually, we need a little more than that." Dr. Luke twisted up his face in such a way as to suggest to Rodrigo that the request for a big favor was coming his way.

"Dr. Artemus and I have a proposed solution, but we need your help."

"With all due respect, stop beating around the bush and tell me what you need from me. If I can help, I will."

"Okay. The solution that we propose is this: Rachel returns to Palm Island, but she moves in with Mrs. Brodie for the short term. What do you think? You know Mrs. Brodie well. Is this possible?"

A surprised look rolled across Rodrigo's face, and he didn't immediately answer. Instead, he turned to look back out of the window at the harbor.

He watched as ruddy-faced men in slickers and thigh-high rubber boots shoveled shrimp from the ships' holding tanks into large coolers. As he watched, he pondered what Dr. Luke had said.

Dr. Luke waited patiently. According to Karen, and he trusted her insight here, Rodrigo knew Mrs. Brodie better than anyone. He wanted Rodrigo to carefully consider the proposed course of action.

After several minutes, Dr. Luke stood up and walked up to the window next to Rodrigo.

"That's why I picked this room as my office," he said to Rodrigo. "I like to watch the boats; see the water. I grew up in New York, out by the harbor. I would pick up odd jobs out on the docks when I was a boy. I find that the water makes me feel peaceful."

"I understand," Rodrigo said. "I grew up on a boat. Live on one now. If God's willing, I'll be on the water the rest of my life."

"As for Rachel," Rodrigo said, "I think that it's a good idea—Rachel moving in with Mrs. Brodie." Rodrigo never took his eyes off of the boats as he spoke.

"I'm glad that you think so," Dr. Luke said. "Because this is where I need your help."

"How so?"

"I don't know Mrs. Brodie, but I am told that you and she are close friends."

"I suppose as close as two loners-at-heart can be," Rodrigo replied wistfully.

"I also know what Karen and Naomi tell me about her," Dr. Luke added. "They tell me that Mrs. Brodie is a generous and compassionate woman. Still, we are asking a lot of her. Do you think that she will agree to have Rachel stay with her for a short while?"

Rodrigo didn't answer right away. He watched the shrimpers and weighed his answer.

Then he said, "I can't speak for her. But my guess is that she will agree. If not for Rachel's sake—and don't get me wrong Mrs. Brodie would help a neighbor—then for the sake of the twins."

Rodrigo turned to face Dr. Luke. "I am not blaming Rachel, but this entire ordeal has affected them. They don't understand death—certainly not suicide. They feel guilty. As if they're to blame."

"Dr. Artemus expressed her concern for the twins as well," Dr. Luke interjected. "She thinks this arrangement will help them as well as Rachel.

"I hope she is right," Rodrigo said. "They are afraid. I think they believe something or somebody hurt Rachel. They can't grasp that she would hurt herself. Since the day they found her on the dock, they haven't gone back into the woods. They never speak of the fort. None of us realized how strongly they had bonded with her."

"Karen tells me that Millie hasn't slept well since that day," Dr. Luke said. "That both she and Mango are clinging to her, to Naomi, to their grandmother. She's tried to talk with them. But like you said, it's difficult for them to grasp what happened. Dr. Artemus and I discussed this exact topic. Rachel staying with Mrs. Brodie could be therapeutic for them as well as for her. Would you be willing to speak with Mrs. Brodie?"

"Sure. I had planned on stopping by the estate tomorrow," Rodrigo said. He shook hands with Dr. Luke and started to leave.

Rodrigo stopped at the door and turning to Dr. Luke, he said, "Now that I have had a few minutes to think about it, you can tell Dr. Artemus that it's settled. I'm sure Mrs. Brodie will take Rachel into her home."

"Thank you, Rodrigo. One down and one to go."

"What?" Rodrigo asked, puzzled.

"It's now Dr. Artemus who has her work cut out for her," Dr. Luke said. "We agreed not to broach the subject with Rachel until we had Mrs. Brodie's answer. I know that you haven't spent any time with Rachel; but according to Dr. Artemus, she is a strong-willed woman."

"So I've heard," Rodrigo said. Now it was Dr. Luke who looked puzzled.

"From her sister," Rodrigo added. "That's what her sister told me at the hospital."

"I'll call you in the morning," Rodrigo said. "But, as I said before, from my end, I believe that it's a done deal."

Rachel was eventually persuaded to move to Mrs. Brodie's. After a week of negotiating, she and Dr. Artemus agreed that she would stay with Mrs. Brodie, but that she was free to visit her home and come and go as she pleased. On those terms, Rachel was released from the facility.

Rodrigo offered to drive over and pick her up; but Dr. Luke politely declined his offer. Both he and Dr. Artemus believed that he was the better candidate. After all, Rachel had only had the one brief conversation with Rodrigo at the hospital.

"It's a trust issue," Dr. Artemus explained to Rodrigo and Dr. Luke. She had asked to meet with them both, and they had driven over to the hospital together.

"Her only relationship with anyone in the household is her friendship with the children. More importantly, she will be depending on others. Rachel's trust of people has been betrayed, and she's anticipating the worst. Add that to the fact that she's leaving the security of the in-patient environment, and she's one anxious lady. Better that she start off with a familiar face.

Rodrigo, it will be your job to help me monitor how well she is adjusting."

"I'm there almost every day. That won't be a problem."

"Then it's settled," Dr. Artemus said, rising to leave. "I will release her tomorrow. Dr. Luke if you could be here at nine o'clock, I will have her ready to go."

CHAPTER FOUR

Rachel was up well before daylight to prepare for the trip. Even with the aid of her sleeping medication, which she had not taken for a long time, she still tossed and turned the entire night. How had she let Dr. Artemus talk her into moving in with perfect strangers?

Dr. Artemus could be very persuasive, that's how, Rachel told herself, regretting her decision to go to the Brodie estate. Dr. Artemus had practically sold the place as a bed-and-breakfast.

Rachel laid awake reliving her earlier conversation with Dr. Artemus. She raised her objections, and Dr. Artemus shot them down. What about privacy? "It is a huge estate, and you will have your own wing of the house." What about payment—she wasn't a charity case? "So pay," Dr. Artemus said. What about solitude? She was accustomed to being alone. "So walk to your house as often as you like," Dr. Artemus suggested. "You are *the running lady*, so running over to your house shouldn't present a problem," Dr. Artemus said, laughing.

Still fretting, she reviewed the positives. She would be close to home and on the island that she loved so much. But, in her heart, Rachel knew the deciding factor had been her concern for the twins.

The welfare of the twins swayed her. She had a lot of guilt about what she put them through. When Dr. Artemus explained that her visit to the Brodie estate would help the twins, she knew that she had no choice but to go.

Now lying awake in the middle of the night, Rachel had her doubts—she had serious doubts. The twins needed this she kept telling herself.

And maybe she needed this living arrangement, too. She wanted some more time on the island. It was much too soon to return to her home in Miami—much too soon!

She wanted to go back to Palm Island. Still, if she was really honest with herself—and after hours of Dr. Artemus and therapy she was learning how to be honest, really honest with herself—she had to admit that facing the house, being there alone, did make her anxious.

She didn't want to go to Susan's. Susan had her own life with Ed and the kids, and Susan had already given her so much time during the cancer. Moving in with Susan was not an option, even a temporary one.

Going to live with Peter in New York was out of the question. She wasn't ready to make another try with Peter. Not yet.

Peter had called fairly often, or what seemed like often to Rachel, while she was in the recovery clinic. Who knew what "often" meant where she and Peter were concerned?

Rachel had not taken his calls—Dr. Artemus had advised against Peter's calls while she was in therapy. Still, Dr. Artemus shared with her whenever Peter called to check on her progress.

When she refused his calls, he sent flowers—a first for Peter. And then, much to her surprise, he wrote her letters. The letters she cherished—reading them and then packing the pages away to read again.

In the letters, Peter asked her to give their relationship another try. But she wasn't ready; not yet. Still, she harbored deep, lingering feelings for him, and she secretly hoped their relationship might work out in time. The letters she shared with no one, not even Dr. Artemus.

At some point in the night, Rachel, in spite of her worry and angst, slept. And then it was morning.

Rachel shook off her fear of living at the Brodie estate and zipped up her small bag. I'm going, and that's that, she told herself. She looked around her room one last time, and then walked out into the lobby to wait for Dr. Luke.

As Dr. Luke approached the main lobby of the facility, he saw Rachel. She looked small and vulnerable to him as he saw her pacing the floor like a high school girl waiting for her first date to arrive.

He hoped that she was ready. Dr. Artemus believed that Rachel was ready to go, and he trusted her professional judgment. Still, he was glad that she was going to the Brodie estate and not home alone.

Rachel didn't even allow Dr. Luke to come into the lobby. As soon as she saw that it was him getting out of the car, she came bursting out of the door.

"Let's go," she said. She opened the back door, threw her small bag inside and was sliding into the passenger's seat before he could even get out a hello.

They rode in silence for quite some distance. Finally, Dr. Luke broke the ice and attempted conversation.

"I think that you will really like Mrs. Brodie," he said. "I've never met her, but I am told by a very reliable source that she is a gentle, kind soul and ..."

"Please," Rachel said, abruptly interrupting him. "I don't even know this woman. I'm going to live in her home as a perfect stranger. I only agreed to this absurd arrangement to get out of the treatment center. And to help the twins." Her voice softened a little when she mentioned the twins.

"I'm going back to my house as quickly as possible," she added.

"Of course, you are," Dr. Luke said. "That has always been the goal as I understand it. Nevertheless, I believe that if you'll give Mrs. Brodie a chance, you'll discover that she has lived a full and interesting life. She has wisdom that only old age can offer."

"Of course," Rachel said dismissively.

Dr. Luke was not so easily deterred. "I know you're skeptical, Rachel. But if I may give you some advice, try to stay open. Give this living arrangement a chance."

"I won't be there long enough to get to know her," Rachel replied, while looking out of her window at the pine forest flashing by. It felt good to be outside, riding in a car.

"And I intend to pay," she added. "I won't be some charity case." Dr. Luke couldn't help but chuckle at this suggestion.

"Mrs. Brodie has enough money to buy Palm Island a couple of times over, or so I am told," he said. "It's not money that she needs. If you try, Rachel, you may be able to repay Mrs. Brodie's kindness with something other than dollars. She has had some troubles of her own."

Dr. Luke turned onto the beach highway. He and Rachel fell silent once again.

The sight of the water glimmering in the bay and the warmth of the sun pouring through the window on her face lifted Rachel's spirits. She dug around in her purse, looking for her sunglasses. I'll get through this, she told herself.

The drive by the water reminded her of the day that she and Peter had driven along the beach together in Miami. She had telephoned Peter to tell him that she was being released from the facility.

It took her several failed attempts before she was able to actually dial the number. When he answered, it felt strange to hear his voice; although, thorough all of the awkwardness, he seemed genuinely pleased that she had called.

When she told him that she was leaving the facility, he insisted that she come to New York and stay with him. The line went silent when she didn't accept his offer. But, if he was upset, he quickly recovered. The island might be good for her he finally admitted. His offer would stay open.

It took a lot of strength on her part to refuse his offer. A part of her wanted desperately to feel the security of her old relationship with Peter; but things had changed.

At this point, if they had any chance at all, they would need to form a new relationship. And she wasn't ready for that.

She feared that any dependence by her upon him now would ultimately frighten him off. He had bailed out quickly enough during her illness. She blamed herself for that, at least partially—always putting her work ahead of him.

Dr. Artemus had worked with Rachel to help her to understand Peter's affair wasn't her fault. She was not to blame. In some ways, Rachel agreed with Dr. Artemus; but not entirely.

She knew Peter; Dr. Artemus didn't. He had fallen in love with an independent, strong-willed trial attorney, not some sniveling baby. Peter abhorred any signs of weakness.

She would take some time on the island and rest, before returning to Miami to try and salvage her career. Only then, would she be ready to try and reignite her relationship with Peter.

Dr. Luke interrupted her thoughts. "Would you mind if I pulled over to the side of the road and put the top down on the car? We could feel the salt air on our faces. There's nothing that makes me appreciate God's good earth like a salty breeze in my nostrils."

"Sure," Rachel said. "I'm not some fluffy female who worries about the wind mussing up her hair."

"I didn't think you were," he said.

Dr. Luke pulled over to the side of the road and popped the switch on his side of the car that fastened in the convertible top.

"This car is the one luxury that I allow myself," he said. He leaned across her to release the switch on her side of the car. She sat stiffly in her seat. He pressed a button, and the top started to lower.

As Dr. Luke maneuvered the car back onto the road.

"My work keeps me mostly inside," he said, "and this car is my way of relaxing. Sometimes, even in the winter months, I lower the top while driving on the beach road. I grew up in the city. I promised myself early on in life that one day I would find a way to leave all of that asphalt and concrete behind. And here I am riding along a country, beach road in the morning sunshine."

Rachel looked at Dr. Luke with curiosity. She had been so self-absorbed for so long that she hadn't thought much about the people around her.

This man probably had a very interesting story. She realized that he had been very kind to her. He had gone above and beyond the call of his duties as a doctor, and here she was treating him like he didn't exist.

"I bought this car from the Hillmans," Dr. Luke said. The cool breeze and the sunshine now pelting down to warm her face felt wonderful. She scratched around in her purse again, pulled out a rubber band and fastened her hair back into a ponytail. A few stray strands still whipped about in the wind.

"I got it at a steal, too."

"What?" She had lost the flow of the conversation, distracted by shoring up her fly-away hair.

"The car. I got it at a steal. A small-town doctor doesn't make a lot of money. People in Trinity don't have much cold, hard cash. But I didn't come here for the money. If I was about money, I could have stayed in Raleigh.

"Don't get me wrong; they do pay. Just not in dollars. I have a freezer full of seafood and a century's supply of firewood. Most folks won't come back unless I let them pay.

"I take what they have to offer. It's my way of making sure they get the medical treatment they need. One woman insisted on bringing me over a hot supper every night for a month after I treated her baby for the croup. Now imagine that."

Rachel smiled over at him. "I really don't know much about the people who live in this part of the country. I kept to myself. I rarely left my house."

Dr. Luke smiled back, a big happy grin, which flashed all of his perfect white teeth and made his eyes sparkle in the sunlight. "Anyway, I was telling you about this car. Bought it from *the Hillmans* at a steal."

"The Hillmans? Who are they?" Rachel asked, taking his bait.

"Only the richest people in town."

"By town, I assume that you are referring to Trinity."

"Well, sure, I am. What other town would I be talking about?"

"I don't know. Like I said, I rarely left home. Almost never left the island. I don't know anything about Trinity or the people who inhabit it."

"I haven't been in Trinity that long myself," Dr. Luke said. "But I've been there long enough to figure out the ropes."

"Seriously?" Rachel asked. He was quite engaging.

"You bet. A country doctor gets all of the gossip and carries many a secret. You asked about the Hillmans, so I'll tell you what I know. The Hillmans are by far the richest *folks* in this town or this part of the Panhandle—excluding the Plantation. Folks—I just love that word. Don't you?"

"I suppose. What about these folks named Hillman?"

"The old man and his wife live in one of the two mansions that Trinity can call its own. They own the timber company. Logging the forest surrounding Trinity has apparently been an extremely lucrative endeavor for the Hillmans."

"A logging company is lucrative."

"You probably aren't familiar with the landscape for this part of the country, but there's nothing but thousands of acres of forest between Trinity and the next town. The Hillmans have done their best over the years to cut that forest to the ground; but that job has proved to be too much, even for them."

"What stopped them?" Rachel said, admitting to herself that the story really was a bit interesting. Plus, it felt so good to ride along in the open air. Her mood was improving with each mile, with each spoken word.

"Tate's Hell—that's what stopped the Hillmans."

"Tate's Hell? What sort of place is that?"

"Tate's Hell—that's what folks call the swampland situated close to Trinity, and it's a lot tougher than even old man Hillman. Not much timber cut out of Tate's Hell. It doesn't matter. With the money that he made off of the timber in the surrounding forest, Mr. Hillman managed to get his finger in about every other pie in town. Mr. Hillman even got himself elected to the state senate."

"*You don't say,*" Rachel said, mocking the local vernacular. She decided to show Dr. Luke that she wasn't completely out of touch with her environment.

"Tate's Hell. That name sounds familiar." Rachel searched her brain, trying to remember where she had heard that name. "Oh, yeah, now I remember," she said. "The twins told me that they lived in Tate's Hell."

"That's right. They live in a clearing about ten or so miles from Trinity right in the heart of Tate's Hell."

Rachel opened her mouth to ask him some more about Tate's Hell, but he stopped her.

"Oh, no, you don't," he said, wagging his finger back and forth with a devilish grin. "I know you want me to tell you more about Tate's Hell, but I'm not done talking about the Hillmans. First things first."

She laughed. "You win," she said, throwing up her hands as a sign of surrender. "So tell me more. What about the Hillmans?"

Dr. Luke, encouraged by her enthusiasm, picked back up on his story. He was as good a storyteller as he was a doctor. He enjoyed the two endeavors about equally. And Rachel had laughed.

He pushed his fingers through his hair, and he pulled on a baseball cap that had been tossed on the seat between them. Resting his left arm on the doorframe, he drove with his right hand on the steering wheel. He stole a glance over at Rachel, whose ponytail was swatting her face like a cow's tail swats flies, only faster, much faster.

"Go on," Rachel said, while still smiling. "Tell me about the Hillmans."

"The Hillmans have two children, a daughter, Melissa, 'Missy' for short—the folks are big on double names and nicknames. It's either Melissa Annnn or Missy." He mimicked the southern drawl that was so prevalent in the area. Rachel laughed out loud.

"Melissa Annnn, settle down and let the doctor take a look at you." Rachel and Dr. Luke laughed together.

Dr. Luke waited a few minutes, a dramatic pause. "Oh, and substituting initials for names. The folks just love that one. There are a lot of J.B.'s, K.B.'s, and R.B.'s in Trinity. I don't know what the 'B' stands for, and I don't ask.

"And Trinity also has a lot of men called Buddy, Bud or Bubba. Again, I don't ask. *'Bubba here has took a bad cough lately, Doc.'"* Rachel couldn't remember the last time that she felt so carefree. She liked, really liked, this young doctor.

"Settle down, Rachel Rochelle," Dr. Luke said, "or I'll never be able to finish my story."

"Rachel Rochelle? How did you know? That is a well-kept secret."

"I read your medical records."

"Let me go on the record," Rachel said, chuckling, "you are not free to disclose that information."

"My lips are sealed."

"Then, please go back to relaying our local folklore," Rachel said.

"Don't get me wrong," Dr. Luke said, "I'm not making fun of these people. They are good, decent people. It's just funny to a boy from New York City, that's all. I'm quite sure they poke a little fun at me behind my back. I don't mind *a'tall.* I must sound and look a bit strange to them, too. What matters is they have, for the most part, accepted me."

"Go back to the Hillmans."

"Oh, yes, the Hillmans. As I said, they have one daughter, Missy, and one son, Trey. From what I hear, other than being a smidgen on the haughty side, Missy has never caused the family much trouble. Now Trey; he is a different story."

"How so?"

"The way the locals talk about him, Trey Hillman has been nothing but trouble since the day he was born. I even heard a story early on when I moved here that he shot and killed a boy while still in high school.

"The incident was officially ruled an accident, but the person telling me the story said that most of the town knew that version of the story wasn't true. It was Mr. Hillman's money and power that got his boy off. Or so the locals say. After the shooting episode, Trey supposedly settled down. He married a local girl. No surprise there. But it's the local girl he chose to marry that makes the story."

"Do tell."

"I will," he replied, delighted that he had an attentive audience. "Trey's wife didn't come from any money herself. She couldn't have. The only money in Trinity is the Hillman money. The only other families that have any money to speak of is Doc Adams' family—the young Dr. Adams is my partner at the Clinic—and the Sedman family.

"Ernie Sedman is the only successful lawyer in town, and he is probably the second richest man in Trinity. Still, he is far behind the Hillmans. His money doesn't hold a candle to the Hillman money. Unfortunately, for the Hillmans, neither the Adams family nor the Sedman family had any daughters—only sons. No match for Trey there. So he married Susan Akers."

Dr. Luke stopped talking and put both hands on the wheel. A logging truck lumbered along on the road ahead, fully loaded, gears grinding.

"Here is the one disadvantage of this car," he said, shouting over the noise of the truck. "Shield your face. Look out for flying wood chips. I'm going to pass, or we won't reach the island before midafternoon."

Rachel read "Hillman Lumber Company" on the side of the truck as Luke sailed around it.

"Back to Susan Hillman," Dr. Luke said. "That is, if you're still interested. Don't let me bore you."

"No. Please. This is good stuff."

"Susan Hillman. She may not have come from money, but she hasn't let that slow her down since she married the Hillman heir. To hear the townspeople talk about her, you'd think that she's the queen of England."

Rachel rested her head on the back of the seat, closed her eyes, and took a long, deep breath. She could feel the tension melting away, like the packed snow after a long, bleak winter.

"*They say*," Dr. Luke said, chuckling, "and I am going to quote here, 'she rides 'round town in that fancy new car of hers, dressed fit to kill even when it ain't Sunday or a special occasion, like she was the Queen of Sheba.'"

Rachel said, "This is getting better by the moment."

"The Queen of Sheba is responsible for me having this sporty car that you and I have the pleasure of riding in this very moment. I bought the car from the Hillmans shortly after I arrived in town. Trey sold the car for almost nothing when his wife decided that she needed to upgrade to something new.

"Susan Hillman's career, and again, I am relying on local gossip as my source, is to run the First Baptist Church. Her involvement with the church gives her an opportunity to showcase her wealth and status in a town that offers few opportunities for showcasing either.

"Folks say that all the preacher does at the First Baptist Church is preach his sermon on Sunday. The rest of the First Baptist activities are dictated by Mrs. Trey Hillman."

"And have you met Mrs. Hillman?" Rachel asked.

"I can't say that I've had the pleasure," Dr. Luke replied.

"Blacks are not invited to the Hillman social events, notwithstanding the fact that I am a doctor. Blacks are still blacks in this town. But I have driven by her house on several occasions, and it's a sight to behold."

"Don't leave me hanging. How so?"

"I'm so glad that you asked. 'Lady Astor'—that's another name the locals have for Susan Hillman—together with her husband, built this monstrosity of a house out on the river. It looks like a carbon copy of Tara from *Gone With the Wind*."

"This Lady Astor sounds like quite a character."

"Oh, and there's more. After marrying Trey, she managed to have her brother appointed sheriff of the county when the county's sheriff 'passed on.' In case you are wondering, 'passed on' is a popular euphemism for dying in this area. Later, with the backing of the Hillmans, Susan Hillman's brother was elected sheriff and serves in that official capacity to date. Now there's another interesting story."

"I'm taking the bait. Go on."

"The story of Bud Akers—that's the sheriff's name— ascension to the office of sheriff, falls into the category of a chicken and the egg scenario."

"What do you mean by that?"

"Well, Trey Hillman and Bud Akers have been the best of friends since they were boys. Nobody knows for sure if Bud landed his sister the job of being Trey's wife, or if she captured that prize on her own, and then landed her brother the job of sheriff.

"Doesn't matter either way. Everybody in Trinity knows the Hillmans have the law in their back pocket. After Trey's brief settling down phase, he went back to being as wild as before. Mostly, it's alcohol and women.

"The only thing that keeps him in check at all is his father. According to the folks who fed me this story, Trey is intimidated by nobody, except his father. Folks say that Trey has spent his life bullying everybody else because his father bullies him so much. And in front of the whole town. Old man Hillman makes sure that everybody knows that he's the top dog, and he regularly makes his son heel. Makes for a very angry young man, or so I hear."

Rachel smiled and then laughed aloud at Dr. Luke, who had taken his eyes off of the road long enough to look at her.

"Sounds like the Panhandle's version of a soap opera—*As the Tide Flows,*" she said.

"Well, I'll be," Dr. Luke said. "The Hillmans and their salacious saga have managed to do one good deed in their otherwise self-centered lives. They have managed to make you laugh today. Good and hearty laugher is, after all, the best medicine. I see a ray of hope for you."

"I forgot how good it feels," she said, giving Dr. Luke's arm an affectionate punch. "I'm sorry that it's taken me so long to say this to you, but thanks, Dr. Luke. Thanks for all that you've done for me. You have gone above and beyond the call of duty."

"Seeing you laugh is thanks enough. It helps me to remember why I chose to come to Trinity to set up a practice. I like getting to know my patients."

"Getting back to our earlier conversation," Rachel said, "you seemed to have gleaned a lot of history from your short stay in Trinity."

"As I pointed out to you earlier, it goes with the territory. A small-town doctor is definitely in the loop when it comes to getting the latest scoop on the gossip."

"And what do you know about Naomi and Mrs. Brodie? So far, you have proved to be a wealth of information. Since I am going to be a guest in Mrs. Brodie's home, I would like to know a little more about her and Naomi as well."

"I don't know much," Dr. Luke said. "Apparently, Mrs. Brodie came to the island many years ago with her extremely wealthy husband. He had a debilitating illness, and then he died. Mrs. Brodie stayed on Palm Island, alone, after her husband died."

"Sad," Rachel interjected.

"Naomi has worked on the estate as a housekeeper since the Brodies moved to Palm Island permanently. Before Mr. Brodie's illness, it was a vacation home for them. After he died, Mrs. Brodie became a recluse. She has not left her estate since his death. Naomi was her only companion for years. Then came Rodrigo and next the twins."

"What about Naomi?"

"I've only known her for a short while. Met her at church. I've been to her house in Tate's Hell a number of times. As they say around here, she's 'good people.'"

"Tate's Hell. You promised to tell me about that place. What kind of place would merit a name like Tate's Hell?"

"You should ask Naomi about Tate's Hell. She's spent the last fifty years of her life there. Suffice it to say that Tate's Hell deserves the name. It consists of acres of dense forest and swampland bordering the river."

"People really live there?"

"A few. Some of Trinity's poorer, but braver souls, have settled on the outskirts and managed to call it home. According to Naomi, she wouldn't live any place else, but I, quite honestly, do not see its appeal. The few times that I've been called out there, even in the daylight hours, it has given me the *heebie-jeebies*. You do know the heebie-jeebies, don't you?" Dr. Luke asked.

"Oh, yes," Rachel replied. "The twins schooled me on the heebie-jeebies. *"*

"This much I know to be true: Tate's Hell is not for the faint of heart. I admit that I'm city born and raised in an area that bears some resemblance to what I think of as hell. And I'm not easily spooked; but the few times that I have driven out there at night, I was downright terrified."

"You're teasing me, right?"

"Admittedly, a little. But honestly, as soon as you leave Trinity, it feels like you've been dropped into the heart of some primitive jungle. Highway 27 is the only way out to Tate's Hell, and to get to anybody's house, you must travel down several winding, dirt roads.

"One night I was out there for the twins' birthday party. It was a blustery night. The road leading away from the Ivey house and back to Highway 27 is cut right through an oak forest. The moss blowing in those trees took on some eerie shapes, like Dante's lost souls floating in purgatory. I didn't relax until the friendly lights of Trinity came back into view."

"Heebie-jeebies?" Rachel asked playfully.

"Sorta," Dr. Luke said.

"And the twins? Where do they fit in?"

"What little bit that I know about the twins I have learned from Karen and my partner, Dr. Adams. Everybody is very close-mouthed about them."

"Please, tell me what you do know."

"Okay, but it's not much. Naomi and Karen live in a small house, almost like a cabin, in a clearing carved out of one of the more remote parts of Tate's Hell. There's nothing or nobody even close to them except for an old couple, who are the twins' grandparents."

"Granny? The twins did mention their granny to me."

"Granny is Bessie Whatley, married to Ephram Whatley. According to Karen—and I'm surprised that she even told me this much because she's not one to talk about other people— Ephram Whatley has been on the verge of drinking himself to death for the last thirty years, but he has always managed to fall just shy of dying. He's down to one good leg and no sense and, pardon my language here, he's one mean son-of-a-bitch."

"Sounds like an awful man. He is the twins' grandfather?"

"So it would seem. Ephram and his wife Bessie—remember that is Granny—had only one child. A daughter named Lily. She died giving birth to the twins when she was only seventeen."

"That would explain the twins never mentioning their parents."

"Yes, that topic is off limits, at least with Karen and Naomi. Well, almost off limits. Karen did tell me that up until Lily's death, Bessie Whatley drank as badly as her husband. Karen also told me that when Lily was a child, Karen's family looked after Lily when the Whatleys went off on one of their drinking binges, which happened frequently."

Dr. Luke waved to a few residents on the streets as he and Rachel passed through Trinity.

"Don't forget to bring Jesse in for her shots," he called over to a young black women, when they stopped at the one red light.

"Vaccinations," he said to Rachel as they pulled away. "Childhood vaccination is one of my crusades here. But back to the story.

69

"Almost six years ago, just days before Christmas, Bessie Whatley called old Dr. Adams, my partner's father, to come out to Tate's Hell. Lily Whatley had gone into labor. The weather was bad out. It was snowing."

"Snowing? I thought the twins created the story of being born on a snowy night in their imaginations."

"No. It was indeed snowing on the night they were born. Karen told me that herself. That's only happened twice in the last forty years, or so I'm told. Lily had the twins and died before Doc Adams could get out there. Bessie took the newborns over to Naomi and Karen. Naomi's husband had died, I think in the spring of that year. Naomi and Karen have lived alone since his death."

"In Tate's Hell!"

"In Tate's Hell. But back to the story. Bessie needed help with the babies the night they were born. So she took them over to Naomi and Karen's home."

"What happened next?"

"This is where the story gets strange and a little light on details. Bessie took the twins to Naomi's cabin that snowy night in December, and that's where they've been ever since."

"Really?"

"Yes. According to Karen—and she is quite skimpy with details on this topic—Bessie tried to look after the twins after Lily died, but it was too much for her. She even quit drinking, but caring for two babies was simply more than she could handle."

"So they stayed with Naomi and Karen?" Rachel asked. "Isn't that a bit odd, for here?"

"Odd or not, it is where they live. From what I can tell, it's Naomi who looks after the lot, including Bessie. Ephram, the grandfather, is still alive and living in Tate's Hell. Thus far, I have avoided an encounter with him. Bessie technically lives with him, but spends most of her time with Naomi and Karen."

"This is true? You aren't making this up?"

"Seriously, Rachel, would I make this up?"

"I don't suppose you would."

"I would not. I am quite fond of all of these people—except Ephram, of course. I have been a visitor in Naomi's home on numerous occasions and each time Bessie was there. Naomi and Karen guard those twins like lionesses with cubs. I know it sounds strange, but it's true. And it seems to work. Every time I've been out there, things run smoothly."

"That comports with what I've learned about them. When I asked them about their mother and father, they told me they had a Granny, Naomi and Karen. The twins seemed to think that qualified as a family unit. And from what you say, I suppose that it does."

"Nobody ever mentions the grandfather, Ephram. The only way I know that he exists is from what Walter Jr.—that Junior business is also a big part of the name game here—told me about him. Remember, I told you earlier that, Walter Jr.—young Doc Adams—is my partner.

"Anyway, to make an already very complicated story even more confusing, Karen and the grandmother, Bessie, cared for the twins out in Tate's Hell while Naomi worked for Mrs. Brodie over on the island up until last year. That's when Karen came to work for me."

"Oh, my gosh, I am so lost."

"Be patient. It took me quite some time to wrap my mind around all of the details. Karen wanted or needed a job. A little of both, I suppose. I offered her a job for three days out of the week."

"She started to work at the Clinic, and the grandmother—Bessie, also known as Granny—cared for them alone the days Karen worked. The children were older, and this arrangement worked out well. Then Granny suffered a fall and hurt her back. I was called out to Tate's Hell myself for that emergency. At that point, the kids started to go to the island with Naomi on the days Karen worked."

Rachel stared over at Dr. Luke. "That's quite a story. Two black women taking in two white children. Maybe, a little strange elsewhere, but believable. But in this little isolated pocket of the south, very strange, and almost unbelievable, but for the fact that you are telling me the story."

"I agree. But then you've never met Naomi and Karen. They're extraordinary women. I know Karen quite well because she works for me. She is as pure and as gentle of a spirit as you'll ever meet. Smart as a whip, too. That's another little colloquial phrase I picked up here."

"Sounds like you're very fond of this Karen," Rachel said, looking over for his reaction.

"I am indebted to her. When I first came to Trinity, I spent days on end with little to do other than clean and reclean my instruments and review my medical journals. Patients didn't exactly flock to my door, although there was plenty of need for a doctor."

"This little pocket of the south situation?" Rachel asked.

"Pretty much. The whites didn't trust a black doctor, and the blacks, although I was the same color as they, didn't trust an outsider. Karen helped to change all of that."

"How so?"

"The blacks in Trinity have a great deal of respect for the Ivey family. Did I tell you 'Ivey' is Naomi and Karen's last name? Once the word got around town that Karen was my assistant, the patients started to come in, and with her help, I've managed to build a respectable practice. I even have some white patients. I have you."

"You do," she said, "and I couldn't be more pleased with my doctor. Besides being a good doctor, I now realize that I have benefited from one of your other talents: you are one hell of a good storyteller."

"And Rodrigo?" Rachel asked "You seemed so well informed on everybody else; what's his story?"

"I'm afraid that I can't help you there. All that anyone knows about Rodrigo is that he showed up here a few years back and bought a shrimp boat. He and Mrs. Brodie became friends when they rode out a hurricane scare in her house. Oh, I do know this. The twins adore him. I suppose he's a father figure to them."

"Which brings up another question. The twins' father. I haven't heard him mentioned in all of this."

"And you won't. He's the best kept secret of all. If anybody knows, they are not telling. Maybe the twins' mother took that secret with her to the grave."

"And one last question. How do you figure into this story? How did you get to Trinity?"

"That's easy to answer. I came to Trinity looking for peace. Walter Adams Jr. was my best friend when we were at Duke Medical together. When he asked me to come here and join his practice, I never thought twice. I came on down, and I'm here to stay, the good Lord willing."

"Just one more question."

"You already said that," Dr. Luke said impishly.

"I promise this is the last one."

"It has to be. I don't mind answering questions, but in case you haven't noticed, we're close to home. I hate to drop you off and run, but I do have a practice, which requires my attention."

"I know. And I appreciate you taking your valuable time to drive me."

"I'm glad that I did. You're a good listener, and I love to talk. I'm sure you've gathered that by now."

"My question is this: have you found peace here in Trinity?"

Dr. Luke took his eyes off the road just long enough to look over at Rachel.

"I have. And if you let yourself, you can find some peace here too, Rachel Edwards."

Rachel turned away. Through the blur of her tears, she saw Palm Island as they crossed over the bridge. She thought she was better, but seeing the island brought so much of her emotional baggage to the surface.

She turned her head to try and prevent Dr. Luke from seeing her crying. The drive had been so much fun.

Her ruse didn't work.

"Oh, Rachel," he said, squeezing her hand. "Please try. You can find peace here if you try."

She turned back to look at Dr. Luke. "I hope you're right," she said.

"I am. This may sound presumptuous of me, but you appear to me to be like a bird who, for a very long time, has had no place to light. Give yourself a chance, Rachel. Light here on this beautiful estate, and let yourself rest. Peace will find you. Be grateful to God for this opportunity."

"I'm not sure that I would even know peace if it came my way. My life has been mostly about turmoil. I haven't known many peaceful moments."

"That's part of your problem. Your concept of true peace may be flawed. Peace is not about moments in time. It's a feeling that you carry inside yourself, even in the worst of life's moments. Obstacles become opportunities to grow, if you open yourself up to that possibility. Open your heart up to these people and this place, and you'll find your peace, Rachel. I promise you that."

"You shouldn't make promises that you can't keep, Dr. Luke."

"I know. What you make of this opportunity is all up to you."

"You pack your own parachute. I heard all of that stuff in therapy."

"Don't be flippant, young lady. Use whatever analogy you like, but the truth is always the truth. Be true to yourself and those around you, and you'll find your peace. Learn to trust, Rachel. Learn to trust yourself and others around you."

"I've made such a mess of things so far. I'm afraid to trust anyone or myself ever again."

"The past is simply that, Rachel. The past. Let all that has happened before this moment go. Forgive yourself and others, and then go forward. Let this be your new beginning."

"Easier said than done."

"Not really. It is far more difficult to hold on than to let go. Try it."

The car slowed down.

"We're here," Dr. Luke said, turning into the Brodie driveway. "Rachel, before we part may I please ask you for two favors?"

"I suppose," Rachel said. "After all, I do owe you my life."

"Then do this for me. But, more importantly, do this for yourself. Try. Give these people, this island and yourself a chance. God will lead you to your peace, if you will let him."

"I'll try, I promise," Rachel said. "And what's the second favor?"

"Stop this 'Dr. Luke' nonsense. I, quite frankly, intensely dislike how people in the South stick a title in front of everybody's given name—Miss Trudy, Mr. Fred, Dr. Luke. Call me Luke. After our drive today, I feel as if we're friends. So how about we call each other Luke and Rachel."

"Done, Luke. Oh, and for somebody who professes not to know very much about what's going on around here, you're a regular town crier. Thanks for the information."

"Thanks for the compliment, I think."

The car rolled to a stop. Rachel had never seen the Brodie estate, only a sideview from the woods. It was magnificent. A stately mansion surrounded by what appeared to be acres of manicured grounds. Millie and Mango sat perched on a fountain, scanning the driveway for the first sign of a car.

"The twins must be your welcoming committee," Dr. Luke said.

At the sight of the car, both twins jumped off of the fountain and came at a full gallop down the drive. Rachel wiped the tears from her eyes and smiled. Maybe this wouldn't be so bad after all. She opened the car door and stepped out. The twins threw themselves into her waiting arms.

"Hold on there, you two wild stallions," Dr. Luke called out. "You're going to knock our running lady on her back."

"I'm fine," Rachel said over her shoulder to Dr. Luke, hugging the children as hard as she possibly could. "I'm just fine."

Rachel released the children and held them at arm's length. She gave each of them a kiss on the cheek.

"I guess I have you two young heroes to thank for coming to my rescue. I'm sorry if I frightened you when you found me sick."

Rachel wasn't sure what the twins had been told about that day, but at their age, explaining attempted suicide couldn't have been an option. "I'm so glad that you two were there, and I'm so proud of both of you for knowing what to do."

"I ran," said Mango. "I ran as fast as you. I ran like those devils Millie talks about was right on my heels." Millie scowled over at her brother. She was tired of hearing about devils in the woods.

"And I held your hand 'til Rodrigo got there," Millie said, "because when I'm sick, Naomi or Karen holds my hand."

"You were wonderful. Both of you," Rachel said, giving them another hug. "And look at you. I do believe that you've grown."

"We're taller," Mango said. "Naomi measures us in the kitchen, and she marks with a pencil how tall we get. Yesterday, she gave us both a new mark! We're higher up!"

"So you are," Rachel said, tousling his hair. She could never resist that shiny cascade of unruly curls. Millie slipped her small hand into Rachel's hand, a timid show of affection.

"Come on," Mango said, taking Rachel's other hand. Mango was bold and boisterous. "Naomi said we 'pose to bring you right into the house. We gonna have a special lunch."

"Mrs. Brodie is takin' a rest to meet you," Millie said. "Rodrigo's gonna be here, too. He's really nice."

"I met your Rodrigo, Millie," Rachel said. "And yes, he is oh so kind."

"And your invited, Dr. Luke," Mango piped in.

"We set the table with Mrs. Brodie's special dishes, and we helped her pick flowers for the table this mornin'," Millie chirped.

"We picked flowers for your room, too, Rachel," Mango said.

"That was 'pose to be a surprise, and now you done gone and told." Millie scolded her brother.

"I love fresh flowers. The surprise is not spoiled at all," Rachel said. "I love flowers, and knowing that you two picked them for me, makes them extra special."

"We told Mrs. Brodie that you liked flowers 'cause you had them all over your yard," Millie said. "At first, Naomi was mad at us for goin' all the way to your house, but then she said that she reckoned the Good Lord sent us there to help you, so it was alright. But that we should never go that far again without tellin' her."

The children walked Rachel down a sidewalk that circled around to a patio at the back of the house. Through an open door, Rachel could see an older black woman bustling around the kitchen.

Mango held the door for Rachel and Millie. "That's what a gentleman does," Mango said proudly. "He holds the door for ladies. Mrs. Brodie teached me that."

"Taught," Millie said. She rolled her eyes at her brother. "Mrs. Brodie says we ain't 'pose to say teached—the right word is taught."

Mango was going to respond to what Millie said, and then he spotted Naomi, who had come to stand at the back door.

"Look," Mango and Millie called out to Naomi. "We got her." They stood proudly, one on either side of Rachel, as if they had captured a trophy. "Here she is!"

"So I see," Naomi said, a big grin erupting on her face. "But you youngens use your manners. You know the proper way to introduce people."

"Allow me," Dr. Luke said, stepping forward and planting a kiss on Naomi's forehead.

"Mrs. Naomi Ivey may I present Miss Rachel Edwards." Naomi wiped her hands on her apron before taking Rachel's outstretched hand into both of her own.

"Welcome, Miss Edwards. We done all looked forward to havin' you here with us. Why these two youngens 'bout worried me to death this mornin' askin' ever five minutes when you's gettin' here. I spent most of the mornin' makin' up chores for 'em to do. Most times, I can't keep 'em inside. But this mornin', they been nothin' but underfoot."

"Thank you, Mrs. Ivey. I'm glad to be here. It's very kind of you and Mrs. Brodie to have me as a houseguest."

"Now none of this 'Mrs. Ivey' stuff. I'm Naomi to everbody 'round here, includin' these youngens. You go on and call me Naomi."

"And you must call me Rachel, not Miss Edwards," Rachel said, returning Naomi's smile.

"For a spell, we didn't know you as nothin' but the runnin' lady. We thought you's somethin' that these kids done gone and made up. These two got 'em some mighty powerful 'maginations. That they do. We shoulda asked you over sooner. It weren't very neighborly of us to leave you over there alone."

"I wasn't very neighborly myself. Please forgive me," Rachel said.

"Enough of this foolishness," Naomi said. "We're all here now. That's what matters. And I 'bout got lunch ready. If you don't mind me sayin' so, from the looks of you, Rachel, you could use a good home-cooked meal or two."

"Well, she has come to the right place for that," Dr. Luke said. "Naomi is a wonderful cook. Her fried chicken is second to none."

"I don't know 'bout that," Naomi said, "but I'm glad that you think so. We're havin' fried chicken today, and I done set you a place, Dr. Luke."

"Naomi, I appreciate your kindness, but I really should be getting back to work."

"Nonsense. I done called Karen, and your first patient ain't 'til two o'clock. Nobody's dyin' in Trinity, and even if they was, Dr. Adams can tend to 'em. There's a bathroom down the hall if you want to wash up."

"I never could say no to your fried chicken. It's a whole sight better than that chicken of Bertha Sparks," he said, with a wink.

"You go on," Naomi said, shooing Dr. Luke down the hall, obviously pleased at his compliment.

"And Millie and Mango, ya'll show Rachel to her room," Naomi said. "She's done had herself a long ride. She is probably tuckered out. Needs a few minutes of peace to herself 'fore lunch. Ya'll got plenty of time to bother her later. Now scoot, all three of ya'll 'fore I burn this here pot of peas, and we left with nothin' but fried chicken for lunch."

"Naomi's the bestest cook in all of the world," Millie said.

"That's 'cause I'm the only cook you two ever knew. I'm quite sure there's many a cook a whole lot better than me. I fix a plain meal, but it's hearty. Sticks to your ribs. Now go. Lunch is gonna be in half an hour. Mrs. Brodie ought to be up and 'bout by then."

The twins led Rachel out of the kitchen and down a long hallway. An elegant oriental rug with an intricate hand-woven pattern of crimson reds and emerald greens ran the length of the hall.

Rachel noticed that original oil paintings hung on the walls. As she passed down the hallway, she looked through an open door into a huge room with a circular glass wall facing the gardens and the ocean. The view was breathtaking; the room was exquisite.

The paintings, sculptures and furnishings in the room were an exotic blend of styles, showcasing an eclectic but elegant design. A baby grand piano dominated the room. Rachel thought that a person might spend hours in this room, and still not take in all there was to see.

"That's the music room," Millie said, when Rachel stopped to have a better look at the room. "Mrs. Brodie teached—I mean taught—us to play the piano."

"Mrs. Brodie says that we are *pro-di-gies,*" Mango crowed. "That means that God gave us special ways to learn the piano."

"Well, I hope that you will play for me some time," Rachel said.

Millie and Mango led Rachel to a wide circular staircase. The stairs were draped with another exotic rug, and the mahogany banisters were polished to a lustrous gloss. A crystal chandelier hung from the vaulted ceiling.

"Your room is upstairs," Millie said. "Mrs. Brodie let us pick out your room all by ourselves. We picked out the one where you can see the bay. It's got a porch, but Mrs. Brodie said the proper name for that porch is balcony. Mrs. Brodie said that we done good. That you would like the room we picked."

"This is it," Mango said, stopping in front of a large door. He turned the knob and, with a bit of fanfare, threw open the door for Rachel.

Rachel stopped and scanned what had to be one of the most exquisite bedrooms she had ever seen. The room was centered by a king-size, four-poster, mahogany bed covered with a brocade spread. Velvet and satin pillows in deep, rich shades of red and green and purple were piled against the headboard.

A Persian rug, woven with strands of strong, vibrant colors, partially covered a stone floor. Fresh flowers adorned every available space in the room.

Rachel walked over to the round, claw-foot table, with a marble top, that sat next to the bed. She leaned over to breathe in the sweet fragrances of roses, mingled with lilies.

A mirrored dressing table filled one corner of the room. An enormous crystal vase, arranged with birds-of-paradise stems and other tropical plants and palms, decorated one side of the table. Mrs. Brodie couldn't have possibly known—birds-of-paradise were her favorite flowers, Rachel thought.

"Look at this," Mango said, taking Rachel's hand and pulling her toward the balcony. The day was cool, maybe 70 degrees, and a balmy breeze drifted in through the open French doors.

Rachel and the twins stepped out onto the balcony where the breeze was strong enough for the moist air to cool their faces.

Potted palms, their fronds flapping in the wind, lush green ferns, and bromeliads of different shapes and colors filled the balcony. A large staghorn fern hung from an oak branch that curved up close by. A teak recliner and a glass table sat in one corner.

"Do you like it?" The twins hopped up and down in their excitement. "Do you like your room?"

"No, I don't like it," she said. The twins eyes opened wide, staring at Rachel. How could she not like the room?

"I love it, I love my room, you silly-willies," Rachel said. She tickled Millie's neck and pushed the hair off of Mango's forehead to give him a kiss.

Rachel sat down on the recliner. She closed her eyes; she felt the breeze; smelled the flowers; heard the children's giggles. And she knew that she was exactly where she should be.

"I love this room, and I love the two of you," she said. She pulled them down into the recliner with her.

"You really are so very special," she whispered to the twins.

CHAPTER FIVE

Ephram Whatley had made a mess of things. He was sober enough to figure that much out. He settled way too cheap with that son-of-a-bitch, Trey Hillman. Hillman was a rich man, and he could afford to pay more. Hell, him and Fred drunk up the money 'fore the month was even over.

He wanted to leave this place. He was fed up with his miserable life. Bessie, his own wife, had all but deserted him. She was always fussin' over them bratty kids.

Why she near 'bout lived with them bitches next door. Never took care of him no more. Lily, when she'd been alive, she'd cooked and took care of 'im. But Lily weren't here no more. And that rich bastard, Trey Hillman, was to blame for that.

Ephram took another swig out of his bottle. "Damn it, this ain't right," he muttered to himself. The time had come for him to take the bull by the horns. Hadn't Fred been tellin' him that for a long time now?

Fred said they oughta go back to Hillman. That Hillman oughta be made to pay more money. But Fred hadn't been the one to get the daylight beat out of him by Hillman neither. He was one mean son-of-a-bitch, that Hillman.

Then again, maybe Fred was right. After all, Hillman hadn't killed 'im when he had the chance. And Hillman had paid the money, right on time, ever month.

Pulling up closer to the heater, Ephram ran over in his mind what Fred had said 'bout movin' down to South Florida.

The weather down there stayed warm year 'round. Or so, Fred said. He'd never been outta Trinity, so he had to go with

Fred's word on the weather part. But warm weather sure the hell sounded good to him. Ephram shivered.

For the right amount of money, 'cordin' to Fred, the two of 'em could buy a trailer in one of them South Florida trailer parks—places that was set up to cater to some bunch of Yankees comin' to Florida in the winter to beat the cold.

As a general rule, he weren't fond of no Yankees. Hardly ever seen any in Trinity. Mostly, them Yankees steered clear of Trinity, 'cept for some of them folks from over on Palm Island that strayed over to the mainland ever now and again.

Them folks from up North had 'em some strange ways, or so he'd been told. But Fred said them Yankees went on back North soon as the winter was over. Besides, livin' with Yankees couldn't be no worse than livin' with Bessie in this run-down, old shack in the bowels of Tate's Hell.

Ephram looked down at the bottle in his hand, which was nearly empty. See, that was the problem, he thought. Always comin' up short. He sure didn't have the money it took to move on to South Florida.

Without Hillman, he didn't have no money a'tall other than his disability check. That weren't enough to keep a dang cat alive. He needed some real money to move. Even Fred had said that. And there weren't but one place to go for some real money—to Trey Hillman.

He couldn't hardly look at them little bastards no more without it turnin' his stomach. The girl, she favored his Lily. He reckoned if it was just her, he could put up with that alright.

That damn boy—now he was a different story. The boy was the spittin' image of Trey Hillman. Lately, just the sight of that damn boy made his blood boil.

Ephram pitched the empty bottle up again the wall. It shattered, and the pieces of glass showered the floor. Then he heard the knock on the door.

"Bessie," he hollered at the top of his lungs. "Come get the goddamn door."

"What bur you got up your ass today?" Fred asked. He pushed on through the door. It wasn't locked.

The lock had busted years back, and Ephram hadn't seen any need to repair the door. "A gnat's fart could blow it down; so what's the use," he told Bessie when she got on his ass to fix it.

"Don't bust a gut," Fred said. "Bessie ain't here. I saw her skedaddling it down the path to that old woman's house next door when I drove up."

Fred held up a paper bag for Ephram to see. "I thought you might need this. What with the weather turnin' off so cold."

"Good thinkin'. I'm out."

"I see that," Fred said, scraping some of the larger pieces of glass to the side of the room with the toe of his boot.

"It's cold as a mother-in-law's heart in here," Fred said, sidling up next to the heater. "What's wrong with this here heater." Fred had started to take off his coat but thought better of the idea. "Hell, you could hang meat in the place."

"The goddamn things don't half-ass work most of the time," Ephram grumbled. "You just 'bout got to be settin' right on top of it to stay warm."

"My heater don't work neither," Fred said, in an effort to commiserate with Ephram.

"I tell you, Fred, I'm plumb wore out with this here old place. I's just sittin' here studyin' on what you said 'bout us movin' to that place in South Florida. It don't make no sense to me no more to keep hangin' round here waitin' for Hillman to pitch me a scrap ever month."

Fred perked up. He liked to hear Ephram talking about moving. Fred had his own reasons for wanting to get out of town.

Fred had more than his fair share of run-ins with the law. Just last week he'd got drunk and sideswiped a car in the parkin' lot of the liquor store. It wouldn't be long 'fore the law caught up with 'im for that.

With his record, Fred thought, he was bound to do some time in the county jail. Might even get sent off to the state prison.

He intended to get out of Trinity, with or without Ephram. But havin' Ephram along, sportin' a pocketful of Trey Hillman's money, would make things go a whole helluva sight easier, or so Fred thought.

Fred took the bottle out of the bag, unscrewed the top and passed it to Ephram for the first drink. An unusual courtesy on Fred's part.

"Yep, Ephram," he said, kicking back in a chair he had pulled up next to the heater, "it's a cryin' shame that you and me ain't got the money to just up and go. If we had us some money, we could be outta here tomorrow. We could be sittin' in the sun in South Florida 'fore dark."

"That was just what I's thinkin'," Ephram said.

Ephram passed the bottle back to Fred, and he took a long pull. Dropping his chair to the floor, Fred leaned in closer to Ephram.

"What you got in mind?" he asked.

Of course, Fred already knew what Ephram was considering. He had planted the seed long ago. They would go after Trey Hillman for a lump-sum payoff.

He'd been pushing Ephram in that direction for some time now. But Ephram was stubborn. Fred had to make Ephram think that it was his own idea and then, and only then, would he be willing to act.

"I been thinkin' that I oughta make Hillman pay up all at once," Ephram said. "This here payin' me by the month just ain't workin' out the way I figgered it would."

"You make a good point," Fred said, by way of encouragement.

Ephram leaned in closer to Fred and said, "The way that I see it, Hillman could get his hands on some money if he tried. A man like Hillman is bound to have some money stored up somewheres."

"You right 'bout that," Fred said. "He sure as hell has got to have hisself a whole shitload of money stuck back somewheres." Fred passed the bottle back over to Ephram.

"My thinkin' was to put the squeeze on him once and for all. Get us enough money to get on outta Tate's Hell. Move on outta here all together."

"Now you're makin' some sense."

"Sheriff Akers," Bud said into the phone.

"We gotta talk," Trey said.

"Why? What's up?"

"Whatley, that's what the hell is up."

"Oh, shit. Meet me at Harley's at three o'clock. I gotta appear in court this afternoon. Testify on that Hingson killin'. You know the one where Hingson caught his wife screwin' 'round. Killed her and the guy she was screwin'."

"I ain't got time to hear this Hingson shit. Hell, I screwed Hingson's old lady way back. Right now, I've got Whatley to deal with. I'll see you at Harley's, at three."

Trey was already well into his fourth beer when Bud arrived at Harley's. Bud spotted him sitting hunched over in a booth. He had one hand clenched around the long neck of a Budweiser, and the other hand stretched out on the table with his index finger tapping up and down nervously.

Bud slid into the booth opposite Trey.

"Where the hell you been?" Trey said. " We agreed to meet at three."

"I know, but I told you that I had the Hingson trial. Jury found the son-of-a-bitch not guilty. Go figure that. Hell, I practically caught 'im with the smokin' gun in his hand."

"How did that happen?" Trey asked.

"Hingson's brother happened," Trey said. "He testified that Hingson had been huntin' with him all afternoon. Jury bought it."

"The jury believed the brother?" Trey asked, surprised.

"Hell no," Bud said, shaking his head. "They knew Hingson did it. Guess they felt like his old lady needed killin'. Tom

Dalson—that's the man Hingson's old lady was screwin'—hell, that poor bastard was just in the wrong place at the wrong time."

"I didn't come here to talk 'bout Hingson's problems," Trey said. "Hell, I got troubles of my own."

"Whatley?'

"Yeah, Whatley."

"What did he do now?"

"Bring me another damn beer," Trey shouted at the waitress. "And bring the high sheriff here one, too."

"I got a call from Whatley last night," Trey said. He called me, at home. Can you believe that? He's one uppity old bastard, I'll give 'im that."

"What did he want?"

"What the hell do you think he wanted? More money. Seems like our man Whatley ain't happy no more with his newfound wealth. He thinks that I ain't been payin' 'im enough all of these years. He thinks that I owe him more—lots more."

"Oh shit!"

"Oh shit is right! He's back on the lump sum again. I told you that somethin' like this was bound to happen when we agreed to pay 'im off the first time 'round."

Bud cringed. This was bad. He had hoped that Whatley would have drunk himself to death or been killed in an accident by now. No such luck.

"We gotta come up with a way to handle Whatley, more permanent this time," Trey said. "I sure as hell can't make no trouble now for my dear old daddy."

"What?" Bud asked. "What's different now?"

"He's up for re-election," Trey said. "He likes being the state senator, and I like havin' him out of my hair. Being state senator keeps him busy."

"I guess," Bud offered, buying some time to think.

"Hell," Trey growled, "If he would just go on and kick the bucket, I'd get the business and the money. But until that happens, I gotta walk the line."

"What does that mean?" Bud asked suspiciously.

"It means that Whatley needs to up and disappear, *pronto*. I could kick my own self in the ass for not doin' it right the first time 'round. I shouldn't have listened to you."

Bud leaned over toward Trey and lowered his voice. "Now you listen up, Trey. There ain't no call to go buyin' more trouble than we already got. You ain't gotta kill Whatley."

Trey picked up his half-full beer bottle and drained it.

Bud said, "Think 'bout it, Trey. Would it be the worst thing in the world, if he told a few folks that the kids were yours. You sure as hell ain't the first man to stray. And this all happened a long time ago. What's it been now? Five, six years? Probably nobody would even believe that old drunken coot after all this time. You been livin' straight. Call his bluff, Trey."

Trey rolled his eyes in disgust. "Have you gone slap damn crazy, Bud? I done told you that my daddy is up for re-election. That's reason enough to kill Whatley."

"Don't talk crazy, Trey."

"Then there's Susan. Me and her been gettin' along better. What with the kids, and whatever the hell it is that she does over at the church, she is keepin' busy. She ain't on my ass day and night no more."

"Susan? When have you ever cared about what Susan thinks?"

"I don't. But so long as we look like the happy little family, my dear old mama and daddy are thrilled. And that means me and Susan keep gettin' to ride the gravy train. I ain't takin' no chances on screwin' things up. Not now."

"Then pay 'im," Bud said, shrugging his shoulders. "Get it over with."

"Nope. Can't do that neither," Trey said. "What's to say if I paid this time, he won't be back later for more. He says that he plans on leavin' town—for good. But even if I believed that bullshit, which I don't, I can't cover the money."

Bud took a long pull on his beer and let Trey keep talking.

"The old man may be richer than shit, but he keeps me and Susan on a short leash. We live good, but he makes us account for ever penny. I couldn't lay my hands on cash money even if I took a notion to. Whatley's gotta go. And I don't mean out of town."

"Trey, it's too damn risky for you to kill Whatley. Just suppose that somebody found out. You being a stone-cold killer would be a helluva sight worse than you being a skirt-chaser."

When Trey didn't butt in, Bud pushed his advantage and kept talking.

"That business with Ronny Diaz could even be brung back up, Trey. I ain't sayin' that you'd be convicted of anything. You wouldn't. But folks like a good piece of gossip. If you're worried about your old man's re-election, you bein' a killer would sure as hell throw a wet blanket over that."

Trey fidgeted in his seat.

"And how you gonna kill 'im?" Bud continued. "He's got that cousin of his, Fred Whatley, and them Seever brothers stuck on him like lead on a magnet most of the damn time. You gonna kill all of them, too."

"I just the hell might," Trey fired back.

"Hell, no you ain't. Forget it, Trey."

"And do what?" Trey retorted.

"If you can't afford to pay Whatley, then we gotta talk some sense into 'im. Scare the hell outta the old bastard. Maybe even offer 'im a small amount of money. He'll fold his cards. I ain't sayin' don't rough 'im up a bit to get your point across, but there ain't no need to kill him or anybody else."

"I don't know," Trey said.

"Well, I do." Bud tried to reason with Trey. "Let me handle this. I'll talk to Whatley. He's scared to death of the law. One visit from the sheriff, and he'll turn tail and run."

"Maybe," Trey said. He was now clearly drunk.

Bud let him ramble on. "Damn it; I shoulda killed that little whore, Lily Whatley, back in the clearin' when I had my chance. That was my first mistake. The second was not killin' the old geezer, Ephram, the first time 'round. But there ain't gonna be no third mistake, Bud. I can promise you that."

Bud finished his beer. He slumped back in the booth, weary. Talking to Trey Hillman was like talking to a fence post sometimes.

"Damn it, Trey, I've got your ass out of worse cracks than this. You make these messes, and then I'm left to clean up after you. But you gotta let me do it my way this time. If you don't listen to me, there's gonna come a day that even I can't save your ass."

Trey motioned to the waitress to bring him another beer. Bud waved her off.

"You already had too much to drink. Go on home, Trey. Let me straighten this out. Come on, let's get out of here."

Trey swilled the last of the beer from his bottle and stood up. "Hell, I don't know, Bud, maybe you're right."

"I know that I'm right. Go on home, Trey. I'll take care of this."

Trey started walking toward the door, and Bud followed closely behind him.

"I promised my wife that I would try to make it home for supper, but I'll call you first thing in the morning," Bud said, when they were outside.

Trey swung himself up into the seat of his truck.

"Go on home now," Bud said. "And don't worry, buddy. I'll work this out."

CHAPTER SIX

Bud left Harley's and drove slowly back into town. He needed to think. He was about as put out with Trey as he had ever been and that was saying a lot. Over the years, Trey's temper had taken its toll on Bud's patience.

Bud realized that Trey's festering anger, combined with his propensity to drink, would make it impossible for him to keep Trey out of trouble forever. At the very most, he was just holding his finger in the dike.

The Trinity City Limit sign rolled past his window. And still Bud had not decided how to handle Trey's latest fiasco. Hell, he thought, the problem with Whatley could wait until tomorrow. A quick stop at the office, and he was going home.

The office was empty, except for the dispatcher, Carol Wiggins, who sat behind a glass partition, thumbing through a magazine.

Bud tapped on the glass, waved at Carol and then went into his office closing the door behind him.

A stack of messages spilled out from his "in" box. Bud hastily thumbed through the yellow slips of paper. Nothing urgent; thank God for that.

Rubbing his temples, he stooped to rummage through his desk drawer for his bottle of Excedrin and a roll of Tums. He had a throbbing headache, and his stomach was pumping acid like a damn oil rig.

Finding the bottles, he swallowed two of the Excedrin and popped several Tums into his mouth. Time to go on home. But first, he had better check on Trey. He didn't want to; but he knew that he should.

Susan answered on the first ring. "Trey ain't here," she said curtly to her brother. She was still harboring a grudge because Bud had reneged on his promise to come for Sunday dinner.

It had been their mother's birthday. "Like it would have killed him and his goody two shoes wife to come," she had complained to Trey. Trey reported Susan's comment to Bud, with a laugh, when Bud asked about the party later.

Bud hung up the phone without saying goodbye. Trey should have been home by now. Snatching up his keys, he bolted for the door.

A quick drive-by of Harry's parking lot, set off alarm bells in Bud's still aching head. Trey's truck wasn't there.

Next, he swung by the Amoco; no sign of Trey. Bud made a quick loop through town—no Trey. Reluctantly, Bud turned onto Highway 27.

"Damnit," he muttered, searching his shirt pocket for more Tums.

Bessie walked back over to the Ivey house. Both kids were recuperating from bad colds, and Naomi thought it best not to take them with her to the island.

Mrs. Brodie was a hearty old bird, but she was still old. No need to take a chance on making her sick. Karen stayed home from work to care for the children, and Bessie spent most of the day over at the Ivey house trying to help Karen cope with the restless twins.

Earlier in the afternoon, Bessie returned home; she needed a break. She wasn't feeling up to snuff herself she confessed to Karen, when Karen found her nodding off by the fire.

"Go on," Karen said, when Bessie mentioned going home to rest. "These kids ain't gonna give you a minute's peace if you stay here. I can manage without you for a spell."

"If you're sure," Bessie said.

"I'm sure. Now go."

But on her return home, Bessie found that she wasn't going to get any peace at her house either. She had hoped that Ephram would be off with Fred, and she could catch a nap on the couch by the heater. No such luck.

She had just dozed off when Ephram woke her up by hollering out to her from his bedroom, demanding that she bring him some food.

Bessie dragged herself up from the sofa and lumbered into the kitchen to heat up a can of beef stew. It was the only way to shut him up. She dumped the stew into a pot and turned the burner on high.

"I ain't had a bite to eat all day," Ephram grumbled. He hobbled into the kitchen, leaning on his crutch. "If my Lily was here, I sure the hell wouldn't be goin' hungry."

Bessie couldn't count the number of times he referred to Lily in one day. If you'd been a daddy to Lily, maybe she'd be here instead of in her grave, Bessie wanted to retort. But she bit her tongue. There weren't no point in gettin' into it with 'im.

"A man could starve to death in his own house," he said. He propped his crutch against the table and lowered himself into a chair.

"Here," she said, pushing a bowl toward him. She slid a spoon across the table where it clanked to a stop against the bowl. "I'm gonna go on back over to the Ivey place and check on the kids," she said.

"What for?" Ephram mumbled, shoveling the stew into his mouth. "We pay them women to watch them brats."

"They've been sick," Bessie said wearily.

"Go on, then; I don't give a damn. I'm lookin' for Fred to pick me up any minute now anyways."

Ephram wanted to make sure them brats stayed good and healthy, especially now that him and Fred had hatched their plan. It took a full bottle of shine for him to work up the nerve to call Hillman, but he had done it—last night.

With any luck, him and Fred would be rollin' outta Trinity any day now. Hillman had been pissed, but he hadn't turned 'im down flat; said that he'd get back to 'im.

Fred took that as a good sign; Ephram weren't quite so convinced. Fred said they oughta haul ass outta Trinity as soon as Hillman paid 'em off. Ephram agreed with Fred on that point. He just weren't as sure as Fred that Hillman would pay.

The door slammed behind Bessie.

"Bitch," Ephram muttered. It would be a fine day when he got shed of that old woman and them youngens. He hoped that Fred was right; that Hillman would pay, and soon.

Bessie simmered as she walked along the path. When she reached the Ivey's porch, she tried to calm herself before tapping on the door.

Bessie gave a couple of little thumps, and the door swung open. All of her anger faded away when she saw Mango smiling up at her. "Hey, sugar pie," she said, kissing him on the head. "Feelin' better?"

"Yep," he said.

"Yes, ma'am," Karen said. "Mind your manners, Mango."

"Yes, ma'am," Mango said. He returned to the table where he climbed up into a chair next to Karen.

Millie was on the other side of Karen hunched over the table, sitting on her knees in a chair, engrossed in a coloring book.

"How 'bout you, sweet pea? You feelin' any better?" Bessie asked. She walked up behind Millie and stroked her hair.

"Yes, ma'am," Millie answered, without looking up.

"What ya'll got?" Bessie asked the twins.

"Colorin' books," Millie said. She picked through her crayons, which sat in a neat pile on the table. "Karen gave 'em to us."

"They're 'bout Christmas," Mango said, holding his book up for Bessie to see.

"Ain't it a little early for that?" Bessie said. She sat down opposite Karen and the twins. "We ain't even digested our Thanksgiving turkey."

"It's my fault," Karen said. "They needed something to keep them busy. So I gave 'em the colorin' books a little early."

Bessie leaned across the table to place her hand on Millie's forehead. "I don't feel any sign of a fever."

"I think the colds are 'bout gone," Karen said. "One more day and they should be good as new."

"I 'spect so," Bessie said.

"Bessie, I need to run into Trinity. I want to pick up some groceries, so I can have a hot supper fixed when Mama gets in from work. Would you mind watchin' the twins while I run to town?"

"Not a'tall," Bessie said.

"Come to think of it. Why don't you just stay on for supper. You could even spend the night with us."

"Are you sure?" Bessie asked.

"Actually, I need you to stay. I was hopin' that you could watch the twins for a few hours in the mornin' while I go by the Clinic. I left Dr. Luke in a bind by stayin' home today.

"Besides that, the radio is callin' for a hard freeze. And you ain't got nothin' but that old kerosene heater at your place. You'd be better off over here with us."

"I don't wanta be a bother," Bessie said.

"You won't be no bother. You never are, Bessie; you know that. Honestly, I could use the help."

"Pleassse," Mango begged.

"Pretty pleassse," Millie added. Both children looked up from their coloring with pleading eyes.

"I guess I could stay over," Bessie said. She flashed back to her recent run-in with Ephram. And Karen was right about the heater; it barely kept the place warm. The idea of staying over with the Iveys sounded good.

"But only if you're sure," she said to Karen.

"I'm sure," Karen said. "So it's settled; you will stay. I'm gonna run on into town 'fore it gets any later."

"I gotta get a few things from my house if I'm stayin' the night," Bessie said. "Maybe the kids could walk over with me. They've been cooped up inside all day. Some fresh air might do 'em good."

"Oh, Bessie, I don't know. It's so cold out. I could wait for you to get back 'fore I go to town. I don't need to be gone long."

Karen did not want the twins anywhere near the Whatley house unless she or her mother was with them.

Bessie sensed Karen's dilemma. "Ain't nobody home. Ephram was 'pose to go off with Fred. I won't stay but a minute. I need that blood pressure medicine Dr. Luke give me and a change of clothes."

"I don't know, Bessie."

"It'll be alright, Karen. These kids could use some fresh air."

Mango had picked up on the conversation, and he was thrilled about the prospect of going outdoors.

"Come on, Karen," he begged, getting up from the table and wrapping his arms around Karen's waist. He gave her his most disarming smile. "Clover, he could go with us."

"It won't take no time to grab up what I need," Bessie said.

Karen wavered. What harm could there be with Ephram gone. She bent down and kissed Mango on the forehead.

"You win," she said to him. "But you and your sister got to bundle up. Hats, coats and gloves. And ya'll mind Granny. You hear."

When Bessie and the twins arrived at her house, there was no sign of Fred's car. She hoped that he had come and then gone with Ephram in tow.

Bessie left the twins out back with Clover while she went in to search the house. Ephram was still home; but he was passed out in the front bedroom.

It was colder out than she had expected, and the children needed to warm up by the heater before she walked them back to the Iveys.

She opened the back door and motioned them inside.

"Shush," she whispered to them, putting her fingers over her lips. They tiptoed together past Ephram's bedroom door. Bessie stationed them by the heater and went to gather up her things.

She was in the back of the house when she heard the ruckus.

First, the dogs started to bark. Probably Fred, she thought, rushing to bundle up the last of her clothes. It would take Fred a few minutes to get out of the car and into the house.

She pictured Fred and Ephram camped out in front of the heater, drinking for the rest of the night. Thank the Lord that Karen had invited her to spend the night. Hurriedly, Bessie grabbed for the pill bottle next to the bed.

She stopped when she heard heavy footsteps on the porch followed by the sound of pounding on the front door.

A man's loud and angry voice boomed through the door. "Whatley, come on out here and show your sorry ass."

Bessie froze. That voice didn't belong to Fred. Dropping her clothes, she dashed into the living room to grab the twins. She managed to make it to the edge of the living room before the front door burst open.

A stranger stumbled inside, tripping over the doorstep, before he regained his footing and stood with his fist extended in the air as if to pound on the door again.

Bessie and the stranger locked eyes. Bessie had never seen the man's face, but she recognized him instantly. The resemblance to Mango was unmistakable.

Trey looked Bessie over, decided she was no threat, and then surveyed the room, his gaze stopping on the twins who hovered together by the heater.

His eyes lingered on Millie as he slowly traced the features on her face. The deep blue eyes; the full, pouty mouth; the blonde hair. All Lily.

He shifted his focus to Mango and blinked his eyes to make sure he was seeing clearly. The boy was the spitting image of Travis, his son.

Bessie made a move to grab the twins, but Trey sprang forward like a striking snake, his fingers clamping down on her arm.

Wincing with pain, Bessie tried to wrangle herself free. Trey tightened his grip and twisted, yanking her face up close to his.

Bessie smelled the stench of beer and cigarettes mingled with the musky scent of the man's sweat.

"Not so fast," he said, nodding toward the twins.

"You want them kids," he snarled, "then you best tell me where to find your old man."

Bessie tried to speak. She tried to nod her head toward the back room where Ephram lay sleeping. But the fear, the heat, the odor, the pain in her arm—it all caused her head to swim. The room floated like a heat mirage in front of her eyes

"You best be tellin' me where to find your old man," Trey said again.

The corners of his mouth curled upward into a smirk. A quick twist of Bessie's arm by Trey, and her brittle old bone snapped like a twig. A searing pain streaked up Bessie's arm and exploded in her head. She screamed out in pain.

"Don't hurt Granny," Mango shrieked. He rushed forward and began to pummel at Trey's legs and body with his small, but determined fists.

Trey dropped Bessie, drew back his arm and slapped Mango with the palm of his hand. The sound of flesh hitting flesh filled the room as Mango spiraled backward, hitting the sofa with a hard thud before he landed on the floor.

When Millie screamed, Trey took two quick steps and throttled her by the throat. Lifting her into the air, he grinned as her arms and legs flapped about like those of a ragdoll.

"Let her be. Ephram's in there," Bessie croaked, barely lifting her good arm to point at the bedroom door.

Trey ignored Bessie as he held Millie at arm's length, admiring his prize.

"Looks just like her mama," Trey said, his voice low like the menacing growl of a dog about to attack.

"Mister, please," Bessie begged. "She ain't nothin' but a baby. Don't hurt her." But Trey was oblivious to Bessie's pleas.

"Looks just like that bitch, Lily," Trey said.

He squeezed down on Millie's windpipe, and the veins in her neck popped out like thick strands of cord; her face turned purplish-blue. Other than a random, involuntary jerk, her arms and legs fell limp at her side.

Bessie scooted across the floor, and using her good arm, she swung with all of the force that she could muster at Trey. The blow connected.

Trey dropped Millie and jerked forward, cupping his crotch with the palms of his hands. Bessie swung at him again. Stumbling backward, Trey pulled a gun from the inside of his coat.

"Get back you bitch," he groaned, waving the gun toward Bessie.

The late afternoon rays of the sun filtered through the window and lit up the gun's long steel barrel. Bessie's eyes fixated on the gun like a magnet on metal.

"Run," she yelled over at the twins.

Millie convulsed on the floor, fighting for air. She couldn't run. Mango tried to pull his sister up onto her feet. When she couldn't stand, he dragged her toward the door.

Trey took another step back, raised the gun and took aim at Bessie.

"Run," she cried out. She forced her eyes away from the gun and turned to look back at the children.

Bessie heard the deafening boom as the gun exploded. But she didn't see Trey as he toppled to the floor like a felled timber.

The asphalt shimmered in the sunlight as Bud raced down Highway 27. He licked his lips and tasted the salt from small beads of sweat.

He rounded the last curve before the turnoff into the Whatley place and swerved to miss a car on the narrow highway. His front wheel dropped off of the edge of the pavement, and Bud pulled hard to get his car back on the road.

He glanced into the rearview mirror, but the other car had rounded the curve and dropped out of sight. Barely slowing down, he snatched the wheel again, and the car fishtailed before it sped down the dirt road that led up to the Whatley house.

Bessie's ears were ringing so loudly that she couldn't hear. She turned her head and saw Ephram, wobbling in the middle of the room, with Trey sprawled out at his feet.

With all of the commotion, neither Bessie nor Trey had seen Ephram peeking out from the bedroom, looking for a way to escape.

Seeing Trey's gun had set Ephram into motion. He weren't worried 'bout Bessie and the youngens. All he wanted was to save his own ass. When Trey pulled the gun, Ephram's gut told him that weren't nobody gettin' out alive. He was forced to make a move.

Ephram saw his chance when Trey aimed at Bessie. Using his crutch, he staggered the few steps forward that separated him from Trey.

Balancing on his good leg, Ephram lifted his crutch up and then brought it down full-force on Trey's head. The adrenaline pumping through Ephram's body gave him the strength to land a good whack. The crutch splintered into two pieces as it connected with Trey's skull.

The shot, which had been intended for Bessie, missed its mark, thrown off course when Trey's arm jerked forward as Ephram's blow hit its mark.

Bessie was trying hard to gather her senses when she spied the gun on the floor next to Trey's outstretched hand. It was only a few feet away from her; she lunged for the gun.

Trey was dazed, but he was not unconscious. Through the rivulets of blood, which trickled into his eyes, he saw a blur of movement as Bessie made her move.

He reacted by rolling to his side, and grasping the handle of the gun. Trey's finger curled around the trigger, and he squeezed.

The bullet from the .357 Magnum exploded into Bessie's chest, propelling her body backward where it slammed into the kerosene heater.

The heater swayed—rocked back and forth several times—and then toppled over, sending kerosene spewing out from the broken pipe. The heater exploded, and as the fire traced the flow of kerosene across the floor, the room erupted into flames.

Trey pushed off of the floor to his feet as the flames curled around his boots. Blood oozed down from his head and dripped in thick, black droplets into his eyes. He was still dazed from the blow to his head.

He swiped at his eyes and tried hard to focus. But the smoke had already started to fill the tiny room, cutting off his air and his view of the front door. He used the wall for support as he felt his away along, searching frantically with his hands in the black fog for the front door.

Ephram, without his crutch to support him, slumped to the floor and started to crawl toward the front door. The flames flickered around his fingers, and he reared up on his one good leg and bayed like a cornered animal.

The faint outline of Trey's body appeared through the haze of smoke. Ephram fell forward and clutched at Trey's legs, hoping that he could hang on as Trey struggled toward the door.

Trey faltered and almost went down, thrown off balance by the pull on his legs. He swung the barrel of the gun, which still dangled in his hand, downward.

The gun smashed into Ephram's shoulder and sent him reeling over onto his back into the flames.

Desperate, Trey resumed his search for the door, but he couldn't find it. Overcome by the black smoke, which now filled the small room, he slid down the wall and collapsed into a heap on the floor.

Bud saw the cloud of smoke first—it was visible before he even got to the clearing—and then the burning house.

He slammed on the brakes to the patrol car, and its four tires ground down into the black dirt next to Trey's truck, sending up a thick plume of dust, which mingled with the ash and soot raining down all around him.

Two dogs circled around him, and then dropped back as he got closer to the burning house. The front door was ajar. Bud kicked it in and a scorching wave of heat and smoke blasted his face.

Then he heard it—a high-pitched, keening wail, like the cry of a bobcat. What he heard was the terrified screams of children. Stepping back, he took in a deep gulp of air, pulled his jacket up to block his nostrils and mouth and stepped inside the front door.

Above the roar of the fire, he heard the screams again. It sounded like the cries were coming from somewhere in the back of the house, but it was hard to tell.

The thick smoke made it impossible for him to see more than a few feet into the room. He squinted, the smoke stinging his eyes as he tried harder to focus. He saw a man, flipped over on his back, his arms and one leg wiggling about like a turtle trapped in its shell.

He tried to go farther into the room, but the heat and smoke drove him back. The room was an inferno. As he backed out the door, he stumbled over an arm. He rolled the body over with his foot and saw that it was Trey.

The roof caved in as Bud, dragging Trey behind him, cleared the porch. A timber crashed only a few feet away showering him with sparks and ashes.

Making one final lunge across the yard, he collapsed on the cold earth, and tried to force the freezing air into his smoke-filled lungs. Beside him, he heard Trey gasping and gagging, trying to find his own breath.

Bud lay motionless on his back, other than the movement of his heaving chest as he inhaled small, shallow swallows of air. Slowly, he opened his eyes.

Smoke drifted aimlessly by overhead before it dissipated into a sky now turned into a brilliant palate, dominated by glowing hues of orange as the first rays of a setting winter sun slipped toward the horizon.

In the distance, he heard the chirping of a bird. For a fleeting moment, Bud felt peaceful, as if he were a young boy, enjoying his final taste of freedom before his mother's voice called him to come in for supper.

His breathing gradually returned to normal, his sweat now cold on his skin. Rolling onto his side, he looked at Trey.

Trey's face was black. Blood, matted with ashes and soot, had crusted on his skin and stuck to his singed hair. His eyes were open, but he stared off into the distance, focused on the woods as if he were on a deer stand with a buck in his sights.

Bud watched as Trey's eyes drifted back and then lingered on his face.

"Bud?" Trey croaked out, his voice as deep as a bullfrog.

Bud rolled back over onto his back. The sight of Trey sickened him.

Startled by a loud pop as the timbers of the house buckled and burned, Bud flinched. And then he heard it again. The screaming. He squeezed his lids tightly shut and put his hands over his ears to block out the sound.

But he could not silence the screams. This time the screams were not coming from the house. They came from inside his head, roaring like an approaching tornado and beating at his temples like a jackhammer.

Trey propped himself up on one elbow, and stared down into Bud's face.

"You alright?" he asked. Trey poked at Bud's ribs. Bud didn't move.

"Bud, say something, man."

Bud opened his eyes, and Trey's face loomed in front of him.

"What the hell happened here?" Bud asked. His throat was raw, his voice raspy and strained.

Trey didn't answer; he turned his eyes away from Bud and looked off into the distance.

Bud's anger swelled up inside him until he felt as if his chest would explode like an over-inflated balloon. Rolling up, Bud straddled Trey, pinning him onto the ground.

"I asked you what happened here, you no-count bastard." Bud spat the words out at Trey like spoiled food.

Trey's answer came back in a hoarse, contrite whisper. "Things got out of hand. I didn't come out here to kill nobody. Goddamnit, Bud, I swear that; I didn't mean to kill nobody. I hollered for Whatley to come on outside. When he didn't, I went in after him, but I didn't intend to kill him."

"What the hell, Trey!" Bud screamed into Trey's face. "Why the hell could you not for just one time in your sorry-ass life listen? Why, Trey?"

"It happened so fast," Trey whined. "I didn't see hide nor hair of Whatley when I first went inside, but his old lady was in there. The kids, too. I hadn't figgered on that."

"Go on." Bud commanded Trey to continue although he really didn't want to hear what he had to say.

"Like I said—his old lady was there. I took hold of the old woman's arm, and told her to tell me where Whatley was at. I didn't count on what happened next."

"And what did happen, Trey? What the hell happened in there?"

"The old woman went to screamin' and hollerin'. Then the boy went for me. He was hittin' and kickin' at me. Both kids went to screamin' at the top of their lungs. All hell broke loose. I went for my gun."

"You pulled a gun on an old woman and two little kids, Trey?"

"It was just to scare 'em. To shut 'em up. I swear to that, Bud. Then I got hit from behind. Whatley, I guess. He musta slipped outta that side room and got the jump on me, while I was wrestling 'round with the old woman and the kids."

"Did you see Whatley?" Bud was trying to figure out exactly who was in the house.

"Not really. I guess I was knocked out. When I came to, the whole damn place was up in flames. Somebody, I think it was Whatley, was grabbing at my leg."

"You *think* it was Whatley? Trey we need to know who was in that house."

"Goddamnit, Bud! I can't be sure. I passed out from the smoke, I guess, because the next thing I knew, I'm out here with you. If you hadn't come along, I'd burnt up in there."

Bud pinned Trey's arms down with his knees. He glared into Trey's bloodshot eyes.

"I heard kids screamin' you bastard. Them kids burnt up alive in that house."

Trey lifted his head and bridged upward with his back. It was enough to break Bud's grip, but not enough to throw Bud off of him. Trey's neck pivoted forward like a turkey scouring the ground for food.

"It was self-defense goddamnit," Trey whined.

Trey licked the corners of his mouth, which were flecked with dried salvia and blood. His next move caught Bud completely off guard.

Trey smiled. Bud was stunned by that smile.

"Self-defense or not? What the hell does it matter, *Sheriff,* 'cause they're all deader than doornails now: Whatley, his old lady and the kids. Which means my troubles are over."

Bud drew back his arm and swung. The back of his hand caught Trey flush on the cheek, making a loud smacking sound as Trey's head spun around and smashed into the dirt.

As quickly and as instinctively as a rattlesnake, Trey's head sprung up, and he coiled to strike. Bridging upward, using all of his strength, Trey managed to throw Bud off balance.

Bud toppled off of Trey and rolled across the ground.

Then both men were on their feet, squared off, eye to eye, fists squeezed tightly, ready to fight.

It was Bud who looked away first. He released his fists and turned away from Trey to gaze at the house. He watched as the chimney crumbled, brick piling upon brick, in the flames.

Trey was right, Bud thought. They were all gone. There was nothing left to do here. As much as it sickened him, what was done was done.

Bud turned back to look at Trey, who stood glaring over at him as he massaged the imprint left by Bud's hand on his soot-covered face.

Bud's anger reignited as that satisfied grin returned to Trey's face.

"Self-defense, you bastard? You kill two old people in cold blood, and you call that self-defense? How 'bout them kids, Trey? Was that self-defense?"

"How was I to know that them damn brats would be in there?" The grin faded from his face, and his voice took on a low, plaintive whine.

"It ain't like I meant to kill 'em. It just happened. That's all."

"That's all?"

"Yeah, that's all," Trey said, defiantly, the whining tone gone from his voice. "Don't go gettin' all self-righteous on me, Sheriff. You're in this pile of shit as deep as me."

Bud didn't answer. He looked away in disgust. Out of the corner of his eye, near the edge of the woods, he thought that he saw something move.

He quickly turned and scoured the edge of the woods. Nothing was there. Or so he tried to convince himself.

"We need to get the hell out of here," Trey said. He stripped off his flannel shirt and used it to wipe his face.

"What?" Bud asked. He was still staring at the woods.

"I said that we gotta haul ass."

"Yeah, right." Bud looked away from the woods and turned his attention back to Trey.

"Go on out to my place," he said. "Sheila's not there. Clean up. Then go on home. And stay there. I mean it goddamnit; don't make a move 'til you hear from me."

"Okay," Trey said. He wiped more grime off of his face and threw the shirt into the bed of his truck.

"I'll wait here a few minutes," Bud said, "so we're not seen together on the road. Then I'll go to my office. I got a clean uniform there. Somebody'll discover this fire sooner or later. I'll let you know what happens."

Bud watched as Trey's truck pulled away. Then he walked toward the woods in the direction of where he thought that he had seen something move. It was a gut feeling; but he felt certain that he had seen something in the woods. He just wasn't sure what.

He found a path and followed it through the woods. It emptied into a second clearing with a house. There was a car parked in the yard.

Bud walked up onto the porch of the small house, no more than a cabin, and he knocked on the door. Nobody answered. He knocked louder. When nobody came to the door, he tried the doorknob. The door swung open; it wasn't locked.

"Anybody home?" he called out, although no lights were on and the house was quiet. The front room was empty, but logs smoldered in the fireplace.

Carefully, he started to search through the house. In the kitchen, he found several grocery bags, still full of food on the table. He searched through the bags. The groceries were fresh. Somebody had set those bags on the table and left in a hurry. Whoever left the bags had not taken the time to put the milk and butter into the refrigerator.

He moved to the back of the house, calling out as he went. Nobody was there. Satisfied that the cabin was empty, he turned to leave.

As he approached the front door, he spied a woman's purse on a table by the door. He shuffled through its contents and pulled out a wallet. There was a driver's license with the picture of a black woman: Karen Ivey.

Bud walked the perimeter of the yard, but found nothing. It was getting dark, and he knew that he should get back into town.

He walked briskly down the path back to his car, fretting as he went along. He was missing something; he was sure of that.

Fred was still shaking even after he knew that Trinity was miles behind him. He wanted to forget what he had seen, and he wanted to get as far away from Trinity as he could get. Fred's fear of prison was second only to his fear of dying.

He had been a worthless son-of-a-bitch all of his life—he was the first to admit that fact—and he wasn't in any hurry to meet his maker. Better to postpone that event as long as possible.

Just a few more minutes, and he woulda been in that house with Ephram when Trey Hillman arrived. Just a few more minutes, and he woulda gone straight from that inferno, which once was Ephram's house, right into the fires of hell. He'd been a lucky man.

He shoulda hauled ass the minute that he saw Trey Hillman's truck parked in Ephram's yard. He would never understand why he hadn't. Whatever had possessed him to walk up on that porch? Curiosity? Greed? Wanted to see what was goin' on. Whatever it was, it had damn near cost him his life.

He heard the scuffle inside before he even made it to the porch. All that hollerin' and cussin' stopped him short of goin' inside. That decision had saved him his life.

Fred never had much of a stomach for violence, mostly because he had pretty much always been on the receiving end. And he was no match for Trey Hillman.

So Fred had watched the fracas from the porch, peekin' in through the window. He knew that he oughta turned tail and run long before the gun went off. But he didn't. God knows why? So now he had to haul ass as far away from Trinity as he could get.

He understood Hillman mighta wanted to kill Ephram. After all, Ephram had been blackmailin' him for years. But honest to God, he never believed that Hillman would go that far. Hell, hadn't he paid the money for years?

And Bessie and them kids killed, too. Now granted, Trey hadn't fired on the kids. But he had hit Bessie point-blank. That weren't no accident.

When that heater exploded, it was over for all of 'em. There weren't a damn thing he could do but run. Fred turned up his bottle and took several long, hard pulls.

There weren't no way he coulda pulled anybody outta that house. He took another couple of swigs from the bottle. Only a crazy man woulda tried to get inside to pull anybody out. That's why he had turned and run. A few more bottles and he might just believe that, Fred thought.

What worried him now was the sheriff. They had just 'bout hit head-on right before the turnoff. The sheriff was goin' wide-open. And so was he. Fred wondered if the sheriff had recognized him. He had looked back just long enough to see the sheriff pull off onto Ephram's road.

There weren't a damn thing to tie him to the fire. Still, he weren't takin' no chances. He stopped at his house long enough to pick up a few clothes and what money he had and then he left. For good. Straight to that trailer park in South Florida. That's where he was headed.

It'd be hard to get by without any money, but what choice did he have now. He sure the hell weren't gonna stay 'round Trinity; in fact, he weren't never goin' back. Fred took another swig from the bottle. It was gonna take a lot of liquor to drink this one off of his mind.

CHAPTER SEVEN

O nly Clover came out to meet Naomi. No heads in the window. No children running out of the door. No smoke from the chimney. And no lights on inside the house. Naomi gave Clover a few pats on the head and quickly went inside. It was quiet. Too quiet. And too dark. The fire had burned down to a few red coals.

"Karen," she called. "Honey, are you here?" There was no answer. Naomi went into the kitchen and pulled on a long cord.

A bulb overhead lit up the room. A single cup sat in the drainboard. The smell of coffee hung in the air. Two bags sat on the table, with groceries poking out of the top.

She walked through the house, turning on lights and calling Karen's name as she went. Nobody was home, but Karen's car was in the driveway. There was only one place that Karen could be—the Whatleys.

Still, that sure was odd, Naomi thought. It was late, the children had been sick and the weather was freezing outside. Naomi hoped that Bessie hadn't had another bad spell with her back.

As she stepped out the back door, Naomi knew that something was wrong. She surveyed the yard. There was hardly any daylight left, but in the pale light of dusk things looked alright. Nothing appeared amiss.

Then it came to her. At first, a mere whiff. The faintest hint of smoke tweaked at her nostrils. She looked up at the chimney, but there wasn't even a puff.

Fear washed over Naomi like a tidal wave. She took off down the path, sniffing at the air like a mother bear as she went.

The closer she got to the Whatley house, the stronger the smell became.

She tried desperately to quicken her pace, but old age has its limitations. Huffing and puffing, she stepped off of the path into the Whatley clearing.

What she saw stopped her dead in her tracks. The Whatley house was burned to the ground, reduced to smoldering flames, some charred remains.

For a few seconds, Naomi's mind refused to process what her eyes saw. The Whatley house was a pile of ashes. She closed her eyes and forced her mind's eye to operate like a camera in slow motion, first in reverse and then forward again.

She tried to erase what she had seen; go back to normal. She had known this feeling twice before: the first time was when she looked at Nathan's body lying in his coffin; the second time was when she had found Washington slumped over his workbench.

Fighting for control, she opened her eyes. The pile of smoldering ashes remained. She took a few tentative steps toward the rubble. The house was gone, and nobody was in sight.

"Please, Lord," she whispered.

Fear ripped at her heart like a hungry animal gnawing at fresh meat. There had to be some reason they were all gone she told herself. Some *good* reason. Some reason that didn't leave her alone. Help. She needed help.

Naomi turned back to the path. It was almost completely dark. She stumbled along, but it was slow going. Finally, she reached the end of the path and spotted a light up ahead.

It was the glow of light from her kitchen window. Naomi felt a surge of relief. Karen and the twins must be home, the lights were on. Then she remembered that she had turned on the light before she started off to the Whatleys.

Still, she hoped as she scrambled across the yard. "Karen," she called out as she entered the kitchen door. But the stillness of the house told her that nobody was home.

111

Naomi rushed to the hallway, to the telephone. A pad filled with numbers, which Karen had prepared for Bessie when she was home alone with the twins, was placed beside the phone.

"You are such a worrywart," Naomi had teased her, when Karen explained the pad to Naomi and Bessie. "You can count the numbers that we call on one hand. Me and Bessie ain't so old and addle-brained that we can't 'member those numbers." But Karen had persisted, and now Naomi was glad that she had.

Scanning the pad, she found the number for the sheriff's office. Her hand trembled so violently that she could barely dial the numbers as she placed her call.

"Sheriff's office," a voice answered after two rings.

"There's been a fire," Naomi's said, her voice quivering.

"Where?" the voice asked in a flat, nasal tone.

"Tate's Hell," Naomi said. She had to steady the receiver by holding her wrist with her free hand.

"You gotta tell me more than that. Tate's Hell covers a lot of territory."

"The Whatley place. Ten miles out. Second road on the left off Highway 27. There's a big oak that hangs out over the turnoff."

"Is anybody hurt. Ya'll gonna need the Davis wagon?" The voice asked these questions without a hint of emotion or concern.

"I don't know. Everbody 'pears to be already gone." A thought flashed through Naomi's mind. Maybe somebody had been hurt. Maybe the wagon had been called, and Karen had gone to the hospital. She would have had to take the kids with her.

"Has anybody else called in a fire?" Naomi asked, silently praying that the answer would be yes.

"I been on dispatch all afternoon. Nobody's called in a fire that I know of. But hold on. Here comes Sheriff Akers. I'll let you talk to him."

Naomi clutched the receiver. She could hear voices in the background. "Somebody's here on the phone. Says there's been a fire out in Tate's Hell."

"Sheriff Akers," a man's voice said.

"This here's Naomi Ivey. I live out next to the Whatley place. I come in from work and found the Whatley's house burnt to the ground. The Whatleys and my girl, Karen, all missin'. Has anybody called it in?"

"Not that I know of. I'll get somebody right out. Stay where you are." The receiver went dead in Naomi's ear.

Naomi placed the receiver back in its cradle. She slowly slid down the wall until she sat slumped on the floor, her knees drawn up with her head resting in her hands. Karen, Millie, Mango, Bessie. She tried to push back the unthinkable.

Then another thought flashed through her mind. She stood up, reached for the phone and called Dr. Luke's office.

"Clinic," Dr. Luke said.

"Is Karen there?"

"Naomi?"

"Uh, huh."

"Well, no. She called in this morning and told me that the kids were sick; that she wouldn't be in to work. I haven't seen her all day. Is something wrong?"

"She's missin'."

"*Missing*?"

"That's right," Naomi said, weakly into the receiver. "I come in from work to find the Whatley place burnt to the ground. Karen's car and purse are here, but I can't find a soul. Everybody's gone. Karen, Bessie and the kids."

"I'll be right out." Naomi heard the receiver go dead in her ear. Luke dialed the phone.

"Sheriff's office."

"This is Dr. Lowry at the Clinic. I want to report a fire."

"If you talkin' 'bout that one in Tate's Hell, the sheriff's done gone out there." Luke dropped the phone, grabbed his medical bag and raced toward his car.

Bud knew there wasn't any sense in calling the fire squad or the Davis wagon. But he needed damage control—a show of a bona fide rescue attempt. No need to arouse any suspicions.

"Sandra," he yelled to the dispatcher. "Send a fire truck on out to the Whatley place. Send the Davis wagon, too."

Bud was the first on the scene. He drove out with his siren blaring. The Whatley shack, which had been a flickering flame when he had left, was now a pile of ashes. All that was left of the house were the bricks from the fireplace.

Kicking at the ashes, Bud looked for Trey's gun. He heard the siren. In a matter of minutes, the fire truck rounded the bend, bounced across the yard and ground to a halt, not three feet from where he was standing, throwing up a cloud of dust and ashes.

"Cut the siren," Bud shouted up at the truck.

The door to the fire truck opened. Doug Greely, one of Trinity's firemen, stepped down onto the running board. "What?" he shouted.

"Cut the damn sirens," Bud yelled. He tried to brush the dirt and ashes off of his shirt. He pulled his shirttail out of his pants and tried to wipe down his face.

Doug leaned into the truck. "Cut the siren, Buck," he hollered.

The siren stopped blaring, its last blast echoing out into the woods. Doug jumped down from the running board and stood next to Bud. Buck followed.

"Doug. Buck. How you boys doin'?" Bud said, spitting on the ground.

"I reckon that we can't complain," Doug said. "Things been a little busy. Always is this time of the year. Folks tryin' to keep warm. Fire gets away from 'em. Accidents happen. Looks like that's what we got here."

"Looks thataways," Bud replied.

Doug nodded over to the remains of the Whatley house.

"Can't do much here but poke 'round in the ashes and see what we can find. I don't 'spect that it'll be much."

114

"Don't bother," Bud said, spitting on the ground again. The taste of soot and ashes lingered in his mouth. Bud propped his foot up on the running board of the fire truck and rested his elbow against his thigh, trying to look relaxed and matter-of-fact, which was difficult considering that his nerves were as raw as fresh-killed meat.

"Gotta make a report," Doug said, "Chief requires it. He's a damn stickler for paper work."

"Ain't no need for you boys to stay out here in this cold. Feels close to freezin' already."

"The bank read 34 when we come through town," Buck said. The First National Bank of Trinity had a thermometer and a clock on its sign.

Bud looked at Doug and said, "Report is this: Whatley shack burnt down. Ephram Whatley lived here with his old lady. They both dead if they was in the house. Ephram's known to drink bad. Runs the bars a lot. I'll ask 'round. But if he don't show up in the next day or two, I'd say that he went up in smoke along with his wife." Bud smiled and spat on the ground again.

"Sounds 'bout right to me, Sheriff," Doug said.

"Ya'll go on back into town," Bud said. "I'm gonna send the wagon on back in, too." They could hear the wail of the Davis siren moving down the lane.

"Stop by in a couple days," Bud added. "I oughta know who was in the house by then. You can do your report then. Sorry that you boys got called out in the cold for nothin'."

"No problem, Sheriff," Doug said. "You just broke up a poker game, that's all. I was losin'. You probably saved me some money and a big fight at home when I come in toting a short paycheck."

"Happy to be of service," Bud quipped, going along with the joke.

"Yep. You done me a big favor, Sheriff," Doug said, slapping Bud on the back. "My old lady's a bitch when it comes to money."

"Ain't they all," Bud said, returning the slap on the shoulder.

Their conversation was interrupted by the arrival of the Davis wagon, which pulled in next to the fire truck.

Bud drew his finger across his throat as a signal to the driver to cut the screaming siren. The driver turned off the siren, but left his engine running as he rolled down his window.

"Bad news, boys," Bud said, leaning down to look in the window. "There ain't no business for you here. Whoever was in that house done gone to meet their maker. Ashes to ashes. Ain't that what the Baptist say." Bud coughed and turned his head to spit in the dirt. They all chuckled at his joke.

"I wouldn't know," the driver of the wagon said. "I ain't no Baptist."

"Ya'll just go on back into town and tell that greedy son-of-a-bitch Davis that he wasted his gas and your time comin' out here," Bud said, grinning wickedly.

"Davis will understand ashes to ashes. He's in the front pew of that Baptist church ever Sunday, I hear."

The driver laughed; he punched the man in the seat next to him in the ribs. They got paid the same, a paltry hourly wage, no matter if they brought in a body or not.

"This oughta piss his Baptist ass off real good," the driver said. They all laughed loudly again. "We're outta here."

"Ya'll go on, too," Bud said to Doug and Buck.

"Sure thing, Sheriff." They climbed back into the truck and eased it down the lane with the Davis wagon following closely behind.

Bud reached down to his waist and retrieved a flashlight from his belt. It was dark and spooky without the light from the fire truck and the Davis wagon.

He scanned the remains of the Whatley home. The chimney had collapsed. It now stood only waist-high, and it looked like a headstone in the beam of the flashlight.

He looked up at the sky. A few stars were already out. It was gonna be a full moon. He remembered hunting possums on nights just like this when he was a boy. Sold 'em to the folks living in the quarters.

A bird screeched in the distance and Bud jumped. He heard the screams of the children in his head. If it weren't for the kids, he just might be alright with this.

It weren't like Whatley didn't have it comin' to 'im. And the old lady—well, she had some guilt by association. But not those kids. They had burnt up alive. Now that was something that Bud just couldn't make right in his mind no matter how hard he tried.

He shook his head. He feared the memory of those screaming, terrified kids would stay with him to his grave.

Bud drove the patrol car over to the Ivey house. He wanted desperately just to go on home; to see his wife; to have a drink of whiskey. Anything to put the sound of those screaming kids out of his mind.

It was that old woman mentioning her girl that kept him out here in this godforsaken place. Better to get to the bottom of that, right now. There were three cars in the Ivey driveway when Bud pulled up and stopped.

As he walked toward the house, he saw two heads through the front window, sitting by a fire. A dog started to bark. Bud tapped on the door.

"It's open," a man's voice called out.

Bud recognized the doctor from over at the Clinic as soon as he walked through the door. Old lady musta called 'im.

The doctor stood up, and Bud thought for a minute that the stupid son-of-a-bitch was gonna try to shake his hand.

Bud ignored him and went to stand in front of the fireplace. He turned his back to the fire and stretched his hands out behind him. His fingers were numb from the cold, and besides that, he wanted the doctor to know that there weren't gonna be no handshakin' goin' on.

"You Naomi Ivey?" Bud asked, clearing his throat. "You the one that called in the Whatley fire?"

"Yes, sir, I'm Naomi Ivey. And I did call in the fire."

"Well then, can you tell me what happened?" Bud was getting impatient. He wanted to wrap this up and go.

117

"Ain't got no idea," Naomi said, shaking her head. "I's hopin' that somebody could tell me. I come home from work and found the Whatley house burnt down to the ground. Weren't no folks 'round the place. They's all gone. I's hopin' that some help done been called. I's hopin' them folks been carried to the hospital or somethin'."

"What folks?" the sheriff asked. "You talkin' 'bout the Whatleys?"

"Yes, sir. Them and my girl, Karen. They all gone."

"Karen?" Bud scrutinized the old woman, remembering the car in the yard earlier and the driver's license in the purse. Trey hadn't said nothin' 'bout some gal bein' in the house.

Bud sat down on the hearth, took off his hat and dropped it between his legs. The fire was blazing. He was hot. His armpits were wet. His scalp itched. But he left on his coat just loosening a couple of buttons. He was bone weary; he didn't plan on staying long.

"Is there any reason for you to believe that your girl was at the Whatley place?" Bud asked, eying the old woman even more closely.

Naomi dropped her head into her hands. "She mighta been. I come home to find her gone; her car in the yard, grocery bags on the table and her pocketbook here by the door. She coulda gone over to the Whatley place. She sure 'nuff ain't here."

Naomi started to rock back and forth. "Lord, Lord," she whispered.

Before Bud could follow up on what the old woman said, the doctor spoke up.

"Sheriff, she can't tell you more than that." The doctor stood up and put his hand on the old woman's shoulder. The old woman looked up at the doctor as if to ask him what she should do. Something was going on between the two of them. Bud was sure of that.

Before Bud could sort matters out in his mind, the doctor spoke to him. "Sheriff, Mrs. Ivey has suffered a terrible shock. I'll walk you to your car."

118

Flipping on his hat, Bud rose from the chair. Hell, he weren't gonna get no more outta of the old lady. Now that the doctor had took over, she was bound to clam up. He'd come back out tomorrow. Hopefully, the doctor would be gone, and he could question her then.

Bud stood up. When he stopped to button his coat, the doctor came up behind him, practically herding him out of the door.

Bud balked, but then he relented and walked on out. Hell, it had been a long day. He was whipped. He didn't have it in him to get into a dust-up with the doctor, not tonight.

Dr. Luke followed Bud to the car. He waited as Bud got in and rolled down the window.

"If what the old woman says is right, my best guess 'bout what happened to her girl is that she burnt up, same as the Whatleys," Bud said. "But if you find out any different you let me know. You hear."

"I hear," Dr. Luke said.

"But Sheriff, if you have the time, I've got a question for you." Dr. Luke didn't wait for Bud to answer.

"What makes you so sure that the Whatleys burned up in the house. Isn't it possible they weren't at home?"

Bud looked up at the doctor scornfully. *He* was questioning him, the sheriff. Bud's voice took on an authoritative tone, the one he used when he was operating from his official capacity.

"Right now, I ain't got one goddamn reason to believe they weren't in the house 'less you know something different. So that's what I'm goin' with, for tonight, anyways. That is, unless them poor bastards come wanderin' up on their own."

Bud spit out the window. The wad of saliva landed next to Dr. Luke's shoe, but he didn't move or take his eyes off of Bud.

"You didn't know the Whatleys, did you, doctor?"

Dr. Luke didn't answer.

"I didn't think so," Bud said. "They was both bad drunks. Poor white trash from out here in Tate's Hell. Never 'mounted to a hill of beans. Who knows what happened to 'em? And who the hell cares?" Bud shoved the car into gear.

"Anything else on your mind, Doc?"

"And what about Naomi's daughter, Karen. How do you explain what happened to her?"

"Accordin' to her own mama, that's her car yonder, she oughta be home and she ain't. My best guess is she musta smelled the fire, saw the smoke and went over to help. Like a good Samaritan and all."

Dr. Luke didn't speak; he just stared at the sheriff.

"You know 'bout good Samaritans, don't you, Doc? Ain't I seen that fancy convertible you bought off the Hillmans parked over at that Shady Grove church on Sunday. Unless, I see some evidence to the contrary, I'm gonna say that she died in that fire, too. A good Samaritan."

"What about the possibility of foul play?" Dr. Luke asked. "With all due respect, Sheriff, the Whatley place didn't look that big to me. It was daylight. Why couldn't those people get out?"

Bud was pissed, really pissed. He spit out the window and this time the glop of spittle landed on Dr. Luke's shoe. Dr. Luke still didn't look away. He held Bud's stare.

"Foul play. What the hell you talkin' 'bout? Robbery? Them Whatleys didn't have a pot to piss in. Lived off a damn government check most of their sorry lives. As cold as it is, they had to be heatin' that shack with something. Kerosene, wood, gas—I don't know. Whatever it was, it musta got away from 'em. Hell, maybe they's passed out drunk when the fire started. I don't know, and I sure the hell don't care. Looks like nothin' but an accident to me, and that's how it goes down in my report. See ya 'round, Doc."

Bud pressed the gas and the wheels spun, slinging dirt on Dr. Luke's pants and shoes. The car sped away, and Dr. Luke went back inside finding Naomi exactly as he had left her—sitting, staring into the fire.

He put some more wood on the fire, shuffled the burning logs with the poker and pulled up the ottoman next to her chair.

He took her hands and stroked them softly. Her skin felt coarse and calloused pressed against the smoothness of his own palms.

"They gone ain't they, Dr. Luke?" she finally said. "Karen, the youngens, Bessie, all gone."

"Naomi, we don't know that for sure."

"I do. If they weren't in that Whatley house, they'd be here."

"I'm sorry, Naomi, so sorry." Dr. Luke had to turn away to hide his own tears.

He stood up and looked out of the window. The light of the full moon flooded the yard with soft light. Frost sparkled in patches about the yard.

The big oak soared up toward the moon. The tire swing looked suspended in midair. The rope invisible. A single leaf fluttered across the porch then floated off in the breeze.

Things looked normal. Karen's car. Naomi's car. His car. The line of trees shielding the clearing like the walls of a fort. Things looked peaceful. If only the world wasn't spinning out of control, he thought.

Dr. Luke walked back and sat down by Naomi. "I'll stay here with you. Or if you want, I'll take you to the island. Mrs. Brodie would be glad to have you, I know."

"This here's been my home for goin' on fifty years. I ain't leavin'. But you go on back to town. Some folks might need a doctor. You can't be stayin' here with me."

"Walter can manage. I'm not leaving you alone."

"Truth is, Dr. Luke, I wanna be alone." She looked up at him with eyes dulled by pain and despair. He had seen this look before on others. Heartbreak eyes, that's what he called this look.

""Naomi, please," Dr. Luke pleaded "I can't just leave you here all alone."

"Go," she said. "I mean it. Go on, now. I 'preciate what you tryin' to do, but I best be alone now."

Dr. Luke knew that he had lost this battle.

"Alright, I'll go. But I'll be back out bright and early to check on you tomorrow. And if you need me, I'm just a call away."

"I know that, and I 'preciate it. I really do. But right now, I need for you to let me be."

Dr. Luke kissed her forehead and reluctantly left.

After he was gone, Naomi slumped back into her chair. The fire burned down to a pile of red-hot embers. And still, she didn't move. The rip in her heart grew larger with each tick of the clock until she felt as her ribs would snap and tear her flesh away from the bone.

It was late when she rose from the chair and slowly shuffled over to the wall where Washington's gun hung suspended between two pegs. She took down the gun.

The temperature was now well below freezing, but Naomi didn't feel the sting of the frost in the air as she opened the door. She let her mind set its own course, drifting along like a sailboat cast about by the wind in a storm.

She walked to the side of the house and stood before the graves of her son and her husband.

Naomi leaned against the headstone of her husband's grave, and then she slid down the marble until she sat on the ground, her back resting against the stone. She looked up at the moon and a sky brilliant with stars.

Looking down, she traced the engraving that etched out Washington's name with the tip of her finger.

An owl hooted close by. An icy breeze blew across the grave. Naomi pressed her face against the cold stone. Clover came over and nuzzled his head down into her lap.

Tears rolled down her face and dropped in soft plunks on the fur of his head. She didn't wipe her eyes. She let the tears flow; small droplets forged a path across her wrinkled skin.

"I spent my whole life trustin' in you, Lord," she said, looking back up to the sky, "but you done put too much on me this time. First Nathan, then Washington, now Karen. Lily, the twins and poor ole Bessie, too. I'm a tired old lady, and I can't walk this world no more. Not all alone."

Naomi leaned back and stared at the gun.

"Naomi, no," Washington's voice whispered to her from the shadows.

"Lord, I need a sign," Naomi whispered back. "I need to know that you're here with me. That I got some reason to go on."

Then she saw it. A falling star streaked across the sky.

Naomi laid across the grave. The sound of her grief pierced the night air as her body convulsed in fierce bouts of weeping.

And then it was over. There were no more tears. Naomi rose to her feet, leaving the gun propped against the headstone.

"You done took me this far, Lord, and I reckon you ain't leavin' me now. So I ain't leavin' you," she said to the night air. "I reckon when the time comes, you gonna take me on outta this world, Lord. I ain't gonna take myself. That ain't right."

She ambled around to the front of the house. The huge oak tree with the tire swing loomed in front of her. She pushed the tire, and in the stillness of the night, she could hear the sounds of her children's squeals.

"Daddy, higher. Daddy, higher," Karen's voice called out. She heard her own voice reply.

"Don't you push them youngens too high, Washington, 'cause if one of them falls and breaks a bone, we ain't got no money for a doctor."

"Hush up, sweet mama," his deep voice boomed back at her. "I don't want my youngens ever to be afraid. There ain't no such thing as reachin' too high."

Naomi walked aimlessly about the yard. When she found herself at Washington's shop, she stopped and pushed on the door. She needed to feel close to him now.

The door was stuck. She shoved harder and it swung open. The moonlight streamed in through the open door, and the workbench and shelves rose up out of the shadows. Naomi started inside and then she froze.

She heard a noise. A rustling in the corner. And she knew that she was not alone.

"Whose there?" she called out. Her heart pounded wildly.

A voice answered, and for the first time in her life, Naomi fainted.

CHAPTER EIGHT

M ama?"
Naomi opened her eyes. A face loomed over her. She tried hard to focus. The face was smeared with soot and dirt and crowned by a few, frizzy, singed strands of hair. Two eyes hooded by swollen lids, the pupils rimmed by red broken veins and floating in a pool of tears, begged for recognition.

"Mama," Karen said again. She cradled her mother's head in her arms.

"Karen?" Naomi stretched out her fingers and stroked Karen's face like a blind person searching for familiar features. Karen pressed her face into her mother's neck.

"Karen, is that you child?"

"It's me, Mama."

"I thought you was gone. Oh, child, I thought you was gone." Naomi sobbed, clutching Karen to her chest.

"Hush now, Mama, I'm not gone. I'm right here with you."

"The Whatley place burnt to the ground, and I thought ..."

"I know what you musta thought, Mama. And I'm sorry for that. But it couldn't be helped."

"You're alive. There ain't no need to be sorry. Thank you, Lord!" Naomi whispered. She choked on her tears as she clung even more tightly to Karen.

Karen pulled away.

"Mama, you got to pull yourself together and listen to me. We ain't got no time to talk, right now. We gotta get outta here."

"What?" Naomi looked into Karen's eyes, confused.

"Mama, we gotta leave Tate's Hell. Now."

Bud hardly spoke a word to his wife all during supper. He pushed the food around on his plate and stared sullenly at the red-checkered pattern on the tablecloth. He couldn't eat; the food tasted like ashes and soot. Sheila wasn't in the best of moods herself.

"Trey was out here when I got home today," Shelia said. "Almost run me over leavin'."

Bud didn't say anything.

"Bud, I'm talkin' to you."

"What? I didn't hear you, honey."

"I said Trey Hillman was leavin' our house today, and he almost killed me. His tires dug a two-foot rut in our yard as he spun outta here. It's no wonder that we can't get no grass to grow."

"I'm sorry, honey. He killed a deer. Dressed it down out back. I told him that he could clean up here before he went home."

"I don't like him havin' a key to our house. For God's sake, Bud! What if I had come home, and he'd been inside. It ain't right. If he wants to cheat on your sister, that's his business. But keep it outta my house."

"It weren't nothin' like that, honey." Bud hated to lie to his wife. He had promised himself that he wouldn't. But how could he tell her the truth—Trey was in their home cleaning up after killing four, maybe five, people.

"Yeah, right," Shelia said, rolling her eyes. "So how was your day, Bud?"

Sheila loathed Trey Hillman, but she wasn't up to getting into a quarrel with Bud over him tonight.

Bud didn't answer. He was thinking about that fifth person—the old woman's daughter. What the hell had happened to her?

"Bud," Sheila said, exasperated. "You're not listenin' to a word I'm sayin'."

"I'm sorry, darlin'." Bud pushed back his plate. "I'm just worn slam out. If you don't mind, I'm gonna go on to bed."

"I don't mind. I'm gonna clean up these dishes. Then I'm goin' to bed myself."

Bud pretended to be asleep when Sheila slipped under the covers. She was warm and soft as he curled up next to her back.

He was bone weary; but he couldn't sleep. The events of the day kept rolling through his mind like a horror movie set on replay.

Nothing added up. There was that car that he had almost hit, just a stone's throw from the turnoff. Who was that? Couldn't been that old woman's daughter hightailin' it out of there; her car was home.

But she was missing. Trey hadn't mentioned any gal being at the Whatley shack. And that old woman had acted mighty peculiar. Too tight-lipped. And what the hell was that doctor doing out there talking about foul play like he was a damn cub reporter or something.

A branch scraped against the windowpane, and Bud jumped. His nerves felt like jagged shards of glass. His headache was back with a vengeance, and he desperately needed his Tums.

Sheila stirred next to him and snuggled in closer. He rolled over on his back and stared out the frosted windowpane.

Had something really caught his eye while he was in the Whatley yard? He thought he saw something on the path. Could it have been the gal? He had walked the path and convinced himself that it was nothing. Now he wasn't so sure.

Bud crawled out of bed. There were too many damn pieces of the puzzle missing. He knew that he sure the hell wasn't going to sleep; not with all of this on his mind.

Better to get up and go back out to Tate's Hell. Have a look around. He was missing something; Bud was certain of that.

"Bud, what are you doin'? Sheila asked groggily. She sat up in bed. "What time is it?"

"It don't matter what time it is," Bud said. "It ain't time for you to get up. But I can't sleep. I got some work to do. I'm gonna run into the office. I won't be gone long."

"You're gonna go to the office in the middle of the night?"

"It ain't the middle of the night. But, honey, I'm the sheriff, not a banker. I gotta work when I'm needed. Now you just go on back to sleep."

"Whatever." Sheila plopped back down on the pillow and pulled the cover up around her neck. "Just be careful."

Trey arrived home after Susan had already gone to bed. After cleaning up at Bud's, he stopped in at Harry's. He thought about going home, but he changed his mind. He felt too damn good; he felt like celebrating.

Finally, he was rid of the Whatleys, kids included. He hadn't gone out to Whatley's place intending to kill the old woman and the kids, only Whatley. But it was better this way. One fell swoop; the slate was clean.

Susan woke up with Trey straddling her.

"Come on, sugar, it's been a long time," Trey cooed. Susan tried to push him away, but then she relented. What the hell. She had to give it up some of the time if she wanted another baby.

Trey pumped his wife while fantasizing about the new waitress he had just met at Harry's. What was her name? Amber. That was it. Amber.

Susan distracted herself by making a mental note of things that she needed to get done for the annual Hillman Christmas party. Time was running short.

Bud parked in the Whatleys' front yard, or what had been the Whatleys' front yard until this afternoon. He got out of his car and looked around.

He reached for his flashlight although he didn't really need it. The full moon lit up the clearing. He could see the outline of the scorched ground where the house had sat.

The musky smell of smoke still clung to the frigid, winter air, although mingled in with the smell was just a hint of the sweet fragrance of evergreen.

The scent of the evergreen mercifully reminded Bud that this too would pass away. In time, Tate's Hell would reclaim this spot and turn it back into wilderness. He hoped that the Whatleys would be forgotten long before that happened.

Bud walked the spot where the Whatley house had stood for the past fifty years, kicking at the ashes and scraps of metal. The toe of his boot caught on something hard.

He looked down at a charred metal pot before moving on. The partially collapsed chimney glimmered in the moonlight, a grim monument to the Whatley clan. There was nothing to be found here.

Bud turned his attention to the path through the woods. Some moonlight filtered down through the bare tree branches, but the light was not enough to suit him.

He flipped on his flashlight as he set off down the path. Dried leaves and pine needles crunched under his boots; an owl hooted in the distance; bushes rustled as a small animal scurried for cover. Bud pulled his pistol out of its holster and let it dangle in his hand.

Something darted across the path in front of him, and Bud flinched, picking up his pace. He was a sensible man; had to be in his line of work. But he was spooked.

He remembered the ghost stories that his grandmother had told him when he was a boy. And the nights when Trey had dared him to walk through the cemetery.

Walking the cemetery never bothered Trey; hell, he seemed to love it. But not him; Bud remembered being terrified each and every time that he had foolishly taken Trey's dare.

And now tonight, walking alone on this dark path in the heart of Tate's Hell, the less sensible side of him halfway expected to see the ghosts of Ephram and Bessie Whatley come swooping down upon him, clutching the hands of their fiery grandchildren.

When a branch snapped under his foot, Bud broke into a trot. He didn't let up until he could see the end of the path.

When he was a few feet shy of clearing the woods, Bud doused his flashlight. It took a few seconds for his eyes to adjust to the return of nothing but the moonlight. He shuddered, trying to discard his fear, but it clung to him like a bad odor. It was time to gather his senses, get a grip, he told himself.

The house sat in the shadow of a large oak tree. There were no lights on inside, and Bud couldn't see much. But he clearly detected the smell of the smoke from a wood fire. And all of his instincts told him that he was not alone.

Two cars, the old woman's car and her daughter's car, sat parked in the yard. They didn't appear to have been moved. But the doctor's car was gone. That bothered Bud.

Bud ran over in his mind the possibility that the old woman's daughter might still be alive. But if that was the case why hadn't she been at home when he stopped in with her mama earlier.

Her mama believed that she was dead; the grief that Bud had seen on the mama's face was real enough. He had already seen enough, as the sheriff, to recognize true grief when he saw it.

Then again, maybe she was dead, which meant that he was out here in the middle of the night freezing his ass off for no good reason. He found the last option to be the most appealing.

Bud stealthily advanced on the Ivey house. At the edge of the porch, he crouched low and listened. The house was quiet, not a sound. He crept up onto the porch and raised his head high enough to peer into the front window. The house was dark except for the faint glow of embers in the fireplace. The room was empty.

The wooden floor creaked under the weight of his heavy boots as Bud moved across the porch toward the door. He tightened his grip on his revolver. His heart danced around in his chest; his skin crawled; and sweat leaked out from every pore on his body. What the hell was he afraid of? At the most, there were two women inside, one of them old enough to be his grandma.

Still he was scared. Until now, being the sheriff hadn't required anything of him more dangerous than arresting a few drunks.

Sneakin' 'round in the dead of night, into some house in the damn middle of Tate's Hell, wasn't what he had in mind when he took on the job. And this on top of what he'd already been through today.

It was nothin' short of a damn miracle that he hadn't burnt up himself in the Whatley shack. Damn Trey Hillman. Home sleepin' like a baby while he was out here in Tate's Hell stalkin' some women like he was a damn Green Beret and they were the Viet Cong.

He had to get a handle on himself. Like it or not, he had a job to do here. He twisted the doorknob and was shocked to find that the door wasn't even locked. He pushed the door, and it opened.

His spine stiffened and goosebumps, big as fire ants, popped up on his arms and neck. An open door wasn't a good sign. If it was him livin' out here in this godforsaken wilderness—which he wouldn't do under any circumstances—he woulda made damn sure that he built hisself a fort.

He sure the hell wouldn't be out here in broad daylight, much less in the dead of night, with unlocked doors. But go figger the kinda crazy folks that would live out here in Tate's Hell. If he lived to be a hundred-year-old man, he'd never understand 'em.

Bud slipped inside and cursorily searched the rest of the house. The search took only a few minutes. The house was empty.

The old woman probably left out with that doctor, he surmised. There were no signs that the old woman's daughter had been here. The house looked 'bout the same as when he had stopped by earlier.

And he was ready to go. Bud had to admit to himself, as he stood in the kitchen, that he hadn't come out here prepared for any kind of a showdown, not even with two women. You never know. Most folks in Tate's Hell could shoot, women included.

Bud made a hasty exit out the kitchen door and then a beeline back to the path. He was disappointed that he didn't know much more than he did when he arrived, but he was also relieved that nothing had happened.

If the girl had survived the fire, and he was now trying hard to convince himself that she hadn't, she wasn't in the house. But that didn't rule out her having left Tate's Hell. He'd question Trey tomorrow, poke around a little bit. See if anything came up.

But for now, all he wanted to do was go home and try to get some sleep. While he didn't particularly relish the idea of tromping back through the woods, it was a helluva sight better than staying out here in Tate's Hell. Even so, he found it necessary to pause at the edge of the woods and gather his courage before striking out on the path.

He took in a few deep breathes in order to try and settle himself down. And then Bud wasn't sure why, but he turned to take one last look at the Ivey house.

That's when he saw her.

In the moonlight, the figure of a woman appeared out of the shadows. She looked like a ghost as she walked hurriedly across the moonlit yard, her shawl fluttering in the breeze. Bud's heart jumped right up into his throat, and he came dangerously close to screaming before he plastered himself behind a tree.

Bud hugged the security of the tree and watched as the figure disappeared into the house. Her size and the stoop in her shoulders reminded him of the old woman he had met earlier in the day. Maybe he hadn't seen a ghost after all.

He stood staring at the house, uncertain as to what he should do next. He wasn't up for rushing the house. Not alone. If it was the old woman, she could have a gun. Not to mention that he was on the verge of a heart attack. His heart was still pounding in his chest like a kettle drum. He had used up his last ounce of courage searching the house.

Then she was back, walking out of the house with a bundle under each of her arms. Bud watched as she got into her car. The interior light came on and then it went out before he could see anything. The motor started, but the car didn't move right away.

Bud thought that he might have heard the sound of a door closing a second time; but he couldn't be sure. The shadows from the forest and the car itself blocked his view of the driver's side of the car. And the motor muffled any noise. He was too far out to really see or hear anything.

As Bud stood staring, the headlights popped on, and the car circled out of the driveway and down the dirt lane. Where the hell was she going at this time of the night?

Bud sprinted across the front yard to the west side of the house where the old woman had stepped out of the shadows. He stopped when he saw the shed rising up in front of him. Damn. He had missed it earlier. It had been concealed by the shadow of several huge oak trees.

He raised the gun in his hand, and stepping to one side of the door, he kicked it open with his foot. Except for the door creaking on its hinges, all was quiet.

Still pressed against the wall, he switched on his flashlight and stuck it through the door. When nothing happened, Bud gingerly poked his head around the doorjamb to have a look. Empty. He lowered his gun and went on inside to poke around.

The place looked like some combination of a work and storage shed to him. Bud ran the light from his flashlight up and down the walls and then along the floor. The only thing that looked out of order was a shovel lying on the floor and a tarpaulin bunched up in one corner. Otherwise, the shed was in perfect order.

He walked over to the corner and kicked at the tarpaulin, flipping it over with the toe of his boot. Stooping in lower, he turned the beam of the flashlight on the underside of the tarpaulin. It was smeared with traces of soot and blood.

"Goddamnit," Bud swore aloud. His first instinct had been right after all. The old woman's daughter was alive. She musta been hid out in this shed. But what did she know? Enough to hide. That much was clear. He had to catch that car.

Bud sprinted across the yard and down the path. He was totally winded by the time he reached his car. Leaning over and clutching his sides, he tried to suck some cold air into his lungs as he assessed the situation. The old woman had a considerable head start on him; she had gained a good fifteen-minute jump already.

Still trying to catch his breath, Bud climbed in the patrol car. He rolled down his window in an effort to cool off and clear his head so that he could think straight.

There was no way to know for sure where the old woman was headed, but Bud thought that a good guess was up Highway 27 toward Trinity.

The opposite direction was nothing but swampland. He doubted that she would head out in the dead of night on that stretch of lonely road, with the next town over fifty miles away.

As soon as Bud hit Highway 27, he opened up the patrol car, full throttle. With speed and a little luck, he might be able to catch up to her.

He was traveling close to ninety miles an hour when he saw some taillights up ahead. But he was closing in on the outskirts of Trinity, and he had to slow down. He couldn't even be sure that it was the old woman.

When the car up ahead made a turn onto the beach road, he followed. What did he have to lose? There were no other cars in sight. He had a hunch that it just might belong to the old woman. So he followed. He needed to think. A night ride would clear his head even if it turned out that he was on a wild, goose chase.

Driving along the beach road, Bud kept his distance behind the car. If it was the old woman, he didn't want to spook her. He just wanted to know where she was going and who, if anybody, was with her.

Bud pondered his options. He could stop the car on some pretense, but then what would he do if he found the girl with her.

He had never killed no damn body, and he sure the hell weren't ready to start now. He weren't gonna kill two women, and one an old woman at that. And not here on a public road.

If the old woman had the girl with her, he could arrest her; hell, he could arrest the both 'em. Think up some bogus crime to hit 'em with. But he didn't want either one of them in jail. That would raise too many questions.

Besides that, the old woman had that damn doctor on her side, who was turning out to be one royal pain in the ass. And him partners with that damn do-gooder Walter Adams. Nope, the two of them would raise a stink if he arrested the women.

Bud tried to focus. He was dead-tired. It was hard to think. Suppose the gal was alive. If she had seen anything, maybe she would be too scared to tell.

She was, after all, a poor, black woman living in Tate's Hell. What could she do? Accuse the richest man in town of murder. And murdering who? Two old drunks. And two little kids.

What if she had seen Trey at the Whatleys? What if she had seen him—the sheriff—out there? He couldn't rule any possibility out. Good god almighty, this was gettin' complicated, Bud thought, and him too wore out to even think straight.

When the car turned onto the bridge over to the island, Bud roused himself out of his thoughts, faced with yet another dilemma. Where the hell would that old woman go on Palm Island this time of the night?

His doubts about whether he was even followin' the right car resurfaced. He had come this far. Might as well keep going. What else could he do other than turn 'round and go home and lay in his bed tossin' and turnin', worried near 'bout to death over he weren't even sure what. That wasn't goin' to happen.

And his gut was talking to him, tellin' him he was on to somethin' although he didn't know what, but somethin'. Bud scoured the glove compartment desperately searching for a roll of Tums. A talking gut required a constant diet of Tums. Hell, he was practically addicted to the damn things.

Bud didn't find any Tums, but he did find a single Excedrin tablet. A cursory search of the front seat and floorboard failed to turn up anything at all to drink. Bud tried to suck up enough saliva to swallow the pill; it stuck in his throat.

Bud put his attention back on the road, only to realize that while he had been fooling around in the glove compartment, he had lost sight of the car. When he reached the crest of the bridge, he should have been able to see the direction the headlights were moving. But he couldn't.

There were only two roads on the island. Bud had been out here enough to know that. The road he was currently on came to a dead end at the beach in less than a mile. The other road ran the length of the island. A right turn off of the bridge led to the Plantation (rich man's land); or a left turn led to the federal land preserve.

"Goddamnit," Bud said, scratching around under the seat for something to drink. He pulled out a half-full bottle of coke. No telling how long that had been there. He unscrewed the cap and took a slug.

Bud turned in the direction of the Plantation. There weren't no house any place else. He didn't come out this way much. The rich folks, who lived on the island, kept to themselves.

Technically, they were within his jurisdiction, but they had their own security and almost never had much need for the services of his office. He decided that if he didn't see anything, that he'd make a U-turn at the guard gate to the Plantation and go on back into town.

As Bud approached the guard gate, he got his umpteenth shock of the night. The car he had been following, after a quick stop, was rolling right through the gate as pretty as you please. The arm to the gate lowered as the taillights disappeared from sight.

What the hell? Black folks weren't allowed on the Plantation 'cept as hired help. He had been followin' the wrong car.

Bud was preparing to make a U-turn, when it dawned on him; one or both of them women could work for somebody out here. Hadn't the old woman said that she had come home from work to find her daughter gone. And he had got fairly close to the car in front of him. The car looked the same as the one he had seen pullin' out of the old woman's front yard earlier.

There was no time left to think. Bud found himself at the entrance to the guard gate. The car rolled to a stop, and Bud rolled down his window.

The guard on duty was Billy Sims. Reluctantly, he ambled out of the guard house; it was cold out and he rarely got cars this time of the night. Now here were two in a row.

When Billy saw that the new arrival was a patrol car with the sheriff himself driving, he put on a fake smile. Bud and Billy had known each other since grade school.

Billy didn't really have any beef with the sheriff. It was just that the sheriff was friends with that bastard, Trey Hillman. And Billy had purely hated Trey since the time several years back when Trey had tried to put the move on his wife.

His wife had been working over at Harry's Tavern tryin' to help him make ends meet. That was before he had landed this good job at the Plantation. Being a Plantation guard paid him enough money to let his wife stay home and keep house and raise up their kids. Billy was especially proud of the fact that his wife didn't have to work no more. Not many workin' men in Trinity could say that.

Bud was thick as thieves with Trey Hillman; that meant Billy didn't have no use for him, sheriff or no sheriff. But you didn't just go pissin' the sheriff off for no good reason.

Swallowing his pride, Billy leaned down and grinned through the window of the patrol car at Bud.

"Well, I be a dang monkey's uncle," Billy said, "if ain't the high sheriff hisself. How the hell you been, Bud?" Billy thrust his arm through the car's window to shake Bud's hand.

For his part, Bud was relieved to see that it was Billy Sims on duty. He and Billy had played football together in high school. Although you couldn't tell by the gut hanging over Billy's belt, he had once been the fastest running back in the region. Bud had no idea that Billy resented him because of his friendship with Trey.

"I'm gettin' 'long good," Bud said, reaching up to grasp Billy's hand. "How 'bout you, Billy? You and your family, ya'll gettin' 'long alright?"

"Can't complain," Billy said.

"Glad to hear that," Bud said, trying to work up some goodwill with the small talk before he asked any questions.

"What the hell brings you out to this neck of the woods, and at this time of night?" Billy asked. "We don't see much of the law out here 'specially the sheriff hisself."

"One of deputies come down with the flu," Bud said. "I'm just fillin' in."

"Yeah, but what you doin' in this neck of the woods?" Billy persisted. Something had brung the sheriff out, and Billy was naturally curious.

"I didn't have much to do to pass the time. I was out drivin' the beach road when I saw a car up ahead of me weavin'. Thought it could be somebody drivin' drunk. I was gonna pull 'em over, but before I could do that, the car turned off onto the bridge.

"We don't usually bother these rich folks out here. You know that, Billy. I decided against pullin' 'em over; instead, I followed the car here. Just wanted to make sure whoever it was got home alright."

"You missed that call, Sheriff," Billy said, chuckling aloud. "If you talkin' 'bout that car what just went through the gate, it had an old woman drivin' it—Naomi Ivey from out in Tate's Hell. She works for one of our *residents*, Mrs. Brodie. She's been with the Brodies for years, or so I was told when I started work here."

"Is that right?" Bud said, doing his best to appear nonchalant, although his mind was racing with this new information.

"Right as rain," Billy retorted. "Oh, and as a general rule, Sheriff, the rich folks livin' at the Plantation don't drive little putt-putt cars like that."

Billy couldn't resist getting this jab in at Bud. The whole town knew Bud wouldn't even be the sheriff if his buddy Hillman hadn't got him the job. It sure weren't 'cause he had any special qualifications or natural talents as a lawman.

Bud recognized Billy's remark as a jab, but he let it pass. It weren't no time to go takin' offense. He needed information that only Billy could give him. "I didn't think 'bout that," he said.

"And I'm pretty sure that Naomi ain't had nothin' to drink any stronger than apple cider," Billy said. He liked Naomi. She was polite and nice to him. Didn't bother a soul. He didn't want the sheriff causin' Naomi trouble just 'cause she was some poor, old woman that he could hassle.

"I 'spect the swervin' was her noddin' off at the wheel," Billy added. "She's way too old to be out workin' this time of night. Said Mrs. Brodie had took bad sick and needed her. Probably that same flu that's got your deputies laid up."

"Probably. Brodie? I don't recollect ever hearin' that name. Do I know them people?"

"I 'spect not, Sheriff. Horace Brodie was the richest man here on the island. Him and his wife moved in here from up North some years ago. He died a number of years back, but his widow she stayed on in that big old house of theirs right by her lonesome."

"You don't say," Bud replied. "Which house is that?"

"I done told you that they's the richest people out here," Billy said, all puffed up with importance. "So it stands to reason that they got the biggest house out here. And that's sayin' a lot. I don't know the last time you was out this way, but there's enough money put in some of these here houses to feed all of the poor folks in Trinity for at least a year, maybe two."

"I ain't been out here in a good long spell," Bud said. "Might as well have a drive through, have a little look-see as long as I'm here. I'm just mostly killin' time 'til the shift is up. Which house is that Brodie house? I wouldn't mind seein' somethin' like that."

"It's the second road on the bay side," Billy said. "First house belongs to some folks outta Miami. One of 'em is a lady lawyer. Can you beat that?"

"Can't say as I can," Bud replied.

"You can't miss the Brodie place," Billy said, starting to hop from one leg to the other to stay warm. "It sits back off the road; but it's big enough that you can't miss it."

"Reckon, I'll cruise on by and take me a gander at the place," Bud said. He was eager to move on. "Good to see ya', Billy."

"You too, Sheriff."

Billy returned to the guard shack and pushed the button to lift the gate. Billy had strict instructions not to let nobody through the gate that weren't a resident, or who hadn't been cleared by a resident. You could be fired for that.

But he didn't see no way 'round lettin' Bud in. Bud was the sheriff, after all. Cleared or not, Billy reckoned that he couldn't turn him away.

And he was warming up to Bud. Hell, the sheriff might be friends with Trey, but he was a working man same as him. They had both grew up not a stone's throw from the quarters. Couldn't blame a man for tryin' to better hisself. Billy waved Bud through.

Bud drove straight toward the Brodie place. He didn't give a flyin' flip 'bout seein' some rich folks' houses out here in *the Plan-damn-tation.* There was only one house he wanted to see— the one belongin' to that Brodie woman.

Billy was right. There was no missin' the Brodie house. Bud whistled under his breath at the sheer enormity of the place. Under the light of the full moon, it soared up to the sky, big as a damn castle. Where the hell do people come up with money like that, he wondered. The President of the United States couldn't live in a house that big.

The house was set way back off of the road up next to the bay. Before turning down the asphalt lane leading up to the house, Bud cut his headlights. There was plenty of moonlight for him to find his way.

He briefly thought about parking the car and walking up to the house but quickly discarded that idea. Rich people like this could have dogs, guards, electric fences—he didn't know what all. He thought back on his trek through Tate's Hell and opted to stay in the car.

Once he got up close to the house, he could see the old woman's car in the driveway. She had pulled in close and 'round toward the back of the house. But he could see the tail end of her car barely sticking out.

After spotting the car, Bud didn't waste any time backing the patrol car out of the drive and heading back to the main road. While he was fully cognizant of the fact that he was the sheriff, he was equally cognizant of the fact that he was intruding on private property, with no good reason for doing so.

A place like this was apt to have some guards, probably armed. Bud wasn't up to an encounter of any sorts, certainly not one with armed guards.

Back on the main road, he pulled the car off of the pavement and stopped on a strip of grass under the cover of an oak thicket. From this vantage point, he could watch the Brodie property, undetected. Bud wanted some time to think about what he should do next. And he wanted to see if the old woman would leave the island, and if she did, where she would go.

In his mind, Bud had pretty much settled on the fact that the girl was alive and had seen something. But just how much she had seen, and who she would tell, that was the sixty-four-dollar question.

And he guessed that the old woman had brung her out here and deposited her behind the walls of that fort. But he couldn't be sure of that. Why would some old rich, bitch who lives out here want to get mixed up in the troubles of that old women.

There were a lot of unanswered questions.

Rodrigo heard the squawk of his radio. The night was cold; and he was tired. Hunkering down farther into his bunk, he tried to block out the noise. But he couldn't. Wrapping himself in a blanket, he stumbled to the front of the boat.

"Rodrigo here. Come back."

"Billy here. Planation Security. Over."

"What's up? Over."

"Mrs. Brodie called. She needs you. Asked if I could get you that message. Over."

"Did she say what's wrong? Over."

"Nope. But Naomi come through earlier. Said Mrs. Brodie was sick. Over."

"Thanks, Billy. Over and out."

Rodrigo pulled on some jeans, a flannel shirt and his boots. Grabbing the keys to his jeep from a peg on the wall, he threw open the galley door. A blast of Arctic air sent him scrambling back for his down coat.

Mrs. Brodie would have never summoned him unless the situation was dire. He gunned the jeep. The Brodie estate wasn't far. His boat was docked only a few miles from the entrance to the Plantation. Glancing down at his wrist, he realized that he had forgotten his watch. It had to be late. He had docked the boat around ten and had gone straight to bed.

As he approached the guard gate, Rodrigo braked hard. He thought that Billy would wave him through, but he didn't. Rodrigo unzipped the window liner as Billy came out the door.

"What's up, Billy?" Rodrigo said.

"Naomi come through 'bout an hour ago. Said Mrs. Brodie was bad off sick. Not ten minutes later, I got a call from Mrs. Brodie asking me to radio through to you. That Mrs. Brodie didn't sound sick to me, but who knows?"

"I told Mrs. Brodie that you guys could get me on the radio if she ever needed me. Hope you don't mind."

"Don't mind a bit. I don't know that Brodie woman myself. But she's good folks I hear. Always sends us guards something to help out at Christmas. That's more than I can say for the majority of these rich bastards up here."

Billy had taken a little leeway talking about the residents of the Plantation. He saw Rodrigo as one of them; one of the working people.

"Thanks, Billy."

"Oh, and Rodrigo, something else. The sheriff is out here. I'd slow down if I was you. He can stop you for speedin' even in here."

"I'll keep that in mind. Thanks again, Billy."

Bud was lost in his thoughts when he realized there were headlights approaching from the direction of the guard gate. It was the dead of winter and the middle of the night. Traffic was the last thing that he expected.

Then he remembered where he was sitting. This was the Plantation where guards were paid to make nightly patrols.

The headlights came baring down hard on him. If this was the guard truck, it was goin' mighty damn fast. The driver had his lights on bright, and for a brief hair-raising moment, Bud thought the vehicle would plow right into him while he sat helpless to move out of its way. He gripped the steering wheel and sat braced for the impact.

But the lights from the oncoming vehicle made a sharp turn to the right and then sped away up the Brodie lane. In the fleeting glimpse that he caught of the vehicle, Bud made it out to be a jeep of some sorts.

Bud stared at the taillights of the jeep as they disappeared down the lane. He was beyond being surprised. So much had happened during the past twenty-four hours that he felt nothing was beyond the realm of possibilities. If the damn Martians landed right on the road in front of him, it wouldn't faze him, not one damn bit.

Now what? Who the hell could be in that jeep? And it most certainly had stopped at the Brodie house. There was no place else for it to go on that road. And Billy had said that this Mrs.

Brodie lived right by "her lonesome." The last time Bud had heard that phrase used it meant "alone." So who was this middle-of-the-night guest who had just stormed this Mrs. Brodie's house like a bat outta hell?

One thing for sure, he wasn't gonna get any answers sittin' here on the side of the road. And he wasn't goin' up to that Brodie house. By now Billy was sure to be wonderin' what had happened to him. It was time to go.

Rodrigo came to a screeching halt directly behind Naomi's car and then ran the short distance to the back door. One knock and the door opened. He was surprised to see Mrs. Brodie. She looked upset but not sick.

"What's wrong?" he asked.

"Come into the study," Mrs. Brodie replied. "Naomi and her daughter Karen are in by the fire. We can talk there."

Karen sat next to her mother on the sofa, her head nestled down onto Naomi's shoulder. When Rodrigo saw Karen, he stopped.

Her eyes were swollen and bloodshot. Her face and hands, though cleansed of the soot and blood, were marred by blotches of burned skin and a myriad of cuts and scratches, which were now smeared with ointment. She had tried to slick back what remained of her hair, but he could see that it was singed off to her scalp and her eyebrows were missing.

Naomi looked up to meet Rodrigo's stare with eyes sagging from fear, fatigue and worry.

"Oh my God! What happened?" he asked.

As Bud exited the Plantation, he honked the horn. Billy pushed open the sliding window to the guard shack; he wasn't going outside. Being polite to the sheriff didn't require him to freeze his ass off twice in one night.

"You leavin'?" Billy asked, trying to stifle a yawn. Bud suspected that he had caught Billy sleeping.

"Yep. Stayed longer than I planned to lookin' at all them rich folks' houses. And most of 'em shut down for the winter. Go figger. I don't know where the hell people come up with that kind of money."

"Beats me," Billy replied. He was trying not to be rude, but he wanted the sheriff to move on. Most nights, especially during the winter months, he pretty much slept through the nightshift.

Not tonight. Tonight this place had been a dang freeway. He hadn't been able to catch a wink. And just when he was dozing off here was the sheriff back wanting to talk. Billy had a part-time day job at the lumberyard. He wouldn't be worth shit tomorrow if he didn't get a couple of hours of sleep.

Billy tried to give the sheriff a hint by sliding the window shut, but Bud reached out and draped his arm across the windowsill.

"Say, Billy. I saw a jeep come flyin' past me back down on the main road. Who the hell is out here rippin' up the roads this time of the night?"

Billy immediately decided that the sheriff was asking a lot of damn questions. One thing for sure, something was going on. The sheriff had moved right on past idle curiosity—Billy was smart enough to know that.

And whatever the hell it was, it had somethin' to do with that Brodie woman. First, Naomi came out in the middle of the night and then Rodrigo. Mrs. Brodie must be mighty damn sick. But what business was it of the sheriff.

Billy worked for the people on this island, Mrs. Brodie included. And the one thing they valued above all else was privacy, especially that Mrs. Brodie. These people buttered his bread, not the sheriff.

He decided not to tell Bud any more. He mighta warmed up to Bud a bit when he first come through, but he had already said too much. Besides that, Rodrigo was his friend.

"I don't rightly know who he is," Billy lied. "He's just some fella that does some work up at the Brodie estate. Like I said earlier, Mrs. Brodie is bad sick. I'm guessin' he took her some medicine or somethin' that she needed."

"You're probably right," Bud said. "What the hell does it matter. See ya 'round, Billy."

"Yeah, see ya 'round, Sheriff."

Billy was holding something back; Bud was fairly certain of that fact. People didn't come and go at a place like this without the guards knowing something about them. Hadn't Billy offered up the goods on the old woman. But he didn't want to say a word 'bout the driver of the jeep.

As Bud turned the bend, he spotted a deserted road leading over to the bay. He backed his car in, just off of the road, and doused his lights. From this spot, he could watch the guard gate without being seen.

Slumping down, Bud rested his head against the back of the seat—to wait. He was turnin' into a regular goddamn Sherlock Holmes, he thought. But he wanted to see who came out of that gate and where they went. That would at least give him some leads to follow tomorrow.

Mrs. Brodie entered the study carrying a silver serving tray, containing a pot of tea and four china cups. Rodrigo was relieved to see her. He had wanted to know what happened as soon as he arrived, but all Mrs. Brodie would say was that Karen had been involved in some dreadful fire in Tate's Hell.

Mrs. Brodie insisted that she make some tea before telling him more. So he had paced the floor looking helplessly on as Naomi tried to comfort Karen.

"Honey, you need to try and sit up," Naomi said to Karen, when Mrs. Brodie came in with the tray. "Mrs. Brodie has made some tea. You might feel better if you could drink just a bit. And we need to talk."

Rodrigo took the cup that Mrs. Brodie passed to him. The dainty china felt awkward in his large hand.

"Please," Rodrigo implored, looking from Mrs. Brodie to Naomi. "Tell me what happened?"

"Sit," Mrs. Brodie said to Rodrigo, pointing to an ottoman next to the sofa where Naomi and Karen sat, before she seated herself in a chair close by.

"Karen, do you think that you can tell Rodrigo what you told us?" Mrs. Brodie asked, leaning in to pat Karen's hand.

"I'll try," Karen said, her voice a hoarse whisper. She sat up and tried to compose herself. "The twins and Bessie were over at our house."

"Bessie?" Rodrigo asked.

"The twins' grandmother," Naomi said. "You know the twins called her 'Granny.'"

"Called?" Rodrigo said. "Has something happened to the twins' grandmother?"

"Rodrigo, it would be best for you to simply allow Karen to tell the story," Mrs. Brodie said.

"Alright," Rodrigo relied. He fidgeted about in his seat.

"Late in the afternoon, about four o'clock, or so, I decided to go into town," Karen said. "I wanted to cook supper for Mama, and I needed to pick up a few things from the grocery store. Me and Bessie had already decided that she was gonna eat supper with us and then spend the night at our house.

"Bessie was gonna watch the twins long enough for me to run to the store. But then Bessie set in for me to let the twins walk with her over to her house. She needed to get her medicine and a change of clothes."

"Her house. Where is that?" Rodrigo asked.

"Bessie lived just a short piece from our house," Naomi said.

Rodrigo caught the use of the past tense again—lived instead of lives—but he remained silent.

"At first, I said no; that I didn't want the twins to go to Bessie's house." Karen went on with her story. "But Mango begged to go, and Bessie promised to come right back. I didn't plan to be gone long." Karen fought back tears. "If only I hadn't said yes. Maybe, none of this woulda happened."

147

"It's alright, honey," Naomi said, stroking her hand. "It's not your fault. There's no way that you coulda knowed what was gonna happen."

"Know what?" Rodrigo said. He looked from Naomi to Mrs. Brodie. "Please, just tell me what happened."

"When I got back from the store, Bessie and the twins weren't home. So I walked down the path to find them."

"Find them?" Rodrigo asked. "Did you find them, Karen?"

Rodrigo felt the first wave of panic course through his body. He looked at Karen's burned and battered body, and suddenly, he felt as if he was on fire—with fear. He crushed the teacup in the palm of his hand as he dropped to his knees in front of Karen.

"Karen, where are the twins?" Rodrigo's eyes pleaded with Karen to give him an answer.

But Karen couldn't speak. She buried her face in her mother's breasts, sobbing. Naomi pulled her in closer as she rocked back and forth clutching her daughter in her arms. "It's gonna be alright, baby girl," she whispered into Karen's ear. "Your Mama is right here. I ain't gonna let nothin' happen to you. Everthin' is gonna be alright."

Mrs. Brodie stood up and placed her hand on Rodrigo's shoulder. He looked up into her face. Her eyes were swimming in tears.

"Where are the twins?" he whispered up to her.

CHAPTER NINE

T he twins are here," Mrs. Brodie said to Rodrigo.

"Here?" Rodrigo asked. "Here where?"

"In there; see for yourself," Mrs. Brodie said. She pointed to the open door of her own bedroom, which was situated off of the study where they were all gathered.

"The twins are asleep in my bed. But they're in grave danger, Rodrigo. That's why I called you."

Mrs. Brodie beckoned for him to follow her, and he rose from the floor and joined her in the doorway of her dimly lit bedroom.

"There," she said, pointing to a hump under the down comforter, which covered a large, mahogany sleigh bed. "You may look in on them, but please try not to wake them. They have suffered an awful ordeal."

Rodrigo crossed the room, the thick carpet muffling the sound of his footsteps. He stooped and lifted the comforter. There, clinging together as they slept, were the twins.

"I was almost too late," Karen said, to Naomi, Rodrigo and Mrs. Brodie, who were all gathered back together in the study. Her voice trembled.

"But you wasn't; and that's what matters," Naomi said. "Try to tell us what happened. I know what you done told me, but I think it's best if Rodrigo and Mrs. Brodie hear the story from you. If you're up to it, that is."

"I'll try," Karen said. Mrs. Brodie poured Karen another cup of tea. Karen's hand shook as she lifted the cup to her lips.

"Just start at the beginnin'," Naomi said.

"Like I said earlier, I had to run into town. Bessie was goin' to watch the youngens. They was gonna walk over to the Whatley place, pick up a few things and come straight back."

"The Whatley place?" Rodrigo asked. "You've lost me, again."

"Ephram and Bessie Whatley's house—the twins' grandparents," Naomi said. "Remember, I already told you the woman the kids called 'Granny' was named Bessie—Bessie Whatley. Ephram was her husband. They lived together in a little shack, a short walk from our place in Tate's Hell."

"Oh yeah, right," Rodrigo said. He was still trying to put the pieces together.

"Go on with your story," Naomi said to Karen.

"I knew somethin' was wrong, almost from the time I pulled into the yard, after gettin' back from the store," Karen said. "I honked the horn, like I always do, but nobody came out. The kids love to help me with the groceries; they always come runnin' when I honk the horn. That bothered me, but I brushed it off. Carried the groceries on inside.

"Our house was deserted. Bessie and the kids shoulda been back from the Whatley place long 'fore I got home. I didn't waste a minute. I dropped the grocery bags on the kitchen table and headed over to the Whatley house.

"I hadn't gone very far down the path when I smelled the smoke. I took off runnin' fast as I could. As I got closer to the Whatley house, I saw the smoke; there was a black cloud of it risin' up over the trees. Lord have mercy, I went to runnin' then. The smoke was thick when I reached the clearin' behind the house. But I could see, plain as day, that the Whatley house was on fire. The whole place weren't nothin' but smoke and flames.

"The next part is mostly a blur. I run up on the back porch. The porch was still standin' then. When I opened the back door, the heat blasted out. It drove me back; the place was a furnace. The flames roared; something crashed inside. I stood there tryin' to get my wits 'bout me, when I heard the screams: terrified, bloodcurdling howls. I knew then that the twins were trapped inside.

"When I heard them little youngens screamin', the Lord just took over. I don't even know how I knew what to do, but I did. There was a spigot by the back steps. I'd seen it before. I don't know how I even remembered that spigot, but I did.

"I jumped down off the porch and yanked on the spigot handle. There was a spurt of orange water, rust in the pipes I guess, and then the water gushed out. I ripped off my coat and drenched it with water. Then I put the coat over my head and shoulders and made another run at the door."

"You done good, girl," Naomi said.

"Daddy, he taught me and Nathan 'bout fire," Karen said. "He made us both practice on how to get out of a burnin' house. All them lessons musta kicked in. Somehow, I knew to drop low below the smoke 'fore tryin' to go back in.

"I could still hear the screamin'. It was hard to tell where the cries were comin' from; but, thank goodness, that Whatley place was small. I crawled down the hall 'cause it was the only way to go. The smoke, pretty much, had my view blocked, but then I saw 'em. I was right on 'em, 'fore I knew it. They was huddled together by the kitchen door.

"There weren't a second to spare. I pulled 'em up under the coat and begged 'em to crawl, tryin' to pull 'em 'long beside me. But little Mango was so confused, he pulled away. Millie, she didn't move a'tall. Both of 'em screamin'—out of their minds with fear.

"For a second, I panicked, too, thinkin' there weren't no way for us to get outta that fire. But I knew that I had to at least try. Pokin' one of them youngens under each arm, I covered us with the wet coat and made a run for the door. All I can say is that the Good Lord had to been with me for us to make it out.

"I cleared the porch, draggin' both youngens along with me. I can't say where I got the strength to do that. I was near 'bout to the edge of the path when I heard a loud boom. I glanced over my shoulder just in time to see the porch roof come crashin' down. Another few seconds, and we wouldn't made it."

"Thank God you got there in time," Rodrigo said. "But what are you doing here? Why haven't you and the children seen a doctor?"

"Just keep listening," Mrs. Brodie said. "There is much more to this story that you don't know."

Karen took a sip of tea before she spoke again. "I drug the youngens as far as I could away from the fire, but I barely got 'em on the path. I was tryin' to catch my breath and see to the youngens when I heard voices. My first thought was that help was nearby. I tried to call out; but I couldn't yell. I could hardly breathe.

"Then I come to my senses some, and I realized that the voices I heard was strangers. It was men talkin'. And their voices was loud and angry, like they was havin' a fight.

"I told the youngens to stay quiet. Then I snuck up behind some trees 'round the side of the Whatley place to try and get a look at what was goin' on. What I saw spooked me, so I moved in a little closer to see if I could hear what they was sayin'."

"They?" Rodrigo asked. "Who are you talking about, Karen? Who was there?"

"It was the sheriff and some other man that I didn't know. I knew it was the sheriff 'cause I seen 'im over at the Clinic. A month back, or so, he come in to pick up some man that Dr. Luke stitched up after the man got cut up in a fight.

"The sheriff was dressed in his uniform. His patrol car and some fancy truck, that I ain't never seen, was sittin' in the Whatley's front yard. I got a good look at both men. The one in the uniform was the sheriff; I'm sure 'bout that. The other man I ain't never seen before."

"What would the sheriff be doing out in Tate's Hell unless maybe somebody called in the fire?" Rodrigo asked.

"I thought that same thing myself," Karen said. "But then who coulda called in the fire. The house was still burnin', and 'less the sheriff was already out thataways, there ain't no way he coulda made it there from town in that short of a time. And besides that, the sheriff and the other man was havin' words. The sheriff was on top of the other man, and they was goin' at it."

"About what?" Rodrigo asked.

Karen pulled in closer to her mother.

"About the fire. The sheriff said the other man had killed Bessie and Ephram—remember, that's the twins' grandma and grandpa. The man was tellin' the sheriff that there'd been a fight; that there'd been a shot fired; that Bessie had been hit; that she musta fell into the heater; that the house caught fire. But it was the next thing that I heard that made my blood run cold." Karen's face clouded over, and she grew still.

"What? What did you hear, Karen?" Rodrigo asked.

"That there'd been *kids* in the house. The sheriff he was accusin' that other man of killin' children. That's when it hit me. They was talkin' 'bout the twins. Both men thought that the twins had died in the fire.

"But that ain't what shook me up the most. The other man, not the sheriff, said that he was glad the Whatleys had been killed in the fire; kids and all. Oh, Lord have mercy, that one man he weren't nothin' but pure evil. I could just 'bout smell the meanness boilin' out of him."

Karen paused and everyone exchanged a troubled look.

"I was hidin' behind nothin' but some brush," Karen continued. "I was studyin' on what to do next, when I heard little Millie cry out. Poor little thing was so weak that she couldn't make much noise."

"Did the men hear her?" Rodrigo asked. He cast an anxious glance over at the partially open door of Mrs. Brodie's bedroom.

"I don't think so. The sheriff he did seem to look over toward the path, but then he looked away. I took that chance to get outta there.

"I stayed low 'til I was outta sight. Then I grabbed up them youngens and hightailed it down the path. I couldn't get far. The kids was hurt too bad, and I didn't have the strength to go far.

So I hid 'em behind a palmetto thicket. Covered 'em with my own body and prayed.

"I don't know how long I was there; it couldn't been very long when the sheriff come walkin' by on the path. I knew it was the sheriff 'cause I recognized the boots from his uniform.

"A little while later he come on back by. I waited as long as I could, prayin' that he was gone, and then I roused the kids. I had to get 'em some better cover. Night was comin' on, and them youngens was cold, hurt and in shock.

"I's scared to take 'em back to our house. Didn't have no notion what the sheriff would do. So I hid out with the youngens in the woods back of the house. I put the twins down in the hollow to a tree and covered 'em with pine straw. Then I laid down over 'em tryin' to keep 'em warm.

"But I knew they couldn't hold out much longer. I decided that I didn't have no choice, but to take 'em on inside the house. Mango he could walk a little, but not Millie. I had to carry her in my arms.

"I got to the edge of the woods, and then I saw Mama and Dr. Luke's car parked in the yard. Lord that was a sight for my sore eyes. I's just 'bout to holler out for 'em to come help me, when I saw the sheriff's car come rollin' down the lane."

"I called the sheriff," Naomi said, taking over the story from Karen. "When I found the Whatley place burnt to the ground and everbody gone, I called the sheriff to report the fire. Then I called Dr. Luke. He was with me when the sheriff come 'round askin' questions.

"The sheriff said nobody had called in the fire 'cept for me. That the best he could figger the Whatleys had died in the fire and so had Karen."

"My God, how horrible for you, Naomi," Rodrigo said. "But Karen, what did you do? Did you go back into the woods until the sheriff left?"

"There weren't no time for that. By the time I saw the sheriff's car, I was cut off from the woods. If I had turned back, we woulda been out in the open, and he woulda seen us for sure. But God was with me once again."

"That he was, baby girl," Naomi said.

"Now you don't know this," Karen said to Rodrigo "'cause you ain't never been out to our place in Tate's Hell. But my daddy built hisself a shed on the edge of the woods. He liked to do woodwork and that was his shop. I played out there when I was a little girl.

"In all of the confusion, it never crossed my mind to hide in that shop. But when I saw the patrol car comin', I looked this way and that, like some kinda animal trapped with nowheres to go. When I looked to my left, I saw my daddy's headstone; and then it came to me. I could hide with the youngens in his shop.

"I didn't waste no time. I grabbed up both the twins and made a run, or as much of a run as I could manage, headed for that shed.

"We made it without the sheriff seein' us. Leastways, I hoped so. Once inside, I hid the youngens in the corner. There weren't no windows, so I couldn't see what was goin' on outside.

"Then I took down a shovel from the wall where my daddy hung his gardenin' tools. I weren't goin' down without a fight. I sat down by the door, shovel at my side and waited. I don't know how long I waited, but it musta been a long time, 'cause I drifted off to sleep.

"I woke up all sudden like when I heard a noise outside. I jumped up and raised that shovel over my head, ready to clobber whoever was comin' through that door. Then the next thing I knowed, I was stoopin' over Mama on the ground beggin' her not to die."

"You hit Naomi!" Rodrigo exclaimed. He looked more closely at Naomi. She didn't appear to have any injuries.

"No. The Lord was with us both that time," Naomi said.

"Right 'fore I let go with my blow," Karen said, "I heard Mama's voice, and I stepped out of the shadows. We faced each other head-on and Mama fainted."

"I would agree that the Lord was with both of you," Rodrigo said. "But still, that doesn't explain how you got here to Mrs. Brodie's estate."

"We had to hide somewheres besides Tate's Hell," Karen explained. "I didn't even take the time to tell Mama what had happened 'til we was in the car. All I told her was that me and the youngens had to get outta Tate's Hell. Mama went back to the house, gathered up her keys, some blankets to cover up the youngens, and we got on outta there."

"So Naomi brought you and the twins here to Mrs. Brodie's house to hide?" Rodrigo asked.

"That's right," Naomi said. "I didn't know where else to go."

"I was sound asleep when I heard the pounding at my back door," Mrs. Brodie said. "When I looked out the peephole—Horace had that thing installed, and I do declare this was the only time that I have ever used it—I saw Naomi.

"I opened the door, and she hurried inside with Karen and the twins. One look at them, and I could tell something horrible had happened."

"God bless, Mrs. Brodie, she just took us right in, no questions asked," Naomi said.

"We put the twins into my bed," Mrs. Brodie said. "Naomi told me what happened while I tried to dress some of Karen's wounds. We didn't know what to do. So we called you."

"And I'm glad that you did," Rodrigo said. He stood up and started to pace the floor, moving between the partially opened door to Mrs. Brodie's bedroom and then back to the fire.

The women sat silently, their eyes following him as he crossed back and forth in the room. All of their hope focused on his being able to help them. Finally, he stopped in front of the fire and turned to face them.

"What baffles me about this whole story, is the *why*. Why would somebody want to kill the Whatleys? From what you have told me, thus far, Naomi, they were two harmless old people living out their lives in Tate's Hell. Why would somebody want them dead? And to kill the twins? And why would the sheriff be willing to stick his neck out and cover-up for the killer? There are a lot of unanswered questions here."

"I think that I know some of the answers," Naomi said.

"You do!" Karen exclaimed. Her head shot up, and her eyes met those of her mother. Until this moment, she had not focused on the reason why any of this had happened. Her mind had been focused solely on survival.

"I do have at least some of the answers," Naomi said, sighing. She rose and stood next to Rodrigo by the fire. "For years I have carried a heavy secret 'round in my heart."

"A secret?" Karen stared at her mother in disbelief. "We never kept secrets in our family. At least, I thought that we didn't."

"I did what I thought was best, Karen," Naomi said. "I kept my secret 'cause I thought that by doin' so, I was somehow protectin' you and the twins. Now I know that I was wrong. The time has come to tell the secret that I have kept buried in my heart since the night that the twins was born. Sit back and listen all of you."

"The man who killed the Whatleys is Trey Hillman," Naomi said.

"Trey Hillman—do you mean one of the Hillmans that Daddy worked for?" Karen asked. "But why, Mama? Why would the Hillmans care 'bout the Whatleys?"

"Because Trey Hillman is the twins' father," Naomi said.

"The twin's father!" Karen exclaimed, bolting up out of her seat to confront Naomi. "The man who killed Ephram and Bessie is the twins' father? But I thought nobody knew who the twins' father was. Bessie always said that Lily took that secret with her to the grave. And you knew all of this time? But why didn't you tell me, Mama?"

"Sit, girl. Don't go gettin' yourself more worked up than you already are. You can judge me when I'm done. I had my reasons for not tellin'. Right or wrong, I had my reasons. And I'm gonna share those reasons with all of you right now."

157

"Excuse me," Mrs. Brodie said. "Just so I'm clear on matters—are you talking about the Hillmans who own the lumberyard? The Hillman who is the state senator?"

Now it was Naomi who had the surprised look on her face. "I'm talkin' 'bout young Hillman. But how would you know the Hillmans, Mrs. Brodie?"

"I may not leave this estate, but I do know what goes on around here," Mrs. Brodie replied. "At least some of it. I have my sources."

Mrs. Brodie poured herself more tea. "I learned about the Hillmans when Horace and I built this house. A despicable family, according to Horace. The elder Mr. Hillman tried to befriend Horace, but Horace wasn't interested. Mr. Hillman supplied Horace with the lumber to build the estate, but that was the extent of their relationship. I didn't think about him again until I heard that he was elected state senator. I never knew that he had a son. But forgive me for interrupting you, Naomi. Please continue. Obviously, both you and Karen know far more about the twins than either Rodrigo or I. Tell us all that you know."

"Lily Whatley, the twin's mother, was the only child of Ephram and Bessie Whatley," Naomi said. "She died the night that the twins was born. Bessie come bringin' the babies to our house that night askin' for help. We took the twins in that night, and we just 'bout had 'em as our own ever since."

"The children's grandmother simply left the children with you?" Mrs. Brodie asked in astonishment.

"Sorta. Let me start at the beginning. Bessie called old Doc Adams when she realized that Lily was 'bout to have her baby. Doc did come; but the weather, it was awful that night. It was snowin'."

"We've all heard the twins say that plenty," Mrs. Brodie said, with a weak smile.

"Doc did come, but Lily died givin' birth to the twins 'fore he could get there," Naomi said. "Bessie, not knowin' what else to do, I reckon, come bringin' them two tiny newborns to us. We agreed to watch them 'til Doc got there.

"Doc eventually did get to the Whatley place that night. He come on over to our place after he saw there weren't nothin' that he could do for Lily. He asked if we'd keep the babies 'til he could get back to town and send help. All the phone lines was out. He said that Bessie was all tore up over losing Lily, and that Ephram was drunk. So we took the little fellas in."

"But help never came," Karen said.

"Not that night," Naomi added. "Doc Adams died 'fore he could get back to town."

"Oh, I recall that night," Mrs. Brodie said. "The weather was dreadful. Doc Adams' car went off of the road. He died of a heart attack going for help."

"That's right," Naomi said, with a tinge of surprise in her voice.

"Perhaps, you have forgotten, Naomi. Horace and I knew Doc Adams. He recommended you for the job here."

"You're right. I did forget that," Naomi said.

"But back to your story," Mrs. Brodie said. "I'm sorry that I interrupted you."

"Where was I?" Naomi asked. "Oh yeah, the sheriff, that was Jonas Tate at the time, he came the next day. But, by then, I'd already gone to town and got the Reverend Taylor and his wife to come help us with the babies. He was the reverend at the Shady Grove Baptist Church back then—that's the black folks' church on the edge of town."

Naomi took a sip of her tea and cleared her throat. "When the sheriff did come," she said, "Bessie begged 'im to let the babies stay in Tate's Hell. It was near 'bout Christmas. He musta felt sorry for her, so he let 'em stay. He was plannin' to send out the welfare people after Christmas, but they never came. I reckon, with all of the fuss of losin' the only doctor in town, that nobody cared 'bout two babies born out in Tate's Hell. We never figgered out why nobody came to see 'bout the babies.

"At first, we just figgered on helpin' Bessie out for a short time. She said that she was gonna take the babies to live with some of her people outside of Trinity. But that never happened."

"And why not?" Rodrigo asked.

"That there is the thorny part of this here story," Naomi said. "That's the secret that I've kept all these years."

"Another secret?" Karen asked. "I thought the secret was that Trey Hillman was the twins' daddy?"

"I wish that was all of it," Naomi said, sighing deeply. "But it don't end there. If you recollect, Karen, when the twins was first born, Ephram Whatley, he didn't want a thing to do with 'em. Wanted 'em outta his sight; outta his house. That, and the fact that the Whatley house weren't fit for no babies to live in, was why the twins stayed on at our place."

"I remember," Karen said.

"We's still grievin' over losin' Karen's daddy," Naomi said, turning her attention to Rodrigo and Mrs. Brodie. "Havin' the twins stay with us was more of a blessin' than a burden. So we didn't see no harm in helpin' out 'til Bessie could go with the twins to her family.

"But then, right out of the blue, Ephram Whatley had hisself a big change of heart. All of a sudden like, he forbid Bessie to take the twins outta Tate's Hell."

"That's right!" Karen said, sitting up erectly. "But I never figgered out why."

"That's 'cause you weren't studyin' on figgerin' out the why of things," Naomi said. "By that time, your heart was done fixed on them babies, Karen. You was just so glad to have 'em stay, that you never looked no deeper for the truth. But I did. I had my notions 'bout what was goin' on."

Karen sat back and stared up at her mother. "I reckon that's true. I loved the twins by then. I wanted them to stay on with us, no matter the reason."

"And the truth of the matter is that I wanted them to stay on, too," Naomi said. "But I weren't blinded to the truth. I knowed that Ephram Whatley hadn't had no change of heart where them babies was concerned. I knowed his wantin' 'em in Tate's Hell didn't have nothin' to do with love. It was 'bout somethin' altogether different. It was 'bout money!"

160

"Money?" Karen asked incredulously.

"Yes, money," Naomi said. "It didn't take me long to figger out that Trey Hillman musta been payin' Ephram Whatley to stay quiet 'bout him bein' the twins' daddy."

"*Blackmail*?" Rodrigo asked.

"I reckon that's the word you white folks would use for it," Naomi said.

"But how did you know that, Mama?" Karen asked.

"Mostly, I just put two and two together," Naomi said.

"Me and your daddy, Karen, we knowed that Lily had been carryin' on with the Hillman boy. But that's another story. Your daddy said it weren't none of our business. Then your daddy died, and I weren't thinkin' on nothin' else but that. But then, when the twins was born, well, it weren't hard for me to figger out who the daddy was."

"But why keep that a secret, Mama, 'specially from me?" Karen asked. The hurt resonated clearly in her voice.

"There just didn't seem to be no good reason to tell you. That was white folks' business. I didn't figger that it mattered none 'til Ephram started actin' strange. He offered to pay you to keep the babies. Remember that?"

Karen nodded that she did remember.

"Ephram Whatley, he never had a red cent to his name," Naomi said. "And he sure weren't 'bout payin' black folks to help 'im. I can't count the times your daddy did one thing or the other round the Whatley place for free. Your daddy was a Christian man, Karen. He didn't take no money for helpin' a neighbor. But it weren't like Ephram Whatley ever offered to pay neither.

"So when he come on with the offer to pay money, I knowed something was up. That, and the fact that he wanted the babies in Tate's Hell, but not in his house, added up to only one thing. Ephram was makin' Hillman pay 'im to keep quiet."

While the others leaned forward to catch Naomi's every word, Karen slumped back in her chair.

Rodrigo noticed. "Karen, are you alright?" he asked.

161

"I guess," she said wearily, "but this is all really too much. How could I have been so blind to the truth?"

"Because we kept you in the dark," Naomi said. "For that, I will never forgive myself."

"We? Bessie knew all of this, too?" Karen asked.

Naomi sighed deeply and said, "I think so. I think Bessie knew, too. We never spoke 'bout it. Once I tried to bring it up, but Bessie clammed up. I'm sure that she knowed the truth, but we let it pass."

"But I still don't understand why you didn't tell me all of this," Karen said.

"I guess 'cause I weren't sure what to do. And then time went on—the twins stayed with us. And 'fore I knew what was happenin', I couldn't bear to see 'em leave no more than you or Bessie. So I fooled myself into thinkin' that it all would somehow work out."

Naomi hung her head. "How could I have been so foolish? Whatever happened between Trey Hillman and Ephram Whatley in that house today, my guess is that it had to do with money—and the twins. I put all of you in danger, and for that, I am truly sorry."

"You did what you thought was right, Naomi," Mrs. Brodie said. "Don't be too hard on yourself. How could you have known how this would turn out?"

"Mrs. Brodie is right, Naomi," Rodrigo added. "You did what you thought you had to do to protect the twins. But now, we have got to focus on the problem at hand, which is the safety of Karen and the twins."

The three women nodded their agreement with Rodrigo's last statement, each looking over to him for answers.

"We think that we know why Trey Hillman would kill the Whatleys—Ephram Whatley was blackmailing him," Rodrigo said. "What we don't know is why the sheriff would cover-up for him, and why he is looking for Karen?"

"We don't know that the sheriff is lookin' for Karen," Naomi said. She looked up anxiously at Rodrigo. "Why would you say that?"

"The guard at the gate tipped me off," Rodrigo said. "After he told me that you were here, he added that the sheriff had come in right behind you. He warned me not to speed. He told me that the sheriff was still in the Plantation. I didn't think much about it, until I heard your story, Naomi."

"I thought somebody mighta followed me outta Trinity," Naomi said. "I didn't want to scare you, Karen, so I didn't say nothin' to you 'bout that."

"Mama, I saw you lookin' in the rearview mirror ever five seconds. So I'm not surprised."

"How 'bout the guard? Did he see Karen and the children?" Rodrigo asked.

"I don't think so. I had Karen hide them on the floorboard under some blankets. I'm pretty sure that he didn't know they was there."

"That's good," Rodrigo said. "The guard is Billy Sims. I know him. He seems to be a decent enough fellow. But we can't trust anyone at this point." The women all nodded their agreement.

"Let's think this through," Rodrigo said. "The sheriff followed you to the Plantation. But he didn't confront you when he saw you and Karen leaving Tate's Hell with the twins?"

"Maybe, that's because he didn't see us," Karen said. "It was dark out even with the full moon. Me and the kids came outta the shed, which is under the cover of the woods. The only way that the sheriff coulda seen is for him to have been close to the shed, which ain't likely, or he woulda probably rushed the shed while he had us trapped inside."

"And there weren't no car out there in that clearin' by the house," Naomi said. "I woulda seen a car. There ain't no place to hide alongside that lane. The woods grow up right next to the road. I didn't see the car behind us 'til we was almost to Trinity."

"Naomi, are you sure a car was following you?" Rodrigo asked.

"Pretty sure. It was the middle of the night. Not many cars out that time of the night. And it stayed in behind me 'til I got here to the island."

"Well, it doesn't really matter," Rodrigo said. "I don't think that it's a coincidence that the sheriff showed up here at the Plantation tonight. It doesn't matter if he followed you or came out on a hunch. We'll have to operate under the assumption that the sheriff knows, or at least suspects, that Karen, maybe even the twins, are alive and hiding here."

"This matter must be reported to the proper authorities," Mrs. Brodie said.

"I agree," Rodrigo said. "The question is who are the proper authorities? It would appear as if one of the culprits is our local sheriff."

"Unfortunately, that does appear to be the case," Mrs. Brodie said, shaking her head. "And while I certainly don't claim to be an authority on the local court system, I do know that when Horace was trying to develop this island, I heard him remark on more than one occasion that the Hillmans had bought the town of Trinity, lock, stock and barrel. And I believe that includes our local circuit judge. We must go outside of Trinity to report the fire, the murders. But go where? Report to whom?"

Rodrigo proceeded to pace the floor again while Naomi cradled Karen protectively in her arms. Mrs. Brodie gathered the china tea cups. A scowl covered her face as she arranged and then rearranged the delicate cups on the silver tray.

Millie moaned in her sleep, and all three women simultaneously flinched.

"I'll see about her," Rodrigo said. He disappeared into the doorway of Mrs. Brodie's bedroom. He returned seconds later and stood at the foot of the sofa.

"I think that I might have a plan," he announced. Naomi, Karen and Mrs. Brodie turned and looked hopefully up at him.

"We could call Rachel," he said.

"Rachel!" Mrs. Brodie exclaimed, almost dropping the tea tray to the floor. Naomi and Karen looked equally shocked.

"Yes, Rachel. Sit," he said to Mrs. Brodie. "Hear me out."

Mrs. Brodie placed the tray on the table and perched herself on the edge of the ottoman. Naomi and Karen remain huddled together on the sofa.

"Rachel is a lawyer," Rodrigo said.

"Oh my, yes," Mrs. Brodie said. "And a well-connected one at that. She would know how to go outside of this jurisdiction and how to get outside of the local law enforcement. The Hillmans may own Trinity, but they don't own this state."

"My thoughts exactly," Rodrigo said. "And she lives far away. With her help, we could move Karen and the children someplace away from here—someplace that is safe—until this matter is resolved."

"Excellent thinking, Rodrigo," Mrs. Brodie said, jumping up and hugging Rodrigo's neck. "I think that you may have hit on a solution. Rachel could be the answer to our problem."

"Do you know how to contact her?" Rodrigo asked hopefully.

"But, of course, I do," Mrs. Brodie said. "I have her number in New York. I can call her immediately."

"That's good," Rodrigo said. "But let's put first things first. We must prioritize. At the moment, we have a more pressing problem. We must move Karen and the children to a safer hiding place—immediately."

"Move them?" Naomi asked. "But why?"

"This place may be a fortress, but it is not impenetrable," Rodrigo said.

Karen and Naomi looked confused.

"The sheriff could find them here. We have no way of knowing exactly what the sheriff knows. Maybe he only suspects Karen is alive? The twins? Who knows? But what we do know is this: something has made him suspicious enough to come snooping around this island."

"That's true," Mrs. Brodie said. "We have security, but that in reality doesn't amount to much."

"Exactly," Rodrigo said. "The sheriff is covering up murder. That makes him a desperate man. And, like it or not, he is the sheriff. He could force his way in here. It is simply too risky to leave Karen and the children here. We must hide them until Rachel can tell us what to do."

"How about your boat?" Mrs. Brodie asked.

"No; wouldn't work. That thought did cross my mind. But it would be impossible to secure the boat. And, if enough questions were asked, I could be connected to this house."

"True again," Mrs. Brodie said. "It is not a secret that you are a frequent visitor here."

"Billy saw me come up here tonight, too," Rodrigo added. "He could give me away without even knowing that he is causing trouble. And, it is also possible that the sheriff himself saw me come in. The boat wouldn't work. If it was searched, Karen and the children would be found."

"Lord have mercy," Naomi groaned, wringing her hands. The fear that she felt for her daughter and the twins was ripping at her stomach like vultures tearing at a fresh kill.

"Now calm down," Rodrigo said to Naomi. "I have a plan. It involves some risk. Some risk is inevitable no matter which way we turn. But I think that what I am about to propose is our safest bet."

"Go on," Mrs. Brodie said. "Don't leave us hanging. Our nerves are far too frayed to be left guessing."

"I know of a little shack. It's up in Tate's Hell. Karen and the twins could be safely hidden there."

"Tate's Hell!" Naomi gasped. "That's where we're runnin' from. How can goin' back to Tate's Hell be the answer?"

"Because I'm not talking about the part of Tate's Hell where people live. I'm talking about another part of Tate's Hell. A place that can only be reached by going up the river."

"The river?" Mrs. Brodie asked. She was not as familiar with the area as the others. As far as she knew, there was only one river in Trinity County. It had a long Indian name, but the locals simply referred to it as "the river." That was the extent of her knowledge regarding local rivers.

But Naomi and Karen knew the river well. They knew the river as a strange and savage mystery. There were countless myths and stories that circulated about the river among the locals. All of them frightening.

Rodrigo knew the river as well; but for him, the river was a friend. While there was no denying that it was desolate and wild, Rodrigo found great peace in the solitude of this untamed wilderness.

The river's headwaters started far back in the bowels of Tate's Hell and then flowed in a winding and unbridled path to the Gulf.

Most people in Trinity were content to fish and swim along the riverbanks, which bordered the southern side of the town. Here the river widened, and its current slowed to a soft meander before it bled into the Gulf.

Few dared to follow the river back into the swamp. Only the staunchest of the locals even considered a trip up river!

"Yes, the river," Rodrigo said, bringing them all out of their thoughts. "I'll explain to you later, Mrs. Brodie. For now simply accept the fact that the river is isolated. The place that I'm thinking about is a shack that sits back off of the river deep in the swamp."

"You have been that far up river?" Naomi asked in disbelief. She and Karen exchanged a shocked look.

"Yes," Rodrigo said. "I was up there fishing a while back when I got caught in a bad storm—thunder and lots of lightning. I had to get off of the river quickly. I stumbled upon this place at that time. My guess is that it once belonged to moonshiners, but nobody but me has used it for years. I'm quite sure of that."

Then women sat in absolute shock as Rodrigo continued.

"The storm came on me late in the afternoon. It was dark when it ended, so I had to spend the night in the shack. The next morning, I was able to find my way back to the main part of the river, but I marked the way in and out of there. Several times since then, I have gone back."

"But why?" Mrs. Brodie asked in total disbelief. Karen and Naomi sat dumbstruck.

"For solitude—a change from the salt air," Rodrigo answered. "It is far too complicated to explain now, but the reason I went back to the shack doesn't matter. What does matter, is that I have spent some nights up there."

The women sat mute. This really was a shocking revelation.

"The shack can't be seen from the river," Rodrigo said. "Unless you know your way in, you can't find it. The shack is totally isolated. Karen and the children would be safe hiding out there for a few days, or at least until Rachel arrives, and we are able to come up with a better plan."

"I don't know, Rodrigo," Naomi said. "The swamp—Tate's Hell. I've heard stories about folks who went up there for whatever reason and never came back. Everybody in the quarters told those stories when I was a youngen." Naomi shook her head skeptically.

"That's my point," Rodrigo said. "Nobody would think to look there. Where else do we know that Karen and the twins would be safe—hidden from the locals?"

Nobody spoke.

"What do you think, Karen?" Rodrigo asked, after a moment of silence. "You're ultimately the one who has to make this decision. And I'll be straight with you. It's spooky back there in that swamp, but nobody could find you there. There's nothing in the lean-to but a fireplace. No furniture. No comforts. But you would be warm and safe. I could take you out there in the fishing boat that I keep at Dawson's Landing."

"I'll go," Karen said. "I grew up in Tate's Hell, and the idea of spendin' a couple of nights in the swamp don't scare me nearly as much as waitin' 'round here for that Mr. Hillman and the sheriff to find me and them kids. I know what them devils can do, and I'd much rather take my chances in the swamp."

"But what about the children?" Mrs. Brodie said. "They have already been through such a traumatic episode. And now to move them out of the security of a familiar house into a moonshiner's shack in the heart of a monstrous swamp."

"Do they have any physical injuries?" Rodrigo asked.

"No, we checked 'em over good," Naomi said. "Other than some burns and scratches, same as Karen here, they appear to be alright. Millie has some bad bruises on her neck."

"That's good," Rodrigo said.

"But they're in a bad way in their minds, 'specially little Millie," Naomi said. "God only knows what them poor little youngens seen and heard today. They need to go to the doctor, not down to some shack in the swamp."

"Mama, it's only for a couple of days," Karen said reassuringly. "I don't see how we got any other choice. If it was just me, I'd stay here and take my chances. But I ain't takin' no chances with Millie and Mango. I saw what that Hillman fella would do. He left them babies to burn up alive in the Whatley place while he saved his own hide. No, ma'am, I ain't takin' no chances where he is concerned."

"Unfortunately, she's right, Naomi," Mrs. Brodie added. "And the children are stronger than you think. They know Karen. They are secure with her. So long as Karen is there to comfort them, I believe they'll be alright. I agree with Karen. I don't see that we have much of a choice. We have got to move them."

"But Karen is hurt, too," Naomi said, taking her daughter's hands into her own. "How 'bout this. I could go along with her and the youngens out to that shack. Be there to tend to 'em."

"I don't think that is a good idea, Naomi," Rodrigo said. "I wish that were possible. I really do. But things need to look normal around here. That means all of us—you, me and Mrs. Brodie—must go about our usual routine."

"I just don't know," Naomi said.

"If the sheriff is suspicious and watching this house, we don't want to do anything that would cause him to believe Karen is alive. If anybody asks, you were distraught after losing your daughter. You came up here to be with Mrs. Brodie so as not to be alone. As difficult as it sounds, Naomi, we all must stick with our routines. Our best bet is to stash Karen and the twins temporarily in the swamp and call Rachel. Once she gets here, she can help us move Karen and the twins to a safer location away from Trinity before she alerts the authorities."

"That's assumin' that Rachel will come," Karen said.

"She'll come," Rodrigo, Naomi and Mrs. Brodie said in unison.

"The twins saved her life," Rodrigo added. "I know Rachel, and she'll do whatever it takes to come the second that we call her. I wouldn't have suggested this plan, if I had even the slightest doubt about Rachel's willingness to help us."

"Then it's settled," Karen said. "Me and the children will go to the shack and hide. So what do we do now?"

"Move. Immediately. The longer that you stay here, the greater the danger that the sheriff and Hillman will discover you. And I want to use the cover of night. That means we have to leave as quickly as possible."

"Then tell us what to do," Mrs. Brodie said.

Mrs. Brodie and Naomi stood at the kitchen table stuffing a basket with bread, cheese, fruit, some fresh slices of ham and a cake that Naomi had baked earlier in the day.

"Mango loves cake," Naomi said. She painstakingly arranged the cake into the basket. Her voice trembled, revealing a fact that she was so desperately trying to hide: Naomi was on the verge of collapsing.

"Oh, he'll like that," Mrs. Brodie said.

"And I put some grapes in for Millie," Naomi added. She was chattering to keep herself from crying. "Now our little Millie, she's a fruit eater. Gets that from Karen. It's Mango whose got the sweet tooth in the family. I never seen a child who likes cake more than Mango 'less it was Nathan. That boy, he'd hang 'round the kitchen all mornin' when he was a little fella on the days that I was bakin'. Lickin' the bowls and spoons. Mango's just like my boy was at that age."

Mrs. Brodie placed her arm around Naomi's shoulders. "Stop your fretting, Naomi. They'll come back to us—Karen and the children—all of them safe and sound. I trust Rodrigo completely. And your Karen is a strong woman. The children are strong, too. Why wouldn't they be? You have brought them up as if they were your very own. Soon, this horrible ordeal will be nothing more than a bad memory."

"I pray that you're right," Naomi said. She continued to fuss over her basket.

A knock sounded at the back door. Mrs. Brodie checked the peephole and opened the door for Rodrigo.

"Are you two ready with the supplies?" he asked. "I ran all the way up to the main road and through the woods over to Rachel's house. If the sheriff is watching this place, he's not doing it from a car. And if he's on foot, which I doubt, I'll get the jump on him. But my guess is that he's gone. I didn't see any sign of him."

"We're ready," Mrs. Brodie said. She placed a bundle on the table. Opening a blanket, she displayed the items stored inside.

"I have some warm clothes for the children, and I even packed a few books and a teddy bear, together with blankets and a first aid kit. Horace always insisted that I keep a first aid kit."

Rodrigo and Naomi looked at Mrs. Brodie with surprise.

"I ordered the warm clothes and books as Christmas gifts for the children," she said, shrugging her shoulders. "I guess they need them more now. And the teddy bear was something for Millie. She doesn't like dolls," Mrs. Brodie added, trying to conceal the fact that she too was on the brink of collapsing into tears.

"Good job, both of you," Rodrigo said. "You two go and rouse Karen and get the twins ready. Dress them in the warm clothes. It will be less to carry, and it will be brutally cold for them on the boat. I'll put these others supplies in the jeep."

Naomi and Mrs. Brodie were zipping the twins into winter jumpsuits when Rodrigo walked back into the sitting room. Neither of the children was quite awake, and they resembled ragdolls as the women poked limp arms and legs into sleeves and pants legs.

"You two are goin' on an adventure with Rodrigo," Naomi said, trying to reassure them.

"No, I don't wanna to go; I don't wanna go," Millie wailed, her small arms clinging tightly to Naomi's neck. "I wanna stay here with you, Naomi."

"Me, too. I don't wanna go neither," Mango whined. "Why do we gotta go, Mrs. Brodie? Why can't we just stay here? Don't you want us?"

"Oh, of course, I want you, my dear," Mrs. Brodie said. She gathered him up in her arms. "It's just that ..." She looked over at Naomi for help.

Naomi spoke firmly, but gently, to the children. "Now hush up 'cause ya'll gotta go. I can't explain everthing to you. But Karen's goin' with you. You don't gotta be scared."

"Karen's goin', too?" Millie asked. She raised her head to look at Naomi.

"Yes, so dry your tears," Naomi said, "both of you. Rodrigo and Karen will take care of you two pumpkin heads. And you won't be gone for long. You'll be home here with us 'fore you know it. And it'll be Christmas and your birthdays. We'll have a big party. Think on the comin' back, not the goin' away."

Rodrigo walked into the sitting room where Karen wrestled with her coat.

"Are you ready?"

"As ready as I'll ever be."

"We can do this, Karen. Just stick with me."

"I know that we can. I trust you, Rodrigo."

"Then, let's roll."

CHAPTER TEN

The whine of the jeep's engine, as Rodrigo shifted gears, woke Bud from a deep sleep. He had left the heater running; the warm air and the drone of the motor had lulled him to sleep. He shook off his grogginess and looked around. For a moment, he was not even sure where he was.

Then he saw the taillights of the jeep pulling away from the guard gate, and it all came back to him. He glanced down at his watch and considered what to do. He had slept for over an hour.

His plan initially had been to see if the old woman came back out—to follow her car. But it couldn't be a coincidence that this jeep was in and out of the Plantation.

Bud eased the patrol car out onto the road behind the jeep, his headlights still off. The jeep did not appear to be in a hurry, and so Bud languished behind, not wanting to tip off the driver that he was being followed.

The jeep crossed the bridge and took the turn on the beach road leading back into Trinity. Out on the main road, Bud flipped on his headlights. Lights in the rearview mirror shouldn't alarm the driver in the jeep. Not here.

This was, after all, the main road into town. It was only a few hours before daybreak, and loggers and fisherman were starting to be up and about. Bud stayed back behind the jeep for the next ten miles or so before he saw it make a turn off of the main road to the left.

Bud recognized the intersection so he lagged behind. He didn't bother to follow the jeep down the road. The road led to only one place, Dawson's Landing, the only marina and boat storage on the river.

If he followed the jeep, he and the jeep's occupants, whomever they might be, would be destined for a face to face encounter. The road was narrow and came to a dead end at the marina. There would be no place for Bud to hide and watch the jeep. And he wasn't up for a showdown. He was out here alone, and whoever was in the jeep could be armed.

So Bud continued on down the highway back into town. He had some questions that he wanted to ask Trey. Then he would return to Dawson's Landing tomorrow and find out who was in that jeep and what they were doing out at the Landing in the early morning hours.

Nothing happened at Dawson's Landing that old man Dawson didn't know about. And he was like a father to Bud. Dawson would tell him what he needed to know.

Peter sat up in bed and turned on the light. "Who was that on the phone, Rach? It's the middle of the night?"

Rachel thought about saying that it was one of his girlfriends, just to get his reaction. He was so smug about his little trysts. Like she was too stupid to figure out what was going on. She hated his condescending attitude more than the fact that he had affairs.

"Rachel," Peter barked, his voice full of aggravation. "I asked you a question. Who was that on the phone?" Rachel wasn't one to lie. And even if she wanted to lie, she couldn't think of one quickly enough to respond to a now seriously impatient Peter.

"It was Mrs. Brodie," Rachel said, crawling back into bed. Peter, who was reaching to turn off the lamp, turned and gave her a bewildered look.

"And why would Mrs. Brodie be calling you in the middle of the night?"

Rachel really didn't want to discuss the phone call with Peter, not tonight. But she knew from experience that he wouldn't give up until he had his answer.

"She didn't say much." Rachel hedged her answer. "She asked me to come to Palm Island. She said that she needs my help. Some sort of an emergency."

"Well, I hope you told that old bag she is crazy calling here this time of the night, and you have no intention of ever returning to that dreadful island."

"As a matter of fact, I told her that I would come. And I would appreciate it if you didn't call Mrs. Brodie names. She is very dear to me."

Peter's arm paused in midair as he turned to face Rachel. "You what? Rachel, have you lost your mind, *again?*"

Stung by the callousness of Peter's remark, Rachel recoiled and sank down into her pillow. She didn't want to take Peter's bait and have a big blowup. Not tonight.

Peter, however, was not giving up.

"You're not going back to that island," he said. "I absolutely forbid it! A trip to the island would only stir up bad memories. Must I remind you, Rachel, that you have not recovered from your last stint there."

Rachel knew it was best not to say anything.

"I blame myself for that; I should never have let you go there in the first place," Peter continued. "And then you pulled that crazy stunt of trying to kill yourself. Whatever problems Mrs. Brodie may have, she has the money to hire someone to deal with them. That is what money is for!"

Rachel turned away from Peter's glare. It was difficult to let his last jab go unchallenged; but she did. Rachel wondered if Peter really believed that money could solve every problem.

When Peter failed to get a rise out of her, he leaned in closer to go in for the kill. Rachel pulled her pillow up around her ears and closed her eyes. But Peter would not be deterred.

Peter pulled the pillow away. "Rachel, you will listen to me. Mrs. Brodie is old. And it would appear as if she may be getting senile. But that is no concern of ours. Whatever the problem, you are not—and I repeat not—going to that island. In fact, I think that it's best that you not even speak with Mrs. Brodie, or anyone from the island, again. And that, my dear, is final. Do you understand?"

"Sure, Peter," Rachel said. Peter missed the sarcasm in her voice. "I understand."

"Well, good," Peter replied. "Now let's try and get some sleep. One of us has to work tomorrow. I have an important meeting, and I need to be rested."

Peter fluffed his pillow angrily before reaching up to switch off the light.

"The nerve of that old biddy," he said in the dark. "Calling our home at this hour."

Rachel lay perfectly still until she could hear Peter's heavy breathing. He had gone back to sleep almost immediately, which greatly irritated her. While she tossed and turned almost every night, Peter slept like a baby. Nothing fazed Peter.

Staring into the darkness, Rachel thought about Mrs. Brodie. Mrs. Brodie refused to discuss the crisis over the phone. But she had insisted that it was a serious matter, and her voice had a desperation in it that Rachel had never heard before.

She had thought of Mrs. Brodie as being invincible since they had met. The fact that she would even ask for help was disturbing. Mrs. Brodie was mentally sharp, certainly not senile as Peter had suggested. She would have never called at this hour asking her to come to the island immediately unless something was terribly wrong.

Rachel fumed as she recalled Peter's words. The nerve of him to forbid her to go; as if she was a prisoner in her own home. Since her move to New York, he had treated her like a child, using her attempted suicide as a sledgehammer to batter away at her self-esteem.

According to Peter, everything was "too much" for her. She didn't even know what too much meant. He didn't want her to work or even leave the house, except to visit some shrink in Manhattan who, for three hundred bucks an hour, prescribed her a handful of pills. Pills that Peter doled out to her daily because she couldn't be trusted with pills.

The pills were antidepressants, and she hated the way the pills made her feel—all nervous and jittery, like she was going to crawl right out of her own skin. After several months, she only pretended to take the pills, in order to placate Peter.

Tears spilled out of the corner of her eyes as she stared at the ceiling. Living here with Peter had become nothing but misery for her.

Somewhere along the way, she had lost the will to leave or even fight back any more. She hoped that stopping the pills would help her regain some of her strength and determination. But, so far, that hadn't happened. Days slipped away and still she stayed. Nothing changed.

Her thoughts drifted to the island. How would it feel to go back to the island? Instantly a picture of Rodrigo flashed into her mind, but she pushed it away.

She thought of the twins. She missed them. And Naomi and Mrs. Brodie. She missed them, too. She had missed all of them desperately since she left.

Rachel closed her eyes, and she was back in the teak lounge on the balcony of her room at Mrs. Brodie's estate. She could hear the faint sounds of birds in the distance; the twins' chatter below her in the garden; Mrs. Brodie's sweet laughter.

"Take off those shoes," Mrs. Brodie called to the twins. "Naomi will have our heads if we track up her floor."

"Our heads?" the twins mocked her, giggling. "But we need our heads."

"Then I suggest you take off those muddy shoes," Mrs. Brodie retorted. Mrs. Brodie and the twins had this same exchange every day.

Those had been good months for her. She had found peace. It came to her like the late spring came to the island after an unusually long and cold winter.

Peace had crept up on her, first in short, surprise respites, and then one day, without any forewarning, the tumultuous storm, which had raged for so long in her mind, subsided into a spring shower.

Happiness took root. It started to grow. It prepared to bloom. A happiness in just being—in that place, at that time, with the small circle of friends who surrounded her.

Then Peter came back. And like a sudden blizzard, which envelops and erases the first visage of a budding spring, the peace was gone, replaced by an ever-deepening depression.

She moved to New York with such high expectations. A bright, happy, imagined future all wrapped up with promises of hope and love.

But Rachel realized all too quickly that promises are easier to make than to keep. That dreams are fragile; a tiny crack here and a chip there, and suddenly dreams can shatter like glass ornaments. Tiny fragments litter the floor, and all you hold in your hand is empty space.

She had arrived in New York in time to savor the last bit of spring; she had endured a long, hot summer; and she had survived a brief, fleeting fall. And now it was winter, again.

Rachel rolled over onto her side and looked at the branches of the trees outside her window. Her life had become as bleak and as barren as those branches.

Like the sap, which had retreated deep within the heart of the tree, so her own spirit had descended deep within her psyche. She was dormant, unable to do any more than gird herself up and wait for the certain onslaught of the winter storms.

Rachel studied the intricacies of the branches and wondered if she would be strong enough to survive the bitter winter. Would she live to see another spring?

Karen felt the jeep stop, and then she saw the outline of Rodrigo's face in the moonlight as he lifted the tarpaulin. He leaned in close to her. "Are you guys alright?" he whispered.

"So far, so good," she replied weakly.

"We've made it to the Landing." He reached back and gently stroked her face. "I'm going to check my boat. I won't be long. Stay down until I come back for you."

Rodrigo opened the door and slid out of the jeep. He looked up at the moon, which now hung low in the sky. Daylight was still a couple of hours away.

The light of the moon glistened on a blanket of frost that covered the ground and crunched under his boots as he hurriedly made his way toward the boat barn.

Old man Dawson and his wife were the only people who lived on this part of the river. Dawson made his living off of the marina. He had a pump for fuel, a barn for boat storage and he did some repairs.

A dog barked in the distance. The sound came from the direction of Dawson's house, which sat up on the crest of a hill overlooking the river. It was at least a half-mile away from the marina. Rodrigo was glad for that.

Rodrigo carried the basket of food in one hand, and the bundle of supplies he stashed under his other arm. He trotted across an open area, then down the length of a long dock that led to the boat barn entrance. The boat barn was little more than a tin roof sitting atop some thick, creosote posts.

A spotlight lit up the dock and the boat barn. Rodrigo could see the surface of the black water shimmering several feet below the wooden planks of the dock.

There had been more rain than usual this winter, and the river was running somewhat high. But not too high to create concern. He picked up his pace, keenly aware that he was visible under the glare of the spotlight to anyone watching the dock.

Rodrigo kept his boat in the water year around, unlike some of the other boat owners, who dry docked their boats during the cold winter months.

He liked to run his boat at least once a month, even during the winter, up the river into Tate's Hell. It cleared his head to get off of the ocean and to go back deep into the woods and the swamp.

When Rodrigo first left Boston and came back to the Gulf, this river in many ways became his saving grace. The long hours of solitude in this strange and savage place gave him the peace he needed to bind up the wounded places in his heart and allow them to heal. It was this river that propelled him forward when all he could do on his own was tread water.

Dawson was careful to keep Rodrigo's boat batteries charged and his tanks full because it was not unusual for Rodrigo to set out on one of his river excursions in the predawn hours.

A seventeen-foot river boat with a 200 hp Mercury engine occupied the first space in the barn. This was Rodrigo's boat. He felt in his pocket for the key, and then jumped down from the dock into the boat.

Positioning himself behind its wheel, he inserted the key into the ignition and turned it to the "on" position. This allowed him to check the battery and gauges without actually cranking the boat. Dawson was usually up long before daylight. Any noise and Dawson would be down at the docks to investigate.

The battery registered charged and the tank gauge indicated full. Rodrigo moved to the back of the boat and lifted up on the spare tank. Its weight told him that this tank was full as well.

Working quickly, he cleared a spot in the back of the boat for Karen and the children. He completed this task, and then hoisted himself back up onto the dock where he lowered the food basket and the bundle of supplies down into the boat.

Satisfied that the boat was ready to go, Rodrigo jogged out of the barn and then sprinted down the length of the dock and across the short span of grass back to the jeep.

"Karen, it's me," he whispered, pulling back the fishnet and the blankets. Karen looked up, relieved when she saw his face in the moonlight.

"I'll carry the children," he whispered, "if you can help me lift them into my arms. We must move swiftly. Old man Dawson is hard of hearing, but if that pack of dogs of his gets wind of us, they'll put up a ruckus that'll surely bring him running.

"I'm not afraid of Dawson. He's a friend of mine. But we would have a lot of explaining to do. I'll lead the way to the boat. You follow. Are you ready?"

"Ready," she whispered back.

"Then, let's go," he said. Throwing off the net and the blankets, Karen sat upright in the cramped space in the back of the jeep. Her arms and legs were stiff from lying crouched in one position for so long; but she ignored the pain. The children felt her sudden movement and stirred.

"Hush now, babies," she said. "Karen's right here."

Rodrigo squatted down next to the driver's side of the jeep and flipped the seat forward. Karen passed first Millie and then Mango into his waiting arms before scrambling over the seat and out of the passenger's door.

Rodrigo stood up, steadied himself on his feet and started toward the boat. Karen followed closely on his heels. As they stepped into the circle of light cast by the floodlight overhead, Rodrigo tried to quicken his pace. Millie whimpered on his shoulder, frightened by the sudden glare of the light.

The shrill yelp of a single dog broke the stillness of the night air. Rodrigo froze. Dawson's dogs had detected them. The single yelp was quickly followed by the sound of the raucous barking of a pack of dogs loping down the embankment toward the dock.

Millie's whimper escalated to a terrified shriek. Mango cried out in Rodrigo's other ear.

Rodrigo started to run, the twins bouncing in his arms. Karen stayed close behind him. The dogs broke into the clearing and bounded down the dock just as Rodrigo and Karen made the turn into the boat barn.

"It's the first boat—the red one. Jump in," he called over his shoulder to Karen.

Karen circled around ahead of him and made the leap into the boat. She landed with a loud thwack, banging her head on the console.

Throwing off the stabbing pain in her right ear, she sprang up and stretched her arms up to Rodrigo, who had dropped to his knees on the dock next to the boat, while still clutching the children tightly in his arms.

He dropped Mango into her outstretched arms. She deposited him hastily on the bottom of the boat, before reaching up for Millie.

The dogs barreled around the entrance to the boat barn, hurling themselves headlong at Rodrigo and the strangers in the boat. Their barking echoed off of the tin roof of the barn, making it sound as if they were a pack of twenty instead of four.

As the dogs closed in on the boat, the children screams blended together into one loud bellow.

Rodrigo rolled off the dock and landed in the boat, certain that the cacophony of barking dogs and screaming children would bring Dawson down on them.

The dogs, who had now reached the boat, strained their heads and necks over the edge of the dock, growling and snapping at the intruders below. Karen cowered in the back, the twins' faces buried in her lap. Rodrigo cast off the line that tethered them to the dock and turned the key in the ignition. The engine roared.

"Get them down in the back," Rodrigo screamed to Karen over the melee. "Cover them up with the tarpaulin."

He put the boat into reverse and maneuvered it out of the slip. As soon as he hit the open water, he thrust the throttle forward to wide open.

The boat lurched, flinging Karen and the children against the back seat. The front end came up out of the water, and the motor bogged and whined as it gathered momentum.

Rodrigo, standing behind the wheel, leaned forward straining with the boat, his bare head and face catching the full brunt of the cold wind. The boat leveled off in the water and then rocketed forward as Rodrigo guided it into the wide bend of the river.

The dark of the night started to give way to the first light of morning, creating a hazy glow over the river. A few bright stars still twinkled in the night sky overhead. A thick fog hung over the river and bled out into the cypress trees, which lined the banks of the river like a flank of giant warriors.

Rodrigo ran the boat in the deep water at the middle of the river. He glanced over his shoulder into the back of the boat. Karen had covered herself and the children under the tarpaulin. But even over the roar of the boat engine, he could still hear the children crying.

Rodrigo kept the boat at full throttle until they had cleared the bend in the river and left civilization completely behind. Past the bend, there were no houses, no humans, just swamp. Here the river narrowed, its banks closed ranks on either side.

Rodrigo pulled back on the throttle, keeping it engaged enough to keep the boat from being pulled off course by the swift current. He moved to the back of the boat and pulled back the tarpaulin. The twins looked up at him with red, puffy, terrified eyes. Even Karen looked overwhelmed.

"I know that you're afraid," he said to the children. "But you must trust that Karen and I will take care of you. And when all of this is over, we will go home to Naomi and Mrs. Brodie."

Karen pulled them in close to her. "Listen to Rodrigo," she said, "he will take care of us."

"For now," Rodrigo said, "I want the three of you to move up to the front of the boat with me. We still have a distance to go."

Rodrigo helped Karen shift herself and the children into the front of the boat. Wrapped in the blankets, but clinging to Rodrigo's legs, the children huddled in the bottom of the boat, out of the wind and next to him.

"Hold on tightly," he said. Rodrigo gunned the boat, and they were back skimming along the river.

Karen couldn't believe that she had actually fallen asleep. The children had nestled down into the floor of the boat while she had stretched out on the seat. She peeked under the blanket at them, relieved to see that both were resting peacefully.

Sitting upright in the seat, she looked over at Rodrigo, who seemed to be concentrating intently on the scenery around them. The boat had slowed to a crawl.

Rodrigo skillfully guided the boat through a maze of small tributaries bordered by huge cypress trees and lily pads. They were in the heart of the swamp. Karen felt her heart sink. This place felt like it was a million miles from home.

Rodrigo felt her stirring and looked over. "Don't be too alarmed," he said. "This place may look like a no-man's-land to you, but I know exactly where we are."

"Actually, we aren't even that far off of the main river. It just looks desolate back here. I think that it's all of the cypress trees. They have a rather oppressive look about them. I have to admit that I was a bit intimidated at first. Imagine me lost here in a storm. But now I have grown to love the tranquility of this place. It grows on you."

"If you say so," Karen said. "Because right now I'm scared as hell. And that's the first time I have ever used a cuss word in my entire life."

Rodrigo smiled over at her, and Karen tried hard to smile back at him.

"We're almost at the shack," he said. "It sits on a small island. The sun actually shines through the trees on the island. It is not quite so foreboding as it is out here."

The boat made a sharp turn to the right. Up ahead, Karen could see a rickety dock drooping out over the water. It appeared to be precariously attached to a small patch of land. Rodrigo maneuvered the boat up next to the dock and threw a line around one of the cypress posts.

"The house is up there behind that clump of trees," he said. "Let's gather up the kids and go."

Karen pulled back the blanket and gently shook the twins.

"Wake up, babies," she said. "We're gonna get off of the boat now, so wake up."

The twins stretched and sat up. The sun pierced through the trees and reflected off of the boat and made the water sparkle.

Cautiously, Mango hopped up into the seat of the boat, rubbed his eyes and looked around. Millie climbed into Karen's lap and buried her head in Karen's shoulder.

"Where are we?" Mango asked. He continued to look around him with a wide-eyed stare.

"We are at my secret fort," Rodrigo said. His voice was upbeat and cheerful. "It's much like the fort that you two have in the woods by Mrs. Brodie's house."

At the mention of Mrs. Brodie's house, Millie started to cry.

"Now now, wildflower," Rodrigo said. He lifted Millie up into his arms. "There is really no reason to cry. This is my secret fort. It's like being up in your tree fort where nobody can see you. And you have me and Karen and your brother here with you."

Karen stood and wiped Millie's tears with a handkerchief that she produced from her coat pocket.

"Blow," she said. She held the hankie to Millie's nose and smiled over at her. Rodrigo placed Millie into Karen's arms.

"Now we are going on an adventure," Rodrigo said. "If the two of you will walk next to Karen, I'll carry this basket and this bundle that Naomi and Mrs. Brodie packed with surprises for you."

Rodrigo held the basket and bundle tantalizing aloft for them to see.

Millie's face clouded over again at the mention of Naomi and Mrs. Brodie, and her eyes welled up with tears.

Rodrigo placed the basket and the bundle on the bottom of the boat. He boosted himself up onto the pier.

"No more tears, wildflower," Rodrigo said. He leaned over and lifted Millie up and out of Karen's arms. He hugged her tightly, planted a kiss on her cheek and placed her at his side.

Mango scrambled out of the boat on his own and wrapped his arm around Millie's shoulders.

Karen passed the supplies up to Rodrigo, and then took his hand to pull herself up next to him.

"Let's go troops," Rodrigo said. He stepped forward to take the lead. Holding the children by their hands, Karen followed behind him down the dock and onto a path.

185

When Karen saw the shack her heart sank once again. It was hardly more than a lean-to, and it sat out in the middle of nowhere. But she braced up. She had to be strong, and at least attempt to put a happy face on the situation for the sake of the children.

Rodrigo sensed her trepidation. "I know that the shack doesn't look like much," he whispered to her over the children's heads. "But it's sturdy. You'll be safe here. And it won't be for long. I'll come back as quickly as possible. I promise you that."

"It's fine," she said. Her voice didn't sound very convincing, even to her. "The important thing is that we're out of the reach of that Hillman man and the sheriff."

When they reached the shack, Rodrigo paused.

"Stay outside and rest," he said. "Spread one of your blankets out, sit in the sun and feed yourself and the children. I'll tidy up a bit inside."

Karen whipped a blanket open and let it flutter down on a grassy knoll. She placed the basket on the corner of the blanket and pulled the children down next to her. Rodrigo disappeared inside.

The interior of the shack was cold and gloomy. With no windows, the room was almost pitch dark. It resembled a cave more than a house.

Along the wall was a makeshift counter, which consisted of a thick plank of wood held up by four wooden stumps. The counter had a porcelain basin and two one-gallon jugs sat on one end.

Other than the counter, the shack was simply an empty room. There was no furniture. Rodrigo always used a sleeping bag for a bed when he stayed here. The shack's one redeeming feature was that it had a large fireplace.

On his last visit here, Rodrigo stocked the shack with dry firewood. He gathered some of these logs and stacked them over a small pile of twigs. Using the matches Mrs. Brodie had packed in the bundle, he lit the kindling wood.

Karen and the twins would need water. He grabbed the two one-gallon jugs off of the counter and hurried out the back door. The shack had both a front and a back door, an architectural feature that its former owners—the moonshiners—must have found appealing, he thought.

Rodrigo set out for the fresh-water spring located about a quarter of a mile up the path behind the shack. He had found this spring on one of his earlier explorations of the tiny island.

He loped toward the spring, leaping over small underbrush and fallen logs. He did not want to leave Karen and the children alone outside for even a few minutes.

When he returned with the water, he peeked around the corner of the lean-to to reassure himself that nothing had happened in his brief absence.

Karen sat with the kids on the blanket. The sun shone down on them as they ate. Both twins seemed to be more relaxed. He went back inside the using the back door.

Placing the water on the counter, Rodrigo went over and stoked the fire. The logs had now caught, and the fire was beginning to turn into a real blaze. Already, it was taking the cold and dampness out of the room.

Rodrigo opened the bundle and examined its contents. Mrs. Brodie and Naomi had done an excellent job.

He took the remaining blankets and spread them on the floor against the wall opposite the fire, making a bed of sorts for Karen and the children. He took a rather large log out of the stack of wood and turned it on its end to make a table next to the bed.

He sat the lantern Mrs. Brodie had packed in the supplies on the table and pulled out its wick. When he lit the lantern, it cast a warm glow over the blanket.

Next, he rolled up the clothes remaining in the bundle and tucked the roll against the wall like a pillow. As a final touch, he propped the teddy bear against the pillow where it sat with a big teddy-bear grin on its face.

After scattering the books on the blanket, he stepped back and studied his work. He rearranged the books and smiled, pleased that the shack would now look a little more inviting to the children.

All that remained of the bundle was the first aid kit. Rodrigo opened the box and examined its contents. In addition to the usual items found in a first aid kit, there was an extra tube of ointment and a bottle of cherry-flavored children's cold medicine.

Rodrigo scanned the bottle. "Caution may cause drowsiness" was written on the label. Rodrigo mentally commended Mrs. Brodie for her quick thinking. One good dose of this medicine, and the children should sleep for hours.

Satisfied that he had done all that he could do to make his little fort presentable, Rodrigo returned to the outside for Karen and the children.

They had finished their meal. The twins were stretched out in the sunshine under a blanket, their heads in Karen's lap. She was telling them a story.

"Hate to interrupt the fun," Rodrigo said, "but the house is ready for guests. Let's all go inside."

Rodrigo stooped and pulled the children up by their hands. All of the while, he kept smiling at them, keenly aware that the children would much prefer to stay put in the sunshine.

"I think that you will find my little fort to your liking," he said. The children looked at him skeptically; nonetheless, they walked beside him. Karen gathered up the basket of food and the blanket. She followed him and the children inside.

The fire was now a roaring blaze throwing heat out into the room. Dancing shadows bounced about the walls.

Millie grabbed Rodrigo's legs when she saw the flames. He lifted her up in his arms and turned her away from the fire to face the bed. The light from the lantern lit up the teddy bear's face.

"How did *he* get here?" Millie asked. Mango advanced cautiously on the bed and picked up one of the books. It was the book about kings and castles. One of his favorites.

"He has a name," Rodrigo said. "His name is ..." Rodrigo looked at the fluffy white teddy bear, wracking his brain for a name.

"His name is Snowball, yeah, that's his name, and the good fairies who live on this island left him here to watch over you," Rodrigo said. "Snowball brought along those books for fun." Rodrigo pointed to the books spread out on the blankets.

"There's no such thing as fairies," Mango said. He looked suspiciously at Rodrigo.

"Maybe not, sport model, I just don't know. But I do know this, for sure. There are guardian angels. So let's just say that a guardian angel left Snowball and these books here for you."

Millie nodded sleepily. "I believe in angels," she said. "Naomi told me all about them."

"Good," he said. Rodrigo sat Millie down on the blanket and pulled Mango over next to them.

"Now I'm going to leave you here for a short while. But there is nothing to fear. Nothing, do you hear me?" The twins nodded that they understood.

"This is my special place, and there is a guardian angel right here with you. Karen will stay with you. So be brave for Karen, and before you know it, I'll be back for you." Rodrigo gave them each a kiss on the forehead before rising to go.

Rodrigo turned to Karen, who stood in the doorway. "The door has a bolt on the inside. Put it on as soon as I leave. I will return as quickly as possible, but I doubt that it will be today."

Karen nodded.

"Hopefully, Rachel will arrive soon, maybe later today. Whatever the situation, I promise not to leave you here for long. You have food and water to last you for several days. I stored enough wood by the hearth."

Rodrigo searched Karen's eyes. She was trying to be brave, but he could tell that she was terrified. Why wouldn't she be? He was leaving her in a lean-to in the middle of the swamp. He held both of her hands in his own.

"Karen, I will come back for you and the children. Do not be concerned about that. Everything is going to work out."

"Thank you, Rodrigo. But go. The sooner you go, the sooner you can return for us."

Rodrigo started out the door when he heard Mango softly call his name. He turned to face him.

"The bad man can't find us here, can he, Rodrigo?" Mango asked. "That bad man, he shot Granny."

Tears began to flow down Millie's cheeks. Mango started to cry, too. First a whimper, then a full-blown wail.

Hearing these words, Rodrigo and Karen exchanged a shocked looked. This was the first time that the twins had spoken about the fire, and Mango's statement confirmed what they had only suspected up until this point. The twins had actually witnessed a murder.

The room was warm and cozy, almost hot from the fire. But Karen started to shiver uncontrollably as she fell on her knees to comfort the twins.

"Don't you worry, Mango, no bad man can find you here," Karen said. "You and your sister are safe."

Rodrigo returned to the blanket. He picked Millie up and rocked her in his arms. "Remember, you have a guardian angel, wildflower. Nothing bad can find you here."

"You will come back for us? Promise, Rodrigo. Promise you will come back." Mango choked out the words. He grabbed Rodrigo around the legs and looked up at him with sad, bewildered eyes. Rodrigo stooped and picked Mango up, too.

"Wild horses couldn't keep me from coming back for you, sport model. I promise you that."

Rodrigo gently placed the children on the blanket where Karen wrapped them in her arms.

"See ya later alligators," he said to them.

Mango looked up. "After while crocodile," he stammered. Mango struggled to catch his breath in between sobs.

Rodrigo fled out the door. If he didn't go immediately, he was afraid that he wouldn't have the courage to leave them. He ran back to the boat while he still had the strength to go. "Wild horses couldn't keep me from you," he whispered to the wind.

CHAPTER ELEVEN

Bud sat upright in bed. All of the events of the previous day converged at once in his head and then exploded like a bomb. But, unlike a bomb, when the dust settled, when he sorted his thoughts out, everything was left standing.

What time was it? He looked at the clock on the nightstand. It was after ten o'clock. He hadn't meant to sleep so long. He needed to talk to Trey. Bud grabbed for the phone.

"He's at work," Susan said, in her usual strident tone, "but I'm glad that you called. What the hell was you and Trey up to yesterday? He come home wearing your clothes. I recognized the shirt Mama gave you for Christmas. And he was in too good of a mood. Now Bud I'm tellin' you ..."

He clicked the receiver in her ear. Stupid bitch, he thought, even if she was his sister.

Trey's new secretary answered on the first ring. She was all of nineteen years old, and her secretarial skills stopped at answering the phone with a sexy voice.

"Trey Hillman's office," she crooned.

"Put him on the damn phone," Bud said.

"I'm sorry, but Mr. Hillman can't be disturbed," she replied.

"Is that right? Well, tell him it's Sheriff Akers. I'm sure he won't mind being disturbed by the law."

"Where the hell you been?" Trey demanded to know, coming on the line. "I've been callin' you all mornin'."

Bud thought he detected a slight slur in Trey's words and grimaced. Trey was probably drinking already. That explained the do not disturb.

"I was home sleepin'. Sheila musta turned the ringer off."

192

"Bud, the last time that I checked you was still the sheriff of this here county. I don't think that you're allowed to cut the ringer off your phone to romance your old lady."

"Shut the hell up and listen," Bud said. "We need to talk. Meet me in Harry's parkin' lot. Now."

"Why, is there ..."

"Yeah, Trey, there's somethin' wrong." Bud slammed the receiver back down in its cradle.

Bud rolled out of bed and trudged into the kitchen. Sheila had left a pot of coffee and a note. He crumpled the note without reading it. He downed a breakfast, consisting of two cups of coffee, two Excedrin and a roll of Tums, before he left for Harry's.

Trey was waiting in his truck when Bud arrived. The sullen look on Trey's face told Bud that he was in a huff. Probably because he had hung up on him and was then late. Too damn bad, Bud thought.

Bud parked the patrol car and climbed into Trey's truck. "Let's ride," he said. Trey jammed the truck into reverse and then turned toward the bay.

"What's up?" Trey asked. "I thought everythin' was just fine when we parted."

Bud let that remark pass. *Oh, yeah, just fine,* he wanted to scream at Trey. But he didn't. He didn't want Trey to go ballistic on him. Instead, Bud calmly replied, "We maybe got a problem."

"How so?" Trey asked.

"After you left Tate's Hell, I went back to the office. I had barely changed into a clean uniform when a call came in about the fire."

"Yeah, I know all that," Trey said. "I was in Harry's when Doug Greely brought the fire truck back into town. You know Doug—he's got to go straight to Harry's and tell his story.

"Nobody seemed too worked up over a shack goin' up in Tate's Hell. Doug reported that it looked like Whatley got drunk and burnt down the house with him and his old lady inside. Nobody thought much 'bout it."

Trey rolled down his window to catch the breeze.

"What the hell is the damn problem, Bud? If this is another one of your attacks of conscience, give it up. You ain't gonna make me feel bad 'bout what happened. Hell, I'm thrilled."

"Well, get thrilled 'bout this shit," Bud said. "We maybe got us an eyewitness."

Bud could see the red flush start on Trey's neck and sweep across his face like an army of fire ants. Trey's smirk faded into a worried frown, and when he spoke, the smugness was gone from his voice.

"An eyewitness? This better not be your idea of a joke, or I'm personally gonna kick your ass."

Trey jerked the steering wheel, turned down a side road on two tires and slammed on the brakes a few feet short of running over a crest, which would have sent them hurling into the river.

Bud's head snapped back against the headrest, and he noticed that, despite the two Excedrin tablets, his headache had returned with a vengeance.

"I wish it was a joke. Trey, think back. Who exactly was in that house?"

"I already told you—Whatley, his old lady and the kids. That's it. I swear."

"Yeah, well, the call reportin' the fire came from some old woman who lives in the clearin' next to the Whatley place."

"So? Did she say that she saw somethin'? Did she see me out there?"

"Not exactly."

"What then? Cut the damn suspense and spit it out."

"Seems like that old woman had a daughter livin' out there in Tate's Hell with her. A grown girl. And here's the kicker— she's missin'."

"Missin'? I don't get it, Bud."

"Her car and pocketbook was there where she lives with her mama out in Tate's Hell—close to the Whatley place. But she weren't nowheres to be found. The girl worked for that doctor in town, Lucas something-or-other. He was out there, too. And him and the mama was all worked up over what happened to her."

"What did they think happened to her?"

"Maybe that she tried to save the Whatleys—got caught in the fire. Hell, nobody seemed to know what to think. That's why I'm askin' you—who was in that damn house, Trey? You done killed four people, so 'fessing up to one more shouldn't matter."

"I killed them people in self-defense. I had to shoot the old woman. Hell, the rest, well . . . it just happened."

"Yeah, right."

"Whatever," Trey said. He rolled his eyes at Bud. "But if that old woman's girl was there, I never seen her."

"You're sure?"

"Sure as I can be. But hell, there was a lot goin' on. And then I was out for at least a few minutes—maybe she showed up after the house caught fire, and I was knocked out."

"Yeah, that's what I'm beginnin' to think happened. While we was in the yard fightin', I thought I saw somethin' move out in the woods. After you left, I walked the path, but didn't see nothin'."

"Yeah, and . . ."

"I didn't think no more 'bout it, 'til that old woman's girl come up missin'. I tried to look 'round but that doctor got in my way."

"Did you see anythin' that looked fishy?"

"No, not really; not then."

"What do you mean, not then?" If Bud was purposefully tryin' to rile him up, Trey thought, he was doin' a damn good job of it, and it was starting to piss him off—big time.

"Cut to the goddamn chase, Bud."

"Okay. Here it is. I went back out there to Tate's Hell later that night. I was watchin' the house when that old woman who called in the fire come walkin' out of the woods like a damn ghost or somethin'. She went in her house for a few minutes, then come back out and got in her car and left."

195

"That's it? She just left. That don't make no sense. Did she have anybody with her?" Trey rolled the window all of the way down. He was starting to sweat. Damn crazy bitches, he thought.

"It didn't look like nobody was with her, but then again, I can't be sure of that. It was dark out, and I was way over on the far side of the yard by the woods. If somebody got in the car with her, they woulda had to come out of the woods in the opposite direction. I went ..."

"Did you follow her?" Trey asked. He was starting to get really pissed.

"No, Trey, I just went on home and crawled into bed like you. What the hell do you think? Of course, I followed her."

"And?"

"And she went to the Plantation out on the island."

"The Plantation! Now I know that you got to be makin' this shit up. What the hell would that old woman from Tate's Hell be doin' up at the Plantation in the middle of the night?"

"She works for some old lady named Brodie up there who is richer than shit. I found that out from the guard at the gate."

"Everbody at the Plantation is richer than shit, Bud. That ain't exactly news."

"I drove on up in the Plantation to check out this Brodie woman's place. You ain't never seen such a place." Bud gave a long, low whistle.

"That Brodie place makes your house out on the river look like a shrimper's shack. The old woman's car was in the driveway."

Trey bristled at Bud's last comment. He was the richest man in these parts. Or at least he needed to think that was true. His whole identity hung on that one fact.

So, as a rule, he tried to ignore the people in the Plantation. He dismissed them as not part of his kingdom. But Bud's reminder that somebody had more money than he had seriously pissed him off.

"Did you go inside this Brodie woman's place and check it out?"

"Check out what, asshole?" Bud said. He was getting seriously pissed, too. The stress of the previous day, combined with no sleep, a gut full of acid and a pounding headache was wearing on him.

"What the hell was I supposed to check out? I'm tryin' to rule the Whatley fire an accident, and let this whole putrid mess fizzle on out. So what was I supposed to do? Go bustin' in on some rich old lady and her maid in the middle of the night, in the Plantation no less, demandin' to search the house for a woman that I just suggested to the doctor is dead."

Trey squirmed in his seat, but he managed to hold his tongue. Bud did have a point.

"Besides all of that," Bud said, his voice now elevated to a high, shrill, agitated pitch, "I couldn't even get inside that Brodie woman's house without a warrant. I guess that you're gonna tell me now that I shoulda woke up old Judge Adler in the middle of the night for a warrant."

Trey flung open the door to his truck to get some cold air. He was now washed down in sweat.

"This whole damn thing could blow sky high," Bud said. "Use your brain, Trey. We're talkin' 'bout the Plan-damn-tation. Even if it is my jurisdiction, I can't treat those people like I treat some trash from out in Tate's Hell. I've got to follow the law with them people. I can't just go bustin' in on some old woman in the Plantation in the middle of the night."

"Alright, alright," Trey said. "Settle down. I get your point." Trey turned to stare out toward the river. Bud saw that Trey's neck and face were now beet red and his nostrils flared out, blowing short puffs of fog into the air like a kettle about to boil over.

Bud saw the danger signals and knew that he had to calm Trey down. If Trey went off on a rampage, that would only spell more trouble.

"Let's get a grip," Bud said. "What's done is done. We've got to stay cool and figger this out."

197

Trey stared out of the truck door as if the river were a drive-in movie screen. Bud waited. After several minutes, Trey squirmed around in his seat and faced Bud. "You're right," he said. His voice was now flat and dejected. "So what now?"

"This is what we know for sure," Bud said. He had thought over all of the possibilities on his drive over to Harry's. "As of yesterday, the old woman's girl was missin'. Either she burned up, in which case we are off the hook, or she saw what happened and is still alive, in which case we're screwed."

"Not necessarily," Trey said. "She is still a black woman from Tate's Hell. This is some mixed-up shit. So if she is alive, do you think that she decided to hide 'til the coast was clear, and then her mama sneaks off with her and stashes her out in the Plantation. You got to admit, nobody would go lookin' for that gal there."

"Hell, I don't know," Bud said. "Maybe we done let our imaginations run away with us. Even if she's alive, chances are she'd keep her mouth shut and get the hell outta Trinity, leastways 'til this thing blows over."

"Yeah, you're right, Bud."

"But still, I'd like to know if she's alive and what she knows," Bud said. He didn't like loose ends.

"I don't give a good goddamn what she knows," Trey said. "If we find her alive, she's fair game. I'm gonna kill her. Then we ain't got to worry 'bout what she knows or don't know, and who she might tell."

"Trey, you done killed four people already, ain't that enough?"

"You're right," Trey said. His sarcasm threatened the temporary truce. "I killed four people already, but I'm gonna just let these bitches go. Forget it, Bud. I ain't goin' soft now."

"And what does that mean?"

"It means, if this woman shows up, I'm gonna assume that she's a witness and that she told her old mama everythin' she saw. I'm killin' her and her mama."

"Right," Bud said.

"Yeah, right, dumbass. Hell, we could dump their bodies down in the swamp. If the gators don't eat 'em, somethin' else will. Nobody's gonna raise a fuss 'bout two missin' women from Tate's Hell. I say let's try to find her if she's out there. And if she is, then kill her and her mama."

"And what 'bout that old woman up at the Plantation?" What do you plan to do 'bout her. Maybe they told her what happened. Do you suggest that we go bust in on her in the Plantation and kill her too, Trey?"

"With them two women dead, ain't nobody gonna pay any attention to any old woman up at the Plantation, no matter what she says."

"Maybe." Bud conceded that Trey might have a valid point.

"Besides, killin' them other two ought to scare her into keepin' her mouth shut, assumin' she's got anything to tell. Without any witnesses, whose gonna believe her?"

"We're gettin' way ahead of ourselves," Bud said. "We don't even know the girl is alive. First, we need to find that much out. I'll do some pokin' 'round this mornin'. As the sheriff I've got a right, hell I've got a duty, to investigate the fire. I'll ask 'bout to see if the girl's been found. Now you go on to work like nothin' has happened."

Bud decided not to mention the jeep that went to Dawson's Landing. Trey wasn't gonna go up to the Plantation to look for the girl, but he wouldn't hesitate to go to Dawson's Landing. And all this talk about killin' more people. He would check this out on his own before tellin' Trey.

"Yeah, well, Bud, get this damn mess straightened out."

Bud stifled the urge to tell Trey that he was the one who had created "this damn mess" in the first place.

"It's my ass, too, Trey, so you'll just have to trust me."

Rodrigo guided the boat back into the boat barn and hurriedly tied off to the dock. As he exited the barn, he said a quick prayer that he wouldn't run into Dawson.

He could explain his being out here easily enough—it wasn't unusual for him to take a run up the river even in the winter. But he didn't want to waste any time. He was eager to get back to the Brodie estate.

Mrs. Brodie and Naomi were sure to be worried sick, and he was anxious to learn if Mrs. Brodie had been successful in contacting Rachel.

Rodrigo stifled the urge to make a run for the jeep. If Dawson did have him in his sights, it was important that nothing look out of the ordinary. Nothing wrong with a quick pace though. It was cold out. As Rodrigo made his way toward the jeep, he scanned the hilltop for any signs of Dawson. The coast appeared to be clear.

Once he cleared the Landing, he gunned the jeep. On the main road, he kept the speedometer exactly at the legal speed limit. Sometimes the local deputies patrolled this area, and he wasn't taking any chances.

He sailed through the guard gate with just a wave, sped up on the main road and whipped into the Brodie estate.

One knock on the back door, and it flew open.

"Thank God, you're back," Naomi said, the fear palatable in her voice. "How's Karen and the children?"

"Well, we made the trip without any hitches."

"Good," Mrs. Brodie said, coming into the room.

"Now Mrs. Brodie you done promised me that you'd lay down and rest up some," Naomi said. She clucked her tongue at Mrs. Brodie in exasperation.

"Naomi, may I remind you that I am only a few years older than you. And like you, I couldn't rest until I knew that Karen and the children are safe. Are they safe, Rodrigo?"

"I believe they are. For now. But there is a new development. Something that you both should know. The twins witnessed a murder."

"What!" Mrs. Brodie exclaimed.

Naomi put her hand up to her forehead as if she could shield off any more bad news. She collapsed into a chair.

"I don't have the details. Of course, Karen and I didn't question them. But Mango told us that 'the bad man shot his Granny.' Millie confirmed it. How would they know about guns, Naomi?"

"I keep Washington's gun. You know livin' in Tate's Hell and all. The kids saw me shoot a rattlesnake last year."

"Based on what the kids saw and what Karen heard, I don't think there is any doubt that Hillman intentionally killed Bessie, probably Ephram, too. Then he left the kids to burn up in the fire."

"Oh my," Mrs. Brodie said, "this is much worse than we thought."

Naomi rocked in her chair. "Lord have mercy," she kept saying.

"Alright now," Rodrigo said. "You two shake it off. We've got to stay focused. Mrs. Brodie, were you able to reach Rachel?"

"Yes, I called her last night."

"And?"

"And she called this morning from the airport. She has chartered a plane to bring her to the island. In fact, she is due to arrive here in about an hour. Could you meet her plane and bring her here, Rodrigo?"

"Of course. But the both of you should try to get some rest while I'm gone. We don't know what the future will bring. We'll all need our strength."

"I aim to spend my time prayin', not sleepin'," Naomi said. "I ain't gonna get no rest 'til this is over."

"Do what you must," Rodrigo said. He pulled Naomi up next to him and stroked the gray hair on the head of his old friend.

"But I must go now. I want to be there when Rachel's plane lands. I'm anxious to see her."

"I know that you are," Mrs. Brodie said, over Naomi's head, which Rodrigo cradled against his chest. "I don't know why you ever let her get away."

Rachel was nervous and jittery on the plane. Even before Peter left for work, she managed to call the airport and charter a plane. She left him a note, but she knew that he would be furious. She would deal with Peter later.

She then called Mrs. Brodie to tell her that she was on the way, but Mrs. Brodie had been reluctant to talk. She would just have to wait until she arrived to find out what was going on.

Rachel picked up the travel magazine stuffed in the back of the seat and flipped through the pages. Her thoughts drifted back to Palm Island.

She remembered the day that she left—how difficult it had been to say goodbye. How hopeful she had been about her new start with Peter.

Peter. Her emotions were quite conflicted about him.

When she first moved into the Brodie estate, she only planned to stay for a few weeks. Weeks turned into months, and nobody seemed anxious for her leave.

Quite to the contrary, they all seemed to relish her company. The children certainly liked having their friend, the running lady, so close to them.

For Naomi she was another soul to nourish and nurture. For Mrs. Brodie she was a much-cherished companion, following the years of lonely exile Mrs. Brodie had imposed upon herself after the death of her husband.

Rodrigo—the protector. What had she become to him? Rachel wasn't at all sure where he was concerned.

Then Peter returned.

First, there were phone calls. Then one day he appeared on the island, wanting her to return to New York with him. This time things would be different he said. They would learn from their mistakes. They had been so in love once. They could have it all again. He still loved her. She loved him. All of the standard lines, and she fell for them.

Despite all of her misgivings, she believed him. At one time, life had been good with Peter. So why couldn't they start again? Why couldn't things be different?

This time they would be living together in New York—no long-distance relationship. This time she wouldn't have her career to interfere. This time she would work, but she would not be wed to her job. This time Peter would cut back on his work as well. This time she would not be sick. This time they would buy a boat, live on Long Island, spend more time together. This time they could make it work. This time ...

She couldn't live on the Brodie estate forever. Returning to her own home alone on the island felt too risky. She never mustered the courage to return there even once after the suicide attempt.

So she convinced herself to believe in "this time" and agreed to go to New York. She packed up the few things that she had at Mrs. Brodie's home, said her goodbyes and left.

When she first arrived in New York, life did seem different with Peter. They both committed to put the past behind them—make a new start. They moved out to Long Island, bought a boat and she started to look for a job. Peter was loving and kind. He spent less time at work and more time at home.

She missed the island, but she started to feel happy again with him.

Then, gradually things started to change. Peter began to work more and come home less. He started to spend nights in the city. If she said anything about his schedule, he became tense and resentful with her.

The problems were compounded by her inability to find a job. Nobody wanted to hire a lawyer who had taken an extended leave of absence for health reasons. And, when she was perfectly honest with herself, she had to admit that her heart was not in the job search.

As time went by, she started to isolate herself at home. Slowly but surely, the depression came creeping back in. She recognized the downward spiral, but she was helpless to stop it.

Rachel sighed, closed her eyes and rested her head on the back of the seat. She couldn't think about Peter today. Mrs. Brodie needed her. That's where she had to put her focus.

She awoke with a jolt, surprised that she had fallen asleep—although she hadn't slept much last night, or the night before. In fact, she barely slept at all lately.

Looking out of the window, she was shocked to discover the plane was circling Palm Island, preparing to land. A tiny mass appeared in the blue-green sea; it grew larger and larger until she could actually see trees and houses and then the runway.

The plane rolled to a stop and the pilot turned to face her. Rachel sat glued to her seat, afraid to move, afraid to face the island again.

"Ms. Edwards," he said. "I don't know how long you plan to stay, but unless you need me, I'll be going back to New York."

"I think that I will be here for at least a few days, but I won't know for sure until tonight. May I call you tonight with my plans?"

"Sure, if you are willing to pay for time on the ground," he answered.

"I am," Rachel said.

"In that case, do you know of any accommodations close by?"

"The Plantation Inn," she replied. Rachel fidgeted, trying to unfasten her seatbelt, while the pilot worked to release the steps to exit the plane.

"I'll call security and send a driver to take you on to the Inn. Then I'll call you later tonight, and let you know of my plans."

The pilot pushed opened the door and dropped the stairs. He exited the plane first.

As Rachel stepped onto the stairs she saw Rodrigo leaning against his jeep. Her body flushed, and despite the chill in the air, she made no effort to put on her coat.

Rodrigo held his hand to his forehead trying to shield his face from the bright sun that glared off of the plane. When he saw her, he smiled and waved.

Rachel's heart pounded as she walked gingerly down the steps to greet him. He wore jeans, a flannel shirt and a down coat. As he walked toward the plane, the wind blew his black hair away from his face. Rachel was surprised to see that Rodrigo's face was windburned and covered in stubble.

She waited for him at the foot of the steps, feeling awkward, unsure of what to do. Then she could see the black sparkle of his eyes, lit up by the bright sun of a clear winter's afternoon, and she relaxed. He was, after all, Rodrigo—the protector. Nothing to fear.

"Rachel," he said, picking her up and pulling her in tightly to his chest. She pressed her face under the down coat and against the soft flannel covering his chest. He radiated heat.

Giving her one big squeeze, he pulled back and looked into her eyes.

"You look great," he said. He planted a kiss on her forehead.

"And you look wonderful yourself," she stammered, horrified that she was blushing.

"Ms. Edwards," the pilot said, clearing his throat. "I have your bags."

"Oh, I'm sorry," she said, regaining her composure. "This is my dear friend, Rodrigo. I didn't realize that he would be here to greet me. Sorry to be so rude."

Rodrigo extended his hand to the pilot.

"Larry Simons," the pilot said, accepting Rodrigo's handshake.

Rodrigo picked up her bag and draped his other arm around her shoulder. "I don't mean to rush you," he said to her, "but there are others who are anxious to see you, too."

"I'll send security over for you," Rachel said to the pilot. He nodded his agreement.

Rodrigo guided Rachel toward the jeep.

"I assume that you are talking about Mrs. Brodie, Naomi and the twins." Rachel said. "I am so excited to see everybody, but especially the children."

Rachel detected a look of distress pass over Rodrigo's face at the mention of the twins. His face became taut, his jaw clenched and his brow furrowed into a deep crease. She stopped and pulled him around to face her.

"Oh my God, Rodrigo. This is about the twins, isn't it?"

"We'll talk on the drive, Rachel." Rodrigo used the arm draped around her shoulders to pull her along.

Her feet remained planted firmly on the tarmac, not budging.

"Rodrigo, am I right? Is this about the children? I have to know. Are they alright?"

The brightness had gone out of the sunshine, and she felt a shiver run through her body.

"They're safe; for now. But we must hurry."

"**Y**ou were right to call me," Rachel said.

Rachel, Mrs. Brodie, Naomi and Rodrigo were gathered together in the Brodie kitchen. Rodrigo had filled her in on what was happening on the drive from the airport.

"This is what I propose that we do," Rachel said. "I'll take Karen and the twins back to New York with me. Once they are out of harm's way, I can use my connections in the legal community to report these murders to the authorities outside of Trinity. One of my close friends from law school is now a United States Attorney in Miami. He'll be able to help. That's no problem. Trust me."

"New York?" Naomi said. "Ain't that a long ways from here? Karen and the twins ain't never been outta Tate's Hell 'cept for Trinity and here."

"That's the point, Naomi," Rachel said gently. She knew this proposition was a giant leap for Naomi. "New York is very far from here. Far enough that this Mr. Hillman and the sheriff can't find them."

"Naomi, I have to agree with Rachel. New York does seem to be the best solution," Mrs. Brodie said. "Karen and the children will be safe with Rachel there."

"And besides," Rodrigo said, "where else can they go? I think that we can all agree they can't stay here. It's far too dangerous."

"But how are we gonna get 'em to this here New York?" Naomi asked. "I don't even know my way past the county line."

"The plane that I chartered to bring me to the island is still here," Rachel said. "I can call the pilot and have him on standby. If we can get Karen and the twins to the airstrip, he can fly us back to New York. Karen and the twins will stay in my home with me until it is safe for them to return to Trinity."

"A plane? Oh my!" Naomi said. "It was a plane that took my Nathan away and then it brought him back in a casket."

"Naomi," Mrs. Brodie said, taking her old friend's hands into her own. "Nathan left to go to war. It was the war that killed Nathan, not the plane. Rachel will be with Karen and the children. She'll watch over them. There really is no other way."

"She's right, Naomi," Rodrigo said. "We don't know how long all of this will go on. We can't hide them here. It's too risky. In New York they will have the comfort and security of a home. And they will have Rachel and Karen with them. The twins need a safe place to heal. We can't offer them that here."

"I suppose that you're right," Naomi said. "I reckon God looks after folks in New York same as here."

"Good! Then we all agree—Karen and the twins go with me to New York," Rachel said. "The question now is how do we get them from Tate's Hell to the airport."

"That'll be my job," Rodrigo said. "If you can have the plane on standby, I'll get them to the airport."

"How?" Rachel asked.

"The only way out to the shack is by boat. I'll be on the river before first light tomorrow, and I'll have Karen and the twins at the airstrip by midmorning."

"I can have the plane ready to take off," Rachel added.

"I'd like to go tonight, but it's too late," Rodrigo said. The frown on his face signaled that he was clearly displeased by the delay. "I wouldn't have time to reach them tonight, even if I left now. I don't want to run the risk of getting lost on that river at night. I'm the only one who knows how to find them. As much as I hate to leave them up there alone tonight, I don't think that we have any other choice."

"I'll go with you in the morning," Rachel said. "We can all go straight from the river to the airstrip."

"Rachel, I think that it would be best if you waited here," Rodrigo said.

"But I won't do that," Rachel replied calmly. "Those children saved my life. Now they need me. Think about it, Rodrigo. My going with you makes good sense."

"How so?" Rodrigo asked.

"Karen and the children are exhausted and in shock. I can help Karen with the children while you run the boat. Time is critical. My help will speed up the rescue."

"She's right," Mrs. Brodie said.

"Plus, I can be an extra set of eyes and ears," Rachel added. "By everyone's account, we don't know who is watching us. We'll save time and have less exposure by going straight to the airstrip."

"You do make a good case," Rodrigo said.

"Of course, I do. I'm a lawyer," Rachel said, giving Rodrigo a quick wink.

"Then it's settled," Rodrigo said. "We'll leave before first light."

"Good," Rachel said. "Now I need to call the pilot."

Rachel stood up and left the room before anyone could disagree with her. An old lawyer's trick. When the judge rules in your favor, pack up your briefcase and go before he has an opportunity to change his mind.

Bud walked the length of the dock at Dawson's Landing and stood staring up the river. Nobody lived up beyond the bend; nothing up there but swamp.

Why would that fella Rodrigo come out here before daylight? If you were going to hide somebody, it wouldn't be here. Nobody, 'specially a traumatized woman, could last very long up in that swamp, and it the dead of winter to boot. None of this made a damn bit of sense to him.

"Bud, is that you boy?" Dawson hollered out.

"Well, you know good and damn well that it's me," Bud shouted back. Dawson hobbled along toward the dock.

Bud walked forward to meet him.

"Now don't tell me, Sheriff, that you was plannin' on sneakin' outta here without so much as a howdy. How many hours did I spend with you as a boy tryin' to teach you to fish? And now you out here at the Landin' and don't even stop for a cup of coffee up to the house."

Bud was now close enough to the old man to reach out and slap him on the back.

"You know that I ain't fixin' to leave outta here without stoppin' in with you."

"Alright then," Dawson said. "Let's head on up to the house and get a cup of hot coffee. Martha ain't able to get out much anymore; particularly, in this kinda cold weather. It's her arthritis. The older she gets, the worser it gets."

"Sorry to hear that," Bud said.

"She mostly stays in by the fire these cold months." Dawson turned to start the walk home. "She'd have my hide if I let the chance for some company slip away—'specially you."

"Well, I don't want that," Bud said, laughing. He fell in beside Dawson.

"Martha thinks the world of you, boy. When it come time to vote you in for sheriff she made me drive her into town. She ain't bothered to vote in years, but when you was runnin' for sheriff that turned her 'round."

Bud smiled. He had always liked the Dawsons.

When he was a boy, Mr. Dawson taught him to fish and Mrs. Dawson spoiled him with free lunches and Coca-Colas. For a poor kid like him, a Coca-Cola was a real treat. And money was scarce out here, too. Those Coca-Colas had been a splurge on her part.

Mr. Dawson pushed open the door, and after he and Bud wiped their feet on the doormat, he led Bud on into the cabin.

"Martha, come on out here now and look who I done brung to visit with you," Mr. Dawson called out.

Mrs. Dawson came out of the kitchen throwing her hands up in surprise.

"Well, I be, if it ain't little ole Bud Akers, now all growed up and in his sheriff's uniform. I'm mighty proud to see you, Bud."

Bud crossed the room and gave Mrs. Dawson a big hug.

"And I'm proud to see you, too," he said. "I was ridin' out on the beach road, and on the spur of the moment, I took a notion to stop in here at the Landin'. Thought I might find a free Coca-Cola."

Mrs. Dawson's face lit up. "I ain't got no Coca-Colas, but I got a pot of fresh coffee, if you can spare the time to take a cup."

"Don't mind if I do," Bud said.

"Sit yourself down over there by the fire and warm up a bit, and I'll bring us all a cup. It won't take but a minute."

"Sit," Mr. Dawson said. He pointed to two rockers by the fire.

Bud sat in one of the rockers and stared at the fire. It felt like years had passed since he stared at the Whatley house going up in flames; but it was just yesterday.

"What really brings you out here this time of year, Sheriff?" Mr. Dawson asked.

"Really, it's nothin', Mr. Dawson," Bud said. He relaxed back into his rocker. "I mostly just wanted a minute's peace."

"Then that's our good luck. Me and the wife get mighty lonesome up here this time of year with just each other for company."

"I 'spect that you do."

"Funny thing, though," Mr. Dawson said as he looked over at Bud.

"What's that?"

"You the second person up here today. We don't see a single soul for months, and now two folks just happen to drop in on the same day."

Mr. Dawson gave Bud a quizzical look as if Bud might have some thoughts on why he would have two visitors in one day.

"You don't say," Bud said. He leaned over to poke at the fire with the wrought iron poker, which rested on the hearth. "Who else has been out here?"

"You probably don't even know this fella. He ain't from 'round these parts. Goes by the name of Rodrigo. I don't even know if that's his first or last name. I just know that's what he calls hisself."

"I don't think that I do know him. I think that I would remember that name."

"He come in here a few years back. He wanted to put his boat at the Landin', and I said fine. You ain't got to be from these parts for me to take your boat in, although most folks who use my boatyard are from 'round here. Them rich people from over at the island, they got their own fancy marina. Don't come in here much a'tall."

Bud propped the poker back against the hearth and sat up straight in his chair to look Mr. Dawson in the eyes.

"Them island people are a standoffish lot. Who's this fella, Rodrigo? What you know 'bout 'im?"

"Likes to fish. He told me once that he lives on his shrimp boat over near the island. Says he likes to come up here to the river for a change—somethin' other than the Gulf."

"Makes sense," Bud threw in.

"He's up here a right smart when the weather's good, but he don't come 'round that much in the winter. Although, he will sometimes come 'round in the winter—just not much."

"You don't mean to say that he's out fishin' on a day like today. Hell, I like to fish good as the next man, but I don't fish when the weather is cold out like it is today."

211

At that moment, Mrs. Dawson came back into the living room carrying a steaming hot cup of coffee in each of her hands. Bud jumped up.

"Here let me help you with that," Bud said, taking the cups from her hand. She handed over the cups to Bud.

"You two drink the coffee. I done had enough coffee to last me for a spell," she said. She took a seat by the window and picked up some knitting.

Bud noticed that her fingers were gnarled, and she struggled to hold the knitting needles in her hands. He made small talk with Mrs. Dawson before he brought the conversation back around to Rodrigo.

"What time did you say that Rodrigo fella was up here this mornin'?"

"I didn't say," Mr. Dawson said, "but I reckon it was several hours after the sun come up." Mr. Dawson used the sun, not a watch, to measure time.

"Did you ask him what he's doin' out here?"

"Nope. Didn't have the chance. When I heard his boat come in, I headed down to the dock. But he was gone 'fore I could make it down to the landin'."

"Close to midmorning?" Bud asked, taking a sip of his coffee.

"Yep. I saw him pullin' off as I topped the hill. I don't move so fast no more, and by the way that jeep swerved outta here, I'd say that he was in a bit of hurry."

"Maybe, he had someplace to be," Bud said. He was eager to keep the conversation going.

"Maybe. I walked on down to the barn. He'd been out on the river. His boat motor was still warm. Strange thing 'bout that is I didn't hear him go out."

Mrs. Dawson chuckled from her spot by the window.

"What you laughin' 'bout old woman," Mr. Dawson said good-naturedly to her.

"You. I done told you, old man, that you goin' hard of hearin'," she said.

"He needs him one of them newfangled hearin' aids." This comment she directed toward Bud. "But he won't have no part of that."

"Martha, I do declare that I don't know why you carry on so 'bout my hearin'. There ain't a thing wrong with my hearin'," Mr. Dawson said.

"Then how come you didn't hear that boat go outta here? I did. It was the dogs that woke me. It weren't even near 'bout light yet, when the dogs started up. I tried to wake him up," Mrs. Dawson said, pointing her knitting needles at her husband.

"But he just rolled over and went on back to sleep. Next, I heard a boat motor. I didn't worry none after that. I figgered as long as they was in the boat, whoever was here didn't mean us no harm. And we ain't never had no stealin' out here as of yet. So I let it be. Then we both heard the boat come back 'bout midmornin'."

"That's when I went on down to the landin'—saw it was Rodrigo," Mr. Dawson said. "I didn't think no more about it. He's come out here in weather worse than this."

"I be damned," Bud said.

"Bud Akers!" Mrs. Dawson exclaimed.

"I'm sorry, Mrs. Dawson," Bud said. His face flushed red.

"Well, I reckon you didn't mean no harm. But you know that I don't abide no swearin' in my home. *Bible* says it's wrong, and I don't stray none from the *Bible*."

"So you can see we've already had us quite a mornin'," Mr. Dawson threw in, trying to change the subject. He wasn't as particular with his religion as was his wife. And he didn't want her fussing to drive the sheriff off. He was enjoying the visit.

"Two visitors in one day," he added. "And it the dead of winter. We had us quite a day ain't we, Martha?"

"That we have, old man," she replied. She put her knitting down on a table next to her chair and rubbed her fingers.

"And how's that pretty wife of yours, Bud?" Mrs. Dawson asked.

"I saw her in the grocery store, oh, it musta been three months back now. She's prettier than ever. I thought you two mighta started on a family by now." Mrs. Dawson smiled and winked at Bud.

"She's gettin' along good, Mrs. Dawson. Thanks for askin'. As for a family, I reckon that will happen when it happens."

"You're right. The Lord will see to that when the time's right," Mrs. Dawson said.

Bud pushed back his chair from the fire and stood up.

"Now I sure do hate to leave this warm fire and such good company, but I got a job to do. I can't be lollygaggin' 'round on taxpayer's time," Bud said, laughing.

"But I thank you for that hot cup of coffee, Mrs. Dawson. It's just 'bout as good as them Coca-Colas use to be in the hot summer. Just 'bout, but not quite." He walked over and gave Mrs. Dawson a little peck on the cheek.

Mrs. Dawson blushed. She wasn't accustomed to so much attention. "Well, I'm sure glad that you come on out here. Say hello to your wife for me, Bud."

"I'll do that, Mrs. Dawson. She'll be glad to hear that you asked 'bout her."

"I'll walk you to your car," Mr. Dawson said.

Bud and Mr. Dawson strolled slowly back to the car.

"What's got you so curious 'bout that Rodrigo fella?" Mr. Dawson asked, when they were halfway down the hill.

"I'd be real surprised if you tell me that he's done somethin' wrong. I'm a pretty good judge of people, and he seems like a decent fella to me. He keeps to hisself, is polite, clean, takes good care of his boat and pays his bill to me on time. He just don't seem like the type to get off in no kind of trouble."

"Now, Mr. Dawson, I didn't say that he was in any kind trouble. I's just curious; that's all. It's part of my nature to be curious. I guess that's why I take to bein' the sheriff like I do. I'm just naturally curious 'bout what's goin' on 'round me."

Bud and Mr. Dawson walked the rest of the way to the car in silence.

After Bud was in the car, he rolled down the window. He said to Mr. Dawson, "I'll see you in the spring for some fishin'."

"You're on, son. Don't be such a stranger 'til then."

Mr. Dawson waved and then turned back up the hill to his house as Bud pulled away.

Bud's mind raced like a wildfire as he drove back into town. All of this was becoming too much of a big damn coincidence.

It was pushing four o'clock by the time that Bud got back into town. He was dog-tired and worried sick. Trey's truck was parked in front of Bud's office.

"Mr. Hillman's in your office, Sheriff," the dispatcher said. "He insisted on goin' in. I tried to stop him."

"It's alright, Sara. Bring me a cup of coffee. Will ya? I'll see what he wants."

Trey was pacing the floor to Bud's office liked a caged animal when Bud walked in and dropped down into his chair.

"Where the hell you been all afternoon?" Trey snarled over at Bud.

"Workin'," Bud growled back. "How 'bout you?"

"Yeah, I went back to work. But I didn't get much done."

"That's not all that unusual for you now is it, Trey? Sittin' 'round your old man's business doin' nothin' all day."

"Look, Bud, I don't need none of your smartass bullshit. All I want to know is what you found out 'bout that missin' girl." Trey was up in Bud's face, and Bud could smell the liquor.

Bud leaned back and put his feet up on his desk. Damn, he was tired. Every muscle in his body ached, and his head hadn't let up all day.

Sara knocked lightly on the door before entering with a cup of coffee. She put it on the desk and glared over at Trey, who had just thumbed his nose at her authority by busting in on the sheriff's office. She spun around and left without saying a word.

"Bitch," Trey said as she closed the door.

Bud let the comment go. He opened his top drawer and took out a bottle of Excedrin and a roll of Tums. Screwing the lid off of the Excedrin, he tapped out two pills and washed them down with the coffee. Slowly, he started to feed himself Tums.

"Well, did you find anything out, Bud? Or have you just been killin' time all day?"

Bud ignored him. He closed his eyes to shut out the light. That helped his headache a little. The rhythm of Trey's pacing boots fell into time with the throbbing of his head.

"Did you go up to that old lady's house at the Plantation?" Trey was getting impatient.

"No."

"Why not?"

Bud didn't answer immediately. All of the way back into town, he had contemplated just how much he was going to tell Trey. There was danger in telling Trey too much or too little. Either way, Trey was a problem.

If Bud told him nothing, then Trey was bound to go out looking for answers on his own. On the other hand, if Bud told Trey what he suspected, Trey would likely try to take matters into his own hands.

The end result was that Bud eventually decided that he would have to tell Trey most of what he had found out. If the girl was up in Tate's Hell, Bud would need Trey's help in going up there to find her. Trey knew that river and Tate's Hell a whole helluva sight better than he did.

When Trey was a boy, old man Hillman had taken Trey back up on that river—fishing, hunting and looking the woods over for timber. He wanted to toughen the boy up. His mama coddled him, the old man said.

Bud reached into the open desk drawer and took out a flask of whiskey. He turned up the flask and took a long pull.

"Sit," he said. He held the flask out to Trey.

Trey pulled up the chair across from Bud's desk and took the flask. He turned it up, swallowed several times, and then slammed it down on the desk in front of him.

"So what's up, old buddy?"

"I think that girl is alive. I think that she saw somethin'; I just don't know what. And I think she's hid up the river in Tate's Hell back up in the swamp."

Trey looked at Bud stunned.

"You mean to sit here and tell me that you think some old woman has managed to squirrel her girl away in the swamp. I thought you said she was up at the Plantation. Now she's back in the swamp. How much of this here damn whiskey have you drunk today, boy?"

Trey held the flask up waving it accusingly in Bud's face.

"Shut up and listen," Bud yelled over at Trey. He dropped to his feet, stood up and walked to the door.

"Sara, you can go on home, now. I'll take dispatch 'til Walter gets here." Bud waited for Sara to leave before he turned back to Trey.

"Trey, do me a damn favor and don't say another goddamn word 'til I'm finished."

Trey stood up, turned and stared out of the window, simmering.

"I didn't say that the old women took that girl up to Tate's Hell, now did I, Trey? Them women got theirselves some help."

"Oh, right. The old rich bitch. She and the other old woman took the girl to Tate's Hell. Now it all makes sense."

Bud slammed the drawer of his desk closed when he couldn't find any more Tums. He took another drag from the flask.

"Fine, Trey, I'm goin' home and get some sleep. You figger it all out you hardheaded bastard."

"Wait," Trey said. He realized that Bud really did intend to leave. "I'm just worried; that's all. I didn't mean nothin'."

"Well, I'm worried, too. I'm in this shit knee-deep and sinkin' fast. So just listen. Sit your ass down, shut the hell up and listen."

Trey slumped back down in the chair. He sipped from the flask as Bud talked.

"The night of the fire, when I was out at the Plantation, I saw a jeep leave outta there a couple of hours 'fore daybreak. I followed it back toward town 'til it turned into Dawson's Landin'. Today I went up to the Landin' and Dawson told me 'bout some fella who goes by the name of Rodrigo that was up on the river 'fore sunup."

"Why didn't you tell me this already?"

"I just didn't. Alright."

"Who the hell is this Rodrigo, and how's he tied up with them women?"

"That I don't know. But I do know this much. He ain't from Tate's Hell, and he does go up to the Brodie estate. Got that from Billy Sims; he's now a guard at the Plantation. This Rodrigo fella runs a shrimper off of the island, 'cordin' to Dawson. But all that ain't important."

"Then why tell me?"

"It leads up to this: for whatever reason, I think that he mighta helped them two women to hide that girl out in Tate's Hell. What baffles me is what they plan to do now? They can't keep her there forever. What they plan to do next, now that's the million-dollar question."

"Assumin' all this crazy shit is true, why Tate's Hell?"

"Why not? Who would go lookin' there? It was just a fluke that I got on to it. Based on what Dawson said, this here fella Rodrigo knows the river and the swamp. But where you reckon he stashed her. Hell, it's the damn swamp. You can't just drop somebody off on the riverbank."

Trey stood up, walked to the window and stared out. Bud leaned back in his chair, propped his feet up on his desk and closed his eyes. A dead silence filled the room.

After a few minutes, it was Trey who broke the silence.

"Me and my dear old daddy use to hunt that swamp. I thought the old man was crazy as a bat for wantin' to hunt up there. But he loved it. Not me. I hated ever goddamn second of bein' up there. Hell, you can kill anythin' you want in the woods 'round Trinity. You ain't got to go back in the swamp. But you couldn't tell the old fool that."

Bud opened his eyes, and Trey was standing in front of him.

"Is there a point to this walk down memory lane, Trey?"

"Just this. We was up there one day when the old man led us back off onto a couple of little creeks. Hell, the old bastard knew that swamp like the back of his hand. We come up on a shack back there that sat up in a little clearin'. Almost like an island. A piece of dry land with swamp on ever side of it."

"No shit!"

"No shit! Daddy said it belonged to Ruddy Waters and his boys. They made moonshine back in them days and run it all over the Panhandle. We didn't go inside. The old man said it was best to leave it be. The name Hillman didn't mean nothin' to them; the shiners figured they owned the swamp and anybody caught in their territory was fair game."

"That was true," Bud said. "The moonshiners ruled Tate's Hell."

"We got outta there, and Daddy warned me off ever goin' back. Like I wanted to go back. Then we stopped huntin' that swamp altogether. I ain't been up there in years, but I reckon that shack could still be standin'."

"Could this fella Rodrigo have hid the woman out there?"

"Hell! Who knows? He would have to know that swamp. That place was set way back off the river."

"But still," Bud said, kneading his forehead with his fingers. "It all adds up. The old woman goes to the Plantation, this guy Rodrigo shows up in the middle of the night, goes out to Dawson's Landing, runs his boat up the river and then comes back late mornin'."

"You think that's where the gal is hid out?"

"Could be. I don't know for sure. Hell, I don't know nothin' for sure. It ain't like I ever had to cover up four murders and a fire."

Trey bristled, but he let the remark go.

"Well, there ain't but one thing to do," Trey said.

"Yeah. What's that?"

"Me and you are goin' huntin' at first light. Go on up into that swamp and have us a look-see. If the gal is up there, that's perfect. We can shoot her, dump the body in the swamp and this whole mess is over."

"And what 'bout them folks at the Plantation?"

"What 'bout 'em? When they go to the swamp lookin' for her, she's gone. Without her, they ain't got no evidence."

Trey took a long pull from the flask. He said, "So what if they come on with some story 'bout us burnin' down the Whatley shack; who's gonna listen to some crazy old woman from Tate's Hell and a couple of outsiders from the Plantation. Nobody. My guess is when she comes up missin' they'll be too scared to say a thing."

"Maybe so. But damn, Trey. I can't shoot down some woman in cold blood, even if she is some trash from Tate's Hell."

"You don't have to. I will. I ain't goin' down 'cause I'm scared to shoot some bitch from Tate's Hell. And don't get some dumb-ass idea 'bout stoppin' me. You can't."

Bud's mind was reeling. The thought of killing anybody, much less a woman was too much for him. But he was already so deep in this shit that he pretty much had to go along with Trey.

Hell, he could lose his job, his wife, he could even go to jail. Maybe Trey was right. Maybe the only way out was to kill that woman. Hell, he just didn't know. He couldn't shoot her, but if Trey did the killin' maybe, just maybe, he could go along with that.

"Do you think that you could find that shack on the river, Trey?"

"Can't really say. It was years back since I was last up there. It might come back to me once we get out on the river. Somethin' might would jog my memory."

"You think?" Bud asked. "The river changes over time."

"Well, I do remember that it took us probably no more than an hour to get back to Dawson's Landin' when we left that shack. I don't know, Bud. But I think that we got to try."

"You're probably right," Bud conceded.

"I know that I'm right." Trey turned up the flask again. "If we can't find it on our own, then maybe we can go after that guy, Rodger. Force him to tell us."

"You mean Rodrigo?" Bud asked. Bud reached for the flask and was pissed when he realized that it was empty—drained dry by Trey.

"Yeah, whatever the hell his name is."

"I agree, Trey. But I think we oughta try and find the shack on our own first. That'll be quicker and easier. The fewer people we get involved, the better. To find Rodrigo, we'd have to ask 'round. Could draw attention to us. Let's have a go on our own first. We can always use him later, if we fail."

"Right. Now you're talkin', Bud."

"Let's think this out," Bud said. "It's 'bout dark now. Too late to get on the river. Let's go home, get a good night's sleep and set out on the river first thing in the mornin'."

"We can run my boat from right here at the dock in Trinity," Trey said. "That way we don't gotta worry 'bout old man Dawson snoopin' 'round. If we leave outta here at first light that'll be soon enough."

"Makes sense to me, Trey."

"How 'bout I get the boat and then pick you up at the first bend in the river. That way we don't gotta be seen goin' out on the river together."

"Do you mean the bend with the sandbar where we use to swim?" Bud asked.

"Yeah, that's it. But don't go tryin' to swim out to meet me. You're liable to meet up with a moccasin and drown like our old buddy, Tommy. You remember that; don't you Bud?" Trey grinned.

Bud realized that Trey was actually lookin' forward to killin' the woman.

"Yeah, I remember that, Trey. I wish I didn't, but I do."

"Survival of the fittest, old buddy." Trey threw back his head and laughed loudly. "That's the way of the world. Right, Bud?"

"Yeah, right. If you say so."

Rachel turned the knob and opened the door to her old room. It was exactly as she had left it—as if nobody had even stepped inside since the morning that she had said goodbye.

She walked slowly across the room and stopped at the foot of the bed. Rubbing her hand along the polished grain of its wood, she let her eyes wander.

This room always had a magical quality about it for her as if nothing bad, not even a thought, could penetrate its portals. She spied a large book with a brightly colored cover on the floor next to the balcony door.

She walked across the room and picked up the book. It belonged to the twins. She recognized it as one of their favorites.

Some afternoons, when the weather kept them indoors, she and the twins would come up to this room, sprawl out on the comfort of the woolen rug, and she would read to them.

Had they come up here after she left? Had they missed her like she had missed them? Had she been wrong to leave them so suddenly? Rachel felt stifled by guilt.

She pulled open the French doors to the balcony. The rush of cold air felt good against her face as she stepped outside.

The moon was full and bright. Her eyes traced the outline of the garden, the meandering line of the woods, and in the distance, she caught a glimpse of the moonlight sparkling on the water in the bay.

She imagined that she heard the giggle of two small children, tiny elf-like spirits as they scurried about the grounds. Rachel recalled the countless hours, when everybody thought that she was napping, when she had actually sat here on this balcony watching them play. She had spied upon them, just as intrigued with them as they had been intrigued with her when they had spied upon her in the woods.

A cloud passed over the moon and she shivered. She thought about Karen and the children, alone and frightened in the swamp. What could a place named Tate's Hell be like anyway, but hell. She didn't hear Rodrigo as he came up behind her.

"Hey," he whispered, touching her shoulder. She wasn't at all startled. His presence on this winter night was as natural to her as the full moon and the scent of pine that swirled around her.

He was a part of this island; the sound of his voice no more surprising to her than the call of a whippoorwill from somewhere deep in the woods, its chant rising and falling on the night air. She didn't turn to face him; she didn't speak.

"Rachel, are you alright?" He rubbed her arms to generate some heat. "It's so cold out here."

Still, she said nothing.

He took her arm and turned her around to face him. In the moonlight, he could see the glimmer of tears in her eyes. He pressed her head against his chest and ran his fingers through the soft curls of her hair.

"I'm just so afraid for them," she sobbed, without looking up at him. "I can't even imagine how they must be feeling tonight: the fear, the confusion, the dread. They're just tiny children, Rodrigo. They're hardly more than babies."

"Rachel, they'll be alright tonight. They have Karen. She'll look after them. And they have something very special; they have each other."

"Rodrigo, if ..."

"No 'ifs.' Stop fretting. We need to get some rest. Tomorrow will be a tough day for everyone." He took her hand and led her back inside, closing the door behind them.

"I'm staying here tonight," he said. "I'll be right across the hall if you need me. Now go to bed."

"Okay." Rachel kissed Rodrigo's cheek before he turned to go. Her eyes followed him out the door. Rodrigo—the protector—was on the night watch.

She found the flannel gown that Naomi had made for her still hanging in the closet. She undressed, pulled on the gown and crawled into bed, snugging the down comforter up around her. Still she was cold.

Thirty minutes later she was still awake, her head buried in the pillow, when she heard a tap on the door.

"Come in," she called out softly.

Rodrigo came inside and sat down on the edge of the bed. "Feeling better?" he asked.

"Not really. It's just that if anything happens to them."

"It won't. Rachel, I promise you that I won't let anything bad happen to the twins. You have got to know by now that I love them just as much as you do."

"I know," she said.

"So trust me. Now sleep," he said.

He sat and stroked her hair until he heard the deep, slow breathes that told him that she had fallen asleep. He tucked the covers once more around her face, rose from the bed and went to stand by the balcony door to have one last look at the night.

Tonight the world looked peaceful. The quiet before the storm, he thought.

He turned to leave the room, but stopped at the edge of the bed and stooped to kiss Rachel's forehead.

"And I love you, too," he whispered, savoring the moist, sweetness of her breath on his cheek. "I love you, too, Rachel."

CHAPTER TWELVE

A heavy fog hung over the river as Bud sat at the sandbar and waited for Trey. Not a good day to be on the water. He took his pistol from its holster and checked the rounds.

He heard the sound of the motor and then saw the boat's running lights cutting through the fog. Bud was at the bank waiting, when Trey ran the boat up close to shore.

"Not much of a mornin' to be out fishin', is it, buddy?" Trey called over. "This wind is colder than a witch's tits. But it's sure as hell a great day for huntin'."

Trey held up his rifle, put it up to his shoulder and aimed it toward the shore.

"How 'bout this fog?" Bud asked. "We gonna be able to run up the river?"

"Yeah. I know the river. As long as I run the middle, we oughta be alright. The river ain't so high enough that there's likely to be much debris floatin'."

"Let's get goin'," Bud said. He climbed into the boat. "I want to get on past Dawson's Landin' 'fore daylight. I don't want the old man to see us out on the river if it can be helped."

"Screw Dawson," Trey retorted. "You the high sheriff, ain't you? That means that you can be any goddamn place you wanta be, and today you wanta be on this here river huntin'. Right, old buddy?"

"Yeah. Right."

Bud and Trey rode in silence as they eased up the river. The noise from the motor made conversation impractical, and there wasn't much either wanted to say to the other. It was still an hour before sunup, but the darkness was gradually giving way to light.

Trey cut the engines after running for about an hour. The fog had lifted on the run up, and the banks of the river were visible.

Bud noticed that the river had narrowed considerably and was now punctuated with small tributaries shooting back into the swamp. He had never been this far upriver, and it made him feel queasy.

"I'm thinkin' this is just 'bout the spot where we oughta turn to get back to that shack," Trey remarked. His eyes searched the river.

"What makes you think that?" Bud asked. He was totally lost, and the place creeped him out.

"Hell, I don't know. It's mostly a guess. It's been a long time since I was out here. The river is always changin'. I can't tell one of these little creeks from the other. I ain't got no earthly idea which way to go."

"Well, that's just great," Bud said sarcastically.

"I guess our best bet is to troll, and hope that I see somethin' that jogs my memory."

Bud merely nodded at Trey. He was beginning to hope that Trey couldn't remember anything. Now that they were up here in the swamp, he was starting to think that this trip had been a bad idea.

He didn't have no stomach for killing. Hell, he hadn't ever killed a soul, much less a woman. Maybe it would be better if they didn't find her. Maybe it was best to just wait and see if the whole thing died down. He sat trying hard to convince himself there was a good chance that the woman would never come forward, and even if she did, that nobody would believe her.

"Trey, this shit ain't lookin' like nothin' but all swamp to me."

They had left the main river, and the boat trolled on a tributary leading deeper into the swamp.

"I hope the hell that you know what you're doin', Trey, 'cause I'm now officially lost."

"Well, I ain't. We ain't made but two turns. Still, I gotta admit though that nothin' is comin' back to me."

"I sure don't see no high ground where a shack could be standin'." Bud stared out into the swamp. "Chances are the damn thing has rotted down. The way this river winds and cuts back in on itself we could get lost in here."

"Simmer down, Bud. I ain't lost—not yet anyways."

"Nobody even knows we're here." Bud was ready to go. "It ain't like somebody would come lookin' for our asses if we did get lost. I say that we head on back into town."

"Yeah, you're probably ..." Trey's voice was drowned out by a loud thump and then the grinding of the motor.

"Damn," Trey moaned. "Sounds like we hit somethin' with the prop."

Trey cut the motor and pressed the lift to raise the motor out of the water.

"Oh hell no!" Bud said, kicking the side of the boat with his boot.

Trey maneuvered around Bud as he moved to the back of the boat to examine the prop. "We're lucky," he said, "it ain't nothin' but some swamp vine."

"I sure as hell don't feel lucky!" Bud said. He pulled his coat up around his neck. He was seriously spooked.

"Calm your ass down, Bud. I got this. But you're right. We oughta go on and get the hell outta here."

"Now you're talkin'."

"Open up the console and hand me that big knife with the serrated edge." Trey leaned over the back of the boat. "I don't think the prop is damaged. Soon as I cut this vine off, we'll head back into town."

As Trey sawed and hacked at the vine, sweat popped out on his forehead. He peeled off his jacket and gloves to work harder. The vine was thick, tough and wrapped tightly around the prop.

Bud noticed that the boat was drifting into a thick stand of cypress trees. He started to sweat, too. But it wasn't from work. Bud's sweat was caused by fear. This damn place was spooky.

"Can I help?" Bud offered.

"Nope. I'm done."

Trey moved back to the front of the boat. "There don't seem to be any damage to the prop," he said. "But we've been driftin'. Let's see if I can get my bearings and get us outta here."

The boat puttered slowly downstream while Trey searched the river for landmarks. He turned up a creek, and there was a break in the overhead foliage as they approached the main river.

"Well, I be damned," Trey said. He slapped his thigh with the palm of his hand enthusiastically. "If luck ain't with us, today."

"What?" Bud asked. Nothing about today felt lucky. He would feel lucky when they made it back to town alive.

"Look out toward that clearin' over there, and tell me what you see."

Bud looked at where Trey was pointing.

"Nothin'," Bud said. "I don't see a goddamn thing but swamp and more swamp."

"No, you gotta look up, Bud. Look up and tell me what you see."

Bud peered through the opening in the trees. He shrugged his shoulders. "Beats me."

"There, to the left," Trey said impatiently.

Then Bud saw it, too. Rising above the treetops was a thin trickle of smoke.

Trey grinned over at Bud.

"Where there's smoke, there's fire, old buddy. We musta missed it earlier 'cause of the fog. If not for that shit with our prop, we mighta missed it altogether."

Bud's pulse quickened as he stared at the thin line of smoke, which was barely discernible in the morning light.

"I think we mighta just found what we came lookin' for," Trey said. "Luck. Nothin' but pure luck."

Bud cussed under his breath. It was luck alright—bad luck. He had Trey talked into going back into town. A few more minutes, and he would have been home free. And now this.

"All we got to do is follow that little creek off to the left," Trey said. "Chances are it'll lead us right to that smoke. And I'm willin' to bet that the smoke will lead us to the shack and one unlucky gal."

Trey followed the creek, and just as he had predicted, a small island rose up out of the swamp. As they moved in closer, a dilapidated dock, its boards rotted out in places and almost hidden by vines, appeared.

"Bingo," Trey said. He pulled the boat up next to the dock. "And, if I don't miss my guess, that path over yonder will lead us right to the shack."

Trey reached out and grabbed at a post on the end of the dock. The post rocked in the water, but it held when Trey tied off the boat. "Let's go huntin'," he said. Trey picked up his rifle.

Bud was as scared as he had ever been. He didn't want to leave the boat dangling from some rickety old dock. The boat was their only means of escape out of here.

And God only knows what they would find on this soggy mound of dirt—wild animals, quicksand. The path was barely a path at all. It wouldn't be hard to get lost in the woods.

Most of all, Bud didn't want to find that woman. That scared him more than all of the other put together.

Bud felt hot and sweaty even though his coat was on the seat beside him, and the air was still so cold that he could see his own breath. His heart raced, his head throbbed and there was a strange ringing in his ears. He thought that he might actually vomit.

"Trey wait. Let's think 'bout this. We ain't sure what we gonna find back in there. And if this boat floats off, we're goners."

"You're right," Trey said.

Bud sat back relieved.

"I better tie off to a tree. Reach in the back there and throw me that extra line."

"Trey, don't be crazy. There ain't no way some woman coulda survived out here. Let's go back."

"Bud, if you aim on turnin' chicken on me, then sit your ass here in the boat. It don't matter to me. Either way, I'm goin' in."

Trey reached into the console of the boat and pulled out a pistol. He tucked it into his waistband, stuck the rifle under his arm and climbed onto the dock.

He stretched his hand out to Bud. "Stay or go, Bud. It's up to you."

Bud took Trey's hand, and Trey pulled him up beside him.

They stood eye to eye as the dock swayed, straining under the weight of the two men. Bud recognized the bloodlust in Trey's eyes; Trey recognized the fear in Bud's.

Bud made one last stand. "Look, Trey. If we find that woman, we ain't got to kill her. I'll arrest her for somethin'. Hell, we can run her out of town. We ain't got to kill her, Trey."

Even as he spoke, Bud realized that his efforts were futile. Trey was going in for the kill.

"I come out here to kill that woman," Trey said in a cold, deliberate voice. "And that's just what I'm gonna do if she's here."

Trey aimed his pistol at Bud's face. "Now you're either with me or you're not. Make up your mind, Bud."

Bud realized in that instant that Trey was capable of killing him, too.

"I'm in," Bud said.

Bud sloshed after Trey in the mud. His mind was flying around in all directions. The path turned a bend, and there in a clearing—the sun glistening off of its roof, smoke curling out of its chimney—sat a shack, no more than a mere lean-to buried amongst the trees.

Damn that smoke, Bud thought. Without the smoke, they would have never found this place.

Trey fell back next to Bud. "We'll creep up to the door, and see if we can hear anythin' goin' on inside," he whispered. Bud nodded.

Trey and Bud eased up onto the porch. Bud felt Trey's breath on his neck, and it made his whole body tingle as if an electric current was surging through him. He strained to hear any sounds from inside, but it was quiet.

For one fleeting moment, Bud thought that maybe luck really was with them; that the place was empty; that whoever built the fire had left; that this had all been a wild goose chase.

He looked down at the gun in his hand. He couldn't even remember taking it out of his holster. But there it was; his knuckles gripping the handle so tightly that they were white.

And then Bud heard it. A sound that made his blood run as cold as ice water in his veins. The sound was faint; barely audible at all.

Trey put the barrel of his guns to his lip to signal Bud that he had heard it, too—not to make any noise.

They stopped and cocked their heads, both listening. Then, they heard the sound again. This time a little louder. There was no mistaking it.

They heard a child crying.

Bud froze. He couldn't move.

When Trey rushed past him, he tried to lift his hand to stop him, but it was attached to an arm that was now heavy and sluggish. He felt his hands slide across the fabric of Trey's shirt, coming up empty.

"Trey, no," he managed to shout, his voice piercing the stillness of the morning air.

Bud watched as Trey coiled his leg like a snake ready to strike, paused to gather his strength and then smashed his boot against the door. The door buckled and then split into two separate pieces, which went crashing to the floor.

Trey spun around to the side of the door, using the wall as his cover. If anybody from inside had fired, Bud would have been hit. He stood a perfect target in front of the gaping hole that was once the door.

He stared inside the lean-to in disbelief. A lamp lit up one corner of the room. In that corner crouched the woman. With outstretched arms, she shielded two small children behind her.

Trey rounded up next to Bud.

"Well, I wish you'd look at that," he said, panting slightly for breath. "Looks like we done found more than we bargained for here. Three for the price of one—the gal and a couple of brats to boot."

"Is that them Whatley kids?" Bud asked. "The ones that you said died in the fire."

"I can't see 'em that good, but they sure as hell look white to me."

Trey leaned his rifle against the wall, pulled his pistol from his belt and moved in closer to Karen. He aimed the pistol at her.

"Back off, gal, and let me have a good look at them youngens," Trey said.

Karen didn't move. She kept the twins pressed back behind her.

"You best do as I say, gal," Trey shouted down at her.

Karen held her ground. Bud could see that she was quivering, but she didn't back down, not even when Trey cocked the pistol.

Trey started to laugh, a mean, sardonic chuckle. He was enjoying himself, like a cat batting around a mouse before the kill.

"Now I wish you would explain somethin' to me," he said. "Why would you women go takin' up with that bunch of nar-do-well Whatleys. Don't ya'll got enough to do lookin' out for your own damn selves?"

Bud came into the room and stood to the left of Trey.

"And them Whatleys was worse trash than I thought," Trey said, glancing over at Bud. "Carryin' on with them bitches. Go figger that!

"It woulda paid for you women to have minded your own goddamn business 'cause your meddlin' in other folks' business is gonna cost you your life."

Trey was staring down at Karen again.

"And the worst part is that it didn't do no good. You done gone to all this trouble for nothin'. I aim to kill them youngens anyways."

Karen didn't answer. Trey took a step closer to her.

"I'm just curious. What did ya'll figger on doin'? Did you aim to try and blackmail me some more? You oughta knowed that weren't gonna work. You saw what happened to Whatley when he tried it—he got hisself burnt up alive. Whatever made you bitches think that you'd ever get the best of a Hillman?"

"Mr. Hillman, we weren't after no money," Karen said. Her voice trembled.

Trey stared down at her in disbelief. He had not really expected her to answer him.

"All we ever wanted was for you to let these youngens be. Please, Mr. Hillman, spare these babies. They can't do you no harm."

"Nope, I can't do that. These so-called babies are old enough to talk. They seen what happened in the Whatley shack. But that don't really matter none 'cause I'd kill 'em anyways. They ain't been nothin' but trouble to me since the day they was born. I aim to kill them and you."

Trey moved forward until he stood towering over Karen. "Now hand me out that little girl. She's pretty. Just like her mama."

When Karen didn't move, Trey pointed the gun at her head.

"Suit yourself, bitch. I'll kill you first, and then I can take my time with the kids. Have me some fun with that little girl."

"Stop it, Trey!" Bud shouted. "You ain't messin' with no little girl. And you ain't killin' no kids. Back off!"

Trey stepped to the right, so he could keep his gun on Karen while turning to look over at Bud. Bud had his pistol pointed at Trey.

"I ain't askin' you to kill nobody, Bud. Hell, I knew that you didn't have the guts to kill this bitch when we come out here. You know, Bud, I was wrong 'bout you for sheriff. You just ain't got what it takes to be the sheriff."

"Maybe your right 'bout that, Trey. I ain't been much of a sheriff this far. Lettin' you run wild. But I'm drawin' the line here. You ain't killin' no youngens. Not with me standin' here."

"Now what you gonna do, Sheriff? Shoot me?"

"Trey, for God's sake listen to me," Bud begged.

"These are children. Your children. Like it or not, Trey, those youngens over there are your own flesh and blood, just like the kids you have with Susan. You can't shoot them down like they're some cur dogs."

Trey started to laugh.

"Why Bud? Are you appealing to my conscience? Because you of all people ought to know by now that I ain't got one."

"Trey, they are Hillman blood, you know that."

Trey lowered his voice, and his smile faded into a sneer.

"Now you listen the hell to me, Bud Akers, and you listen good. It don't make a goddamn difference to me if them brats got Hillman blood or not. That blood has done been tainted by that bitch mama of theirs from Tate's Hell."

"Trey, listen," Bud pleaded.

"No, you listen. Them brats saw me shoot down their grandma in cold blood and burn down the house with their grandpa in it. They're old enough to talk and that means old enough to die."

"Trey, they are babies. Nobody will listen to them."

"Don't matter. I shoulda killed 'em a long time ago. Good sense always told me that. But I listened to you. And that cost me plenty. But it ain't gonna cost me no more. Now go outside if you ain't got the stomach for this. Go on! Get outta here."

Bud's hand shook so badly that he thought he would drop his gun, but he kept it raised and pointed dead on at Trey.

"I can't let you kill 'em, Trey. I just can't."

"Then go on you weak bastard, shoot me! If you got the guts, shoot me 'cause that's the only thing that's gonna stop me."

Tears started to run down Bud's face, blurring his vision. "Trey, I'm beggin' you. Don't do this."

"You are so goddamn weak," Trey said, shaking his head in disgust. "Blubberin' over there like some damn Girl Scout. Stand back now. I'm always the one who's got to do the dirty work for us."

It took Rachel several seconds when she woke up to remember that she was at the Brodie estate, not in New York. She looked over at the clock. She still had a few minutes before it was time to get up. Pulling the cover up around her face, she thought about Karen and the children alone in the swamp.

By this time tomorrow, Karen and the twins would be in New York. Peter was certain to be furious, but she didn't care. In fact, she hoped that he would be angry enough with her to stay in the city.

Rachel rolled out of her warm bed and walked over to the French doors leading out to the balcony. A thick fog hung over the estate. This was sure to complicate matters. She flipped on the light and started to sift through her bag looking for something warm to wear.

When Rachel walked into the kitchen, she was surprised to see Rodrigo, his back turned to her as he stared out the kitchen window. Rachel walked up behind him and placed her hand on his shoulder.

"You okay?" she asked.

"Fine. How about you? Did you sleep?"

"Surprisingly enough, yes—like a baby!"

Rodrigo turned and looked down at her. "I take that to mean that you usually don't sleep."

"Oh, no," Rachel lied. "I sleep just fine."

"Is that so?" he said. "Because when I took your bag up to your room, a bottle of pills must have fallen out of the side pouch. I saw them on the floor. I wasn't sure they were yours, so

I read the label. Sleeping pills. I thought you put all of that behind you."

"Rodrigo, I'm fine, really. I brought them just in case."

"When all of this is over, you and I are going to have a long talk about how you are really doing; I don't believe that things are as rosy as you pretend."

"Okay. But not now, Rodrigo. We have a bigger problem to worry about other than me."

"Nothing is more important than you, Rachel. This problem is simply more immediate."

Naomi walked into the kitchen before Rachel could reply.

"I see that you found my coffee, Rodrigo," she said. "What about you, Rachel? Don't you want a cup?"

"Yes. But I can get it."

"No, child, let me. My whole life's been spent lookin' after other folks, and it would do me good to look after you a bit, too. By my way of thinkin', you need a little lookin' after."

Rachel sat at the table, and Naomi brought her a cup of coffee.

"Thank you," Rachel said, giving her a smile. "I guess everybody needs a little 'looking after' at times."

"I'm gonna make you two some breakfast. You got a long day ahead of you. You need to eat."

Rachel opened her mouth to protest that she never ate breakfast, but Rodrigo spoke first. "Thanks, Naomi," he said. "But hurry. We need to leave soon. This fog is going to slow us down some."

"You got a bad mornin', alright. Frost on the ground and fog in the air. Still, you gotta eat."

"Good morning," Mrs. Brodie said, walking into the kitchen.

Mrs. Brodie made herself a cup of tea and sat down next to Rachel.

Rodrigo continued to stare out of the window until Naomi called him to the table.

"Come on now, sit," Naomi said. She placed two plates filled with bacon and eggs on the table.

"We should be on the water by first light," Rodrigo said in between bites. "With any luck, this fog will lift, and the cold weather will keep Mr. Dawson in by his fire. It should take us about an hour on the water to reach the shack, if the fog doesn't slow us down. We'll pick up Karen and the kids and head straight to the airport. I'll come back here once the plane is safely in the air."

"When we arrive in New York, I'll call to let you know that we are safe," Rachel said. "At that point, I'll contact my friend in the U.S. Attorney's office."

"Let's go," Rodrigo said, pushing back from the table. Rachel stood up, hugged Naomi and Mrs. Brodie and joined Rodrigo by the door where he was pulling on a heavy coat with a hood.

"Put on your coat, Rachel, we need to go."

"I forgot to bring a heavy coat," she said.

"Wait here," Mrs. Brodie said. In a matter of minutes, she was back with a heavy coat, a hat and gloves.

Rachel suited up and Rodrigo opened the door. The cold air hit them like an Arctic blast, stinging Rachel's cheeks and nose.

"This is as bad as New York," she said, tugging the hat down over her ears.

"Look at the bird bath," Rodrigo said. "There is a layer of ice on the top. It must be well below freezing. But, at least for now, the fog is our friend. It gives us some cover."

"Where's the jeep?" Rachel asked.

"At your house. I parked it there last night. Just in case somebody was watching the Brodie estate. We're going to take the path through the woods. Stay close. I know the way, but it may be a little tricky in this fog."

Rodrigo trotted across the grounds toward the woods. The cold air burned her lungs as she ran, but Rachel managed to stay close behind him. I haven't been working out nearly enough, she thought. This shouldn't be so hard. Once in the woods, Rodrigo stopped and turned to check on her.

"You okay?" he asked.

"So far, so good," she replied.

"Here give me your hand. It's going to be tough going through these woods. I know the path by heart, but it will still be rough in the dark. This flashlight won't penetrate the fog."

Rodrigo grabbed Rachel's hand, and they started through the woods.

Rachel couldn't make out anything, but Rodrigo held her hand firmly. He seemed to know exactly where he was going. He was moving quickly, and every few steps Rachel had to break into a jog to keep pace with him.

They reached her yard.

"Stay low and make a run for the jeep. It's parked at the top of the driveway," Rodrigo said.

She hesitated. The fog was so thick that she couldn't see a thing.

"You know your yard," Rodrigo said, reading her mind. "Trust yourself. Now let's go."

Rachel moved as quickly as possible. She stumbled and fell, but she was back on her feet in seconds. She could barely make out Rodrigo moving ahead of her. The jeep emerged out of the mist.

Rachel climbed inside. Rodrigo was ahead of her. By the time she was in her seat, he had the motor going.

"We made it," he said.

"So far, so good," she said.

"If I can remember correctly, there is nothing behind us. Right, Rachel?" Rodrigo put the jeep in reverse.

"Right."

Rodrigo inched down the drive without the aid of the headlights.

"I don't want to use any lights at all—if that is possible—until we are on the main road. Somebody could be watching this house, too."

"Rodrigo, do you really think somebody might watch my house? Who could connect me to all of this?"

"I don't know what is and what is not possible anymore. I just want to take as many precautions as possible. Pay attention. I need your help navigating in this fog."

Rodrigo pulled out onto the main road and turned on the lights. They drove in silence, both straining to see the road.

"Duck," he said. "The guard gate."

Rachel sank down low in her seat and put her head between her legs. She felt the jeep slow down, come almost to a stop, and then pick up speed.

"The coast is clear," he said. "The guard waved me through. Too cold for him to come out and chat."

They crossed the bridge and turned onto the beach road. Rodrigo sat hunched over the steering wheel, his eyes glued to the road. Rachel could tell that he was concentrating, so she sat quietly, not wanting to distract him.

"Why are you so quiet over there?" he asked "You aren't afraid, are you, Rachel?"

"No, not really. But I am anxious for Karen and the twins. I can't imagine how alone and afraid they must feel."

"Yeah, it had to be a rough night for them. I didn't want to worry Mrs. Brodie and Naomi, but Karen would have had to be up and down all night to keep the fire going. That old lean-to is nothing more than some wood thrown together; it doesn't hold the heat very well. But Karen was brought up in Tate's Hell. She's a survivor. And so are the twins."

"Rodrigo, did you know the story about their mother?"

"Not until the fire. Naomi always seemed reluctant to discuss the situation. Now I know why."

"When I first met them I thought they were Mrs. Brodie's grandchildren. I even asked them once about their parents, but they seemed confused. They simply said that they lived with their Granny, Naomi and Karen. I know that this is terrible, but I assumed that the mother ran off and left them to be raised by their grandmother."

"I thought about the same thing, so don't feel badly."

"Now that I think about it, Rodrigo. I don't know much about any of you. For instance, you never told me how you and Mrs. Brodie got to be such close friends."

"Are you sure that I never told you that story?"

"Quite sure. We talked about a lot of things, but never about you," Rachel said, looking over to gauge his reaction. "I really don't know very much about you either."

"Well, there isn't that much to know."

"Let me be the judge of that."

"Some other time, Rachel."

"You promise."

Rodrigo hesitated. "We'll see," he said.

Rachel was about to make a comment on his last remark when she went hurling forward. If not for her seatbelt, she would have been plastered on the windshield of the jeep. The jeep did a complete spin in the road before it came to rest in the ditch.

"Are you alright?" Rodrigo asked. He looked anxiously over at Rachel.

Rachel locked eyes with him and then sat back, stunned.

"I think so. What about you?"

"Yeah. But that was close."

"What happened?"

"Looks like an accident up ahead. With all of this fog, I was right on top of it before I knew what was happening. Sorry. But if I hadn't slammed on the brakes and swerved, we would have plowed right into the wreck."

"That was lucky."

"Hold your breath. We aren't home free yet. We're in the ditch. Fortunately I have four-wheel drive. Hang tight. Here goes."

Rodrigo engaged the four-wheel drive and pressed hard on the gas. The tires spun and the engine groaned, but the jeep didn't move."

Rodrigo stopped and stepped out of the jeep. After a few minutes, he climbed back in. Rachel noticed that he had mud up to the calves of his legs.

"I'm going to try again. Pray, baby. Otherwise, our whole plan is shot."

Rachel held her breath and prayed. Rodrigo pressed the gas again. When the engine whined and the wheels spun, she prayed harder. Slowly the traction caught, and the jeep started to climb its way out the ditch.

"Thank God," she said, taking a deep breath when she felt the pavement beneath them. They could both now see the accident up ahead. It looked as if the road was blocked.

"Stay here, Rachel. I'm going to see if I can find out what's going on."

"Alright, but hurry."

Rodrigo disappeared into the fog, and that made Rachel even more nervous. He had pulled the jeep off onto the shoulder of the road, but still, the next car might not see them.

She fidgeted in her seat, turning first to see if any lights were approaching from behind and then turning back to see if she could make out anything that was going on up ahead.

The twinkle of flares appeared, and then Rodrigo emerged from the fog and climbed back into the jeep.

"What happened?" she asked.

"Tractor-trailer jackknifed. Nobody hurt badly. I helped the driver put out some flares, but we need to change our plans."

"Why?"

"The road is completely blocked. We'll have to take a different route."

"Are we gonna lose time?"

"Afraid so. But it can't be helped."

Rodrigo turned the jeep and headed in the opposite direction.

"How much time will this cost us, Rodrigo?"

"Well, we won't be there by first light, that's for sure."

"Oh, no!" Rachel groaned. Time was critical.

"Can't be helped," Rodrigo said.

"The back way into the Landing is on an unpaved road that's not traveled much. I wouldn't even know about the road, but the main highway washed out after a big storm a couple of years back. For at least a week after that storm, anybody needing to use the beach road, which included me, had to take a detour. That detour was the back road that we're going to use now. I can't tell how much time we'll lose until I see the condition of the road."

Rodrigo slowed the jeep and made a turn on what appeared to Rachel to be no more than a lane. Certainly not a county roadway.

"Welcome to County Road 119," he said. "Brace yourself against the dashboard; otherwise, you won't be able to hold on."

The ride was rough. The jeep rattled and shook, and even holding on as tightly as she could, Rachel bounced around in her seat. If not for the seatbelt, she felt as if her head would have hit the roof on a number of particularly bad bumps.

The forest rose up like a barricade on either side of the them, and branches scraped against the windshield and the sides of the jeep. The fog was still hanging on which cast the whole scene in a strangely eerie light. Rachel felt as if she had dropped onto the set of one of those creepy, horror movies.

"How are you doing over there?" Rodrigo asked. He was concentrating intently on keeping the jeep on the road and avoiding the more treacherous of the potholes.

"My insides are a little shook up, but I'll survive," she said. "But, Rodrigo, you must admit that this road is just a little spooky."

"Nonsense," he said stealing a brief glance over at her. "Just think of this as an adventure. Here you are deep in the woods on a cold, foggy morning, alone, except for the companionship of a mysterious, tall, dark man. How many of your girlfriends in New York can say that they lead such a thrilling life."

"I'm quite certain the answer is none," she said. "At this moment, they're all soundly asleep in down-covered beds, in climate-controlled houses, with their short, bald, and very predictable husbands."

Rodrigo laughed. She laughed with him. Laughter lessened the tension.

"This is so absolutely insane. None of my friends would ever believe me if I told them this story," she said, laughing even harder.

"Then don't tell them. People always find you more interesting when they know very little about you. Imagination is a wonderful thing."

"And your every bit as wonderful as I imagined you to be," Rachel said. "I'll never forget how you helped save me, and now you are saving Karen and the children. I have a nickname for you."

"Which is?" Rodrigo risked another brief look at her.

"Rodrigo—the protector."

"Seriously?"

"Yes, seriously."

"Don't make me out to be a hero. I'm doing all of this for selfish reasons. I'm a private man. I don't let people into my inner circle. I like life better that way. But for those in my circle, I do all that I can to keep them safe and happy. And that's what I'm doing here. I'm protecting those in my inner circle."

"And does that inner circle include me?"

"Rachel, I'm hurt that you would even ask me such a question. Of course, that includes you. You have been in that circle since the day I first laid eyes on you."

Rodrigo and Rachel rocked along in silence for several more miles. Rachel was becoming convinced that they would never see the end of this road.

"If this is a county road, then I would think that the county would spend a little money in maintaining it," she said, after the jeep plunged into one of the more treacherous potholes.

"Priorities. If you drive down any of the roads leading up to the Hillman homes and property, those roads are well maintained. Trinity County is no different from any other place. It's been my experience that the squeaky wheel gets the grease, or those who can grease the wheels ride, or some other such nonsense."

"I think the saying is 'the squeaky wheel gets the grease,'" Rachel said, laughing.

"All I know is this: the Hillmans have the money, and whatever the Hillmans want, the Hillmans get," Rodrigo stated. "The poorer people who live out in Tate's Hell get what's left over. And when people as greedy as the Hillmans are at the head of the line, there's rarely much, if anything, left over."

"Do the Hillmans really have that much control over this county, Rodrigo?"

"Remember, Rachel. I'm on the outside, looking in, just like you. We weren't born here, we moved in and that means we'll always be outsiders, no matter how long we stay."

"Yes, that has been my experience," Rachel said.

"But to answer your question about the Hillmans' power, from what I can tell, the Hillmans exert a tremendous amount of clout in this county."

"Does that include the Plantation?"

"Not so much. The Plantation appears to be sacred ground."

"Really? Why?" Rachel had never given this topic much thought.

"One word—money. There are people with more money than the Hillmans who call the Plantation home, if only for a few weeks or months during the year. Money equals power."

"Always," Rachel said. Her time as a lawyer had hammered that lesson home.

"The unspoken rule is that the Hillmans and Trinity leave the Plantation alone, and the Plantation ignores them."

"How long have you lived here?" Rachel asked. "You seem to have a good feel for local politics."

"Long enough," Rodrigo replied. "That's why I'm so shocked that the sheriff actually had the nerve to show up at Mrs. Brodie's home."

Rodrigo glanced over at Rachel. "Desperate men will do desperate things, and that was a desperate move by the sheriff.

That's the very reason, it's imperative for us to move Karen and the kids out of here as quickly as possible. When the Plantation is no longer a safe haven, something has gone terribly awry."

"Rodrigo, tell me about Mrs. Brodie. I know that the two of you are close, and you must know something of her background."

"I do," Rodrigo said, stealing another look over at Rachel. "But there are two very important reasons that I can't share Mrs. Brodie's history with you."

"Which are?"

"One is that it's her story to tell to you, if and when she wants to tell it; I never break a confidence. The second reason is that we're almost to the main road, and we need to turn our attention toward making a plan."

"Right," Rachel said. She strained to see the road ahead.

"Around this next bend is the main road." Rodrigo had his eyes glued to the road. "We have a few miles on the main road, and then we're at the turnoff to Dawson's Landing."

Rodrigo glanced briefly down at his watch as he spoke.

"All together we have lost at least a good hour and a half. That means the sun will be fully up when we get there."

Rachel suddenly noticed how light it had become outside. She had been so engrossed in her conversation with Rodrigo that she hadn't noticed the night turning into day.

"The good news is that some of the fog has burned off," Rodrigo said. "That means we can possibly make up some lost time on the river."

As Rodrigo was speaking, the jeep rolled out from under the cover of the trees, and a stop sign appeared announcing the entrance to the main road.

"You're right," she said. "The sun is up, and the fog does seem to be lifting."

"I know that I'm right, Rachel," he said, turning slightly and giving her a wink. "I know these woods."

"On the back road, the trees covered the road and made it appear darker. With any luck, old man Dawson will stay up by his fire and not come down to investigate our arrival. But that's not likely. My guess is that it's now late enough in the day for him to put in an appearance. We'll have to move fast to avoid him."

"I can keep up," Rachel assured him. "You just lead the way."

"When we're actually on the boat and clear the Landing, I'm going to give the boat full throttle, which means that we'll be moving at a fast speed."

"Good." Rachel was eager to make up lost time.

"And I do mean fast," Rodrigo warned her. "Don't be afraid; I know this river, and with the fog burned off, we shouldn't have any trouble."

"Don't worry about me," Rachel said. "My only fear is for Karen and the twins."

"The shack is over an hour up the river. It'll be especially cold in the boat; the wind off of the water can cut through you like a sharp knife. I suggest that you bundle up and stay down low in the back—that will cut the wind some. But trust me, it will be cold."

"I'll be fine, Rodrigo. Don't worry about me. Just get us to Karen and the kids as quickly as possible."

The jeep made a turn off of the beach road onto another dirt road. This one was in much better condition than the other back road, but they still bounced and rolled in their seats as Rodrigo pushed the pedal to the floor. He was trying desperately to make up for lost time.

Rachel could distinguish up ahead what appeared to be a long dock leading to a shed. She couldn't actually see the river, but she could see a break in the landscape and a row of trees, which she surmised must be the bank on the far side of the river. This must be Dawson's Landing, she thought.

As if reading her mind, Rodrigo announced their arrival at the Landing as the jeep rolled to a stop. "We're here. Are you ready?"

"Ready."

"Let's go."

As Rachel stepped out of the jeep, her knees almost buckled when she hit the ground. The bumpy ride had left her with rubber legs.

Rodrigo flipped back the seat and took a couple of gas cans out of the floorboard.

They both heard the noise of barking dogs from up on the hill at the same time. They exchanged a troubled look. By the sound of the barking, it was obvious the dogs were headed their way.

"We need to hurry," Rodrigo called over to her.

"He grabbed up the gas cans and started to trot. Rachel followed closely behind him. They ran down a wooden pier and then made a sharp turn into the boat barn.

As they entered the boat barn, Rodrigo pointed to a boat.

"There she is," he said. "My pride and joy."

The sound of the dogs was much louder now. Rachel hoped they were friendly, but she suspected this was not the case.

Rodrigo ran the short distance to his boat and placed the gas containers on the edge of the pier.

Rachel stood next to the gas cans while watching the door. The dogs were bound to come loping through the door at any second.

Rodrigo swiftly dropped down into the bow of the boat. He lifted the tanks from the dock and placed them in the back before he reached up for Rachel. She took his hand and jumped off the dock down into the boat.

Rodrigo threw off the line securing the boat to the dock and moved to a standing position behind the wheel.

The dogs bounded through the door and up to the boat. Even in the boat, Rachel was terrified. Rodrigo remained focused.

"Sit here next to me," he said, patting the seat beside him.

She obeyed instantly.

Rodrigo turned the key and ran through a quick scan of the monitors on the screen. God bless, Dawson, he thought. Even with the cold, Dawson had replenished the tank with fuel.

"Ready?" he called over to Rachel, returning to his spot behind the wheel.

She nodded her head.

"Here goes." Rodrigo turned the key, and the engine came alive. Rachel jumped, not quite prepared for the powerful roar that reverberated off of the metal roof.

Rodrigo skillfully maneuvered the boat out of the boat barn and into midstream. Rachel was relieved to leave the boat barn and the dogs behind.

"I want to try and make up time," Rodrigo shouted to her over the sound of the idling engines. "Hang on. I'm going to run full throttle."

Rachel nodded to him again that she was ready.

Rachel wasn't at all prepared for the power of the boat. When Rodrigo pushed the throttle to wide open, the force of the takeoff caused Rachel to lurch forward. Rodrigo extended his arm to catch her.

Even with the windshield as a barrier, the wind hit her face like scalding water.

When the boat leveled off, Rachel fell back into her seat.

Rodrigo dropped the arm protecting Rachel, and he put both hands on the wheel, staring ahead intently.

After the initial shock of the takeoff, Rachel relaxed a tiny bit, just enough to look around her. She couldn't even imagine the speed at which they were skimming across the water.

If it were not for Karen and the children being in danger, this would all be a wild and exhilarating adventure. The sun was up bright and clear, and the banks of the river flew past in a brown and green blur.

Rodrigo stood firmly poised, looking over the windshield. Already, his face was blistered red by the wind. His jaw was clenched tightly shut, and he looked determined.

Rodrigo—the protector—was in the zone, and she was glad for that.

Rachel tried to imagine Peter in this situation. She couldn't. The only boat that Peter could manage would be a quiet sail on a Sunday afternoon. Take Peter out of New York, and he was lost.

Rachel wasn't sure how long they had been running, when the boat slowed down. It had been a good while.

She stood up next to Rodrigo and looked around her.

"Why are we slowing down?" she asked.

"The river is narrower here," Rodrigo answered. "We're almost to our first turn into the swamp. If I run the boat over a submerged log or miss the turns, that will cost us even more time. Trust me. I know what I'm doing."

"Of course, you do. It's just that I'm so anxious to get there."

"Me, too. That's why I'm moving cautiously."

Rodrigo bore off to the right following one of the smaller creeks.

The tree branches were so close to the boat that Rachel could touch the limbs. Everything began to feel surreal to her.

She had never been any farther into the wilderness than her brief excursions into the woods surrounding the Brodie estate. She halfway expected natives to attack from the banks or crocodiles to circle the boat like in the old Tarzan movies.

"It really is beautiful here, if you can get over the feeling of being so far from civilization," Rachel said.

"That's what I like about it the most," Rodrigo answered, without taking his eyes off of the course. "Few humans have penetrated the swamp this far back, and we're only on the edge; this swamp encompasses hundreds of acres. But relax. We're almost there."

"I don't see anything."

"That's the beauty of the hideout; it's completely concealed when looking from the river. The only thing visible from the water is the dock. One more turn and we're there."

Rodrigo steered the boat into a narrow creek. It really was so beautiful—and peaceful, Rachel thought.

As they rounded a curve, Rodrigo and Rachel were shocked to see a boat tied to the rickety dock.

They heard the shots at the same time.

ABOUT THE AUTHOR

Roseanna Lee is a native Floridian. She earned a B.A. in English Literature at the University of Florida, an M.A. in English Literature at East Carolina University and a J.D. at the Florida State University College of Law. While she enjoyed her career as a Florida attorney, her passion has always been reading and writing fiction.

She lives in rural North Florida, the "other" Florida of pristine rivers and springs.

When not at home on her beloved Ichetucknee River, she is an avid traveler.

Cover Design and Layout: Isaac Rivera
www.isaacsifontes.com

Thank you for reading *A Watch in the Night*.
This exciting series consists of four books and may be
purchased through Amazon. And, we invite you to leave a
review on Amazon as well.

Give your Angels Charge

Book One

Shadow of Death

Book Two

ISBN: 978-1-945190-73-5

Snare of the Fowler

Book Three

ISBN: 978-1-945190-74-2

Set on High

Book Four

ISBN: 978-1-945190-75-9

Made in the USA
Las Vegas, NV
29 December 2021

39760602R00152